Copyright © 2025 by Q.B. Tyler

All rights reserved.

No part of this publication may be reproduced, distributed, or transmitted in any form or by any means, including photocopying, recording, or other electronic or mechanical methods, without the prior written permission of the publisher, except in the case of brief quotations embodied in critical reviews and certain other noncommercial uses permitted by copyright law.

This is a work of fiction. Names, characters, businesses, places, events, and incidents are either the products of the author's imagination and used in a fictitious manner. Any resemblance to actual persons, living or dead, or actual events is purely coincidental.

Content Editing: Kristen Portillo- Your Editing Lounge
Interior Formatting: Stacey Blake- Champagne Book Design
Cover Design: Pang Thao
Cover Image Photographer: Ren Saliba

PLAYLIST

I've Been in Love (feat. Channel Tres)— Jungle
Wicked Game— Jessie Villa
Beautiful (feat. Pharrell)—Snoop Dogg
Habits (Stay High)—Tove Lo
Let Go—Frou Frou
Tired of Being Alone— Al Green
Crazy in Love (2014 Remix)— Beyoncé
How Does it Make You Feel—Victoria Monét
You & Me (feat Eliza Doolittle)— Disclosure
Call on Me— Litany
In My Mind—Lyn Lapid
Best Part (feat. H.E.R.)— Daniel Caesar
For Once in My Life— Stevie Wonder

Rowan Kincaid hasn't dated in over a year.
Not since the mother of his children unexpectedly passed away leaving him to parent their three children alone.
Exhausted, overworked and feeling like he's failing at every turn he's desperate for help.
The help that shows up?
A gorgeous woman almost twenty years younger than him.
She's compassionate and charming
and the kids fall for her instantly.
And despite the fact that she should be off limits,
he falls for her too.

The NANNY is OFF LIMITS

CHAPTER ONE

Rowan

"Mr. Kincaid, I have your son's school on line two." My assistant's voice bounces off the walls of my office. Panic and a flare of annoyance set in as I wonder what my ten-year-old did this time.

This is the third call this week. There were the fake cockroaches he brought in that incited a riot and screams from practically every fifth-grade girl on Monday. He did the same with a rubber snake on Wednesday. This is on top of his standard daily comedic routine that does nothing but infuriate his teachers for being *disruptive*.

He's already a year ahead, having skipped kindergarten and he does exceptionally well in school, making the school psychologist believe he's the textbook study of a child misbehaving because he's not being *challenged enough*, on top of the trauma of the last year, but he's barely ten years old and in fifth grade. I'm not ready to send him to middle school yet and I'm not about to send him there to force him to a maturity level he is definitely not ready for.

But you're forcing my hand, Sawyer.

They haven't exactly threatened to kick him out of school but the words *better fit* and *elsewhere* have been thrown around a few times in the last principal-parent conference and that was before the rubber snake incident.

Fuck.

I rub my temples in preparation for the headache this phone call is going to cause. "This is Rowan Kincaid."

"Hi, Mr. Kincaid." I hear the voice of his principal, Mrs. Dean, who I imagine has been in early childhood education since before I was born and therefore has the patience of a saint but also doesn't take a whole lot of shit from anyone.

I take a deep breath, preparing for the worst. "Is he okay? Everything alright?"

I hear a sigh and the closing of a door. "Sawyer is fine. We have him here in the office. You're going to need to come down to the school now though."

Unease washes over me and I run a hand through my hair nervously because he's never been sent home from school before. "And why is that?"

"Your son started a fire in the boy's restroom."

Thoughts of my ten-year-old being labeled an arsonist and banned from every private school in Maryland come charging through my brain. "Excuse me?"

"It has been contained and no one was hurt, but we did have to evacuate the building and he is suspended from school for the next three days. We are considering expulsion, Mr. Kincaid." I don't say anything because really what the fuck could I say? "We have been patient and understanding about your…*situation*, and Isla is lovely. She is thriving in first grade," she says in reference to my youngest daughter, "but we need to have a serious conversation about your son's future at Rosewood Academy."

"Is Isla, okay? Does she understand what's going on?" I don't focus on the second part of her statement as I panic thinking about Isla being afraid and also not being able to find her brother when they were evacuated. This is another reason I haven't moved to send Sawyer to middle school. It's Isla's first year at this school and I wanted her to have her brother close while she acclimated.

"Yes, the younger children just think they have a second recess."

I look down at my watch to see the time and know it's going to be annoying as hell getting out of D.C. at the moment. "Give me thirty minutes," I tell her.

"Very well. We will see you soon."

"Thank God," I hear murmured as soon as I push through the door to the administration office. I turn to see my ten-year-old sitting on the couch in the corner with his feet propped up on the coffee table and his arms spread along the back like he owns the place.

"Oh, you better start praying." I point at him and watch as he has the audacity to roll his eyes before standing up and making his way toward me. My son is the spitting image of me with dark hair and sometimes green sometimes hazel eyes, depending on the lighting, but he, like my other two children, has a more olive complexion due to their mother's Italian roots. "You're in big trouble." I point at him before pointing a finger back to the couch. "Every electronic you own is mine for the rest of the month."

"Month!? Dad—" he starts.

I only glare at him. He couldn't possibly think he was getting off easier than that.

"You want to make it the rest of the year?" I glower.

"It's September." He deadpans.

"You're telling me. You've been in school for two weeks."

I watch as he huffs and moves back to the couch. He pulls his hood over his head and crosses his arms, and I already can picture him doing the same as a surly teenager in a few years.

God, help me.

"Mr. Kincaid." Mrs. Dean's voice cuts through the air and I suddenly feel like I'm the one in trouble. "Let's talk in my office. Sawyer will join us in a moment." I follow her into the room where another woman is seated holding a notepad in her lap on top of three textbooks. She gives me a warm smile and a nod. "This is Dr. Courtney Anderson. She's the school's psychologist."

I resist the urge to groan because the last thing I need is her weighing in on all the ways I'm failing as a parent. I don't respond because as an attorney, I know to never show my hand early on.

"I'm just here to try and get a better gauge of the situation. No one wants to expel Sawyer."

"There are several parents in the parent-teacher association who would beg to differ," Mrs. Dean says with a fake smile and a look that makes me believe I won't be leaving this office without writing a check.

"We just want to help," Dr. Anderson adds and I can already picture Sawyer's resistance if they try to make him meet with her once a week. I had all three of my children in therapy throughout the past year and only Isla had a positive experience because she's six and a chatterbox. She was thrilled to have someone else to talk to about the latest drama with her imaginary friends and the latest episode of *Bluey*. "We understand that this past year has been difficult for your family and we are so sorry for everything you've been through."

I swallow past the lump in my throat thinking about my children losing their mother unexpectedly. While we had been divorced for three years at the time of her death, it has affected me in a way I never anticipated. I'm not quite a widower but the grief washes over me like I am one at times. It's a weird feeling that the person responsible for half of my children no longer walks the Earth. I have no one to run things by and I suddenly feel like I'm failing at every turn. While we hadn't worked as a couple, she was a great mom and we co-parented well.

"Yes," Mrs. Dean says, and I hear the qualifier in that one word, "but we can't keep making excuses when it's affecting the other students here. Your son lit a stack of papers on fire and put them in a trashcan. We can't just let that go without consequences even though we understand he is going through a difficult time."

"I get that and I think the *suspension* is more than fair." I nod, doing my best to divert the conversation away from the dreaded "e" word.

"It's not just my decision if he's expelled. My phone has been ringing off the hook for the past hour with angry parents," Mrs. Dean insists.

"How much?" I grunt, giving her a look.

She shuts her eyes like she's planning to chastise me and when she opens them, I can see the fire in them. "This isn't about money, Mr. Kincaid. Your son is disruptive and it does not appear he has any motivation to change that." I sigh in defeat but Mrs. Dean leans forward and laces her fingers together. "However," she starts and I give her a look as if to say, *'uh-huh, that's what I thought, get to it.'* "We would be delighted to move up the timeline on the expansion of our second library."

"As well as meeting with me once a week," Dr. Anderson adds with a weak smile. "We want to get Sawyer on the right track, and I think having someone to talk to will help."

I snort. "He's had someone to talk to. Multiple someones. He doesn't open up to anyone but his older sister or me when he feels forced." My son is my mini-me and up until last year, he didn't want to be anywhere but in my shadow. Yet somehow living with me full time has put a strain on our relationship. Maybe because I wasn't the disciplinarian before. I was the fun parent that never nagged him or made sure he did his homework and now I have to find the balance. I'm struggling with that, especially with these destructive behaviors he's picked up.

"This isn't an option. If he doesn't want to risk expulsion, once a week after school, he'll need to meet with Dr. Anderson."

"Do you want to get kicked out of school? Is that what this is all about? Do you hate Rosewood?" I look at my son through the rearview mirror on our drive home as he stares out his window with a bored expression on his face.

"No." The one-word answer gets under my skin and I want to yell, but that hasn't been working, so clearly I need to try another approach.

"Then why do you keep acting out? They want to expel you, SJ," I say using my nickname for him. He doesn't say anything, and I go for another angle, hoping he'll tell me more about why he's been acting like this. "Did someone make you do this? Are you being bullied? What?"

"Good one." He snorts and I feel a pang of unease that my son is probably the ringleader when it comes to mischief.

"Then what is it?" He shrugs, and I grip the steering wheel tighter as I take a deep breath. "You know I hate that. Try again."

"It's nothing. I thought it would be cool. I wasn't expecting the smoke alarms to go off. I thought I had it under control."

"You're smarter than that. This was a cry for attention and now you have it. Great work," I say giving him a thumbs up.

"I'm hungry," he says, ignoring the topic of conversation completely.

"Are you serious?"

"Yes? I got hauled into the office right before lunch. Can we get Chipotle?"

"You're kidding, right?"

He looks at me through the rearview mirror. "I'm sorry, *may* we get Chipotle?"

"You do realize how much trouble you're in, right?"

"So, that means you're not going to feed me?" He chuckles.

"Man, Dr. Anderson is going to have a field day with that."

"Sawyer Jack," I warn him. I still have a brief to finish and while I do cook sometimes, tonight is not going to be one of them. "Fine, but this is not me rewarding your behavior. I want your PS5, your iPad, and your laptop. When we get home, you need to rake the leaves in both the front and backyard, take a shower, do your homework, and that's it. No television either."

He mumbles something under his breath and begins to chew on one of the strings of his hoodie. "What am I supposed to do?"

"Read a book."

"Oh great, like I don't do that enough," he replies dryly and it's times like this I hate having a ten-year-old with an IQ that very well may be higher than his older sister's. I sometimes struggle with wanting to chuckle at his wit. "Am I allowed to go to soccer tomorrow?"

I want to tell him no because he shouldn't be allowed to do anything he enjoys while he's suspended from school but I don't want to deny him the only healthy outlet I feel he appreciates. While he may be the youngest on the team, objectively he is probably the best and his mom always stressed the importance of nurturing our kids' hobbies. "We'll see."

After we grab his food, we're back at our house just before one in the afternoon. I'm shocked to see my oldest daughter, Margot's, light blue jeep in the driveway because she should definitely still be in school.

"Oooh, someone is in trouble," SJ sings through a mouthful of chips that he's shoving into his mouth by the handful.

I narrow my eyes at her car before pulling up my phone and checking her location which is coincidentally *off*.

"What is with my children today?"

I open the door as quietly as possible to attempt to see what my sixteen-year-old daughter is up to. We have cameras so I am surprised that I didn't see her come home; I'm guessing she disarmed one before she left this morning so it wouldn't alert me when she came back in.

I am hoping, *actually praying*, that when I walk through the front door, I spot Margot lying on the couch watching television with a box of tissues surrounding her because she has a cold. Something that will tell me my sixteen-year-old has a real reason for being home in the middle of the day even if it is without my permission. What I do *not* expect, however, is my daughter and her boyfriend, Gabe—no, *I am not crazy about this term*—in the horizontal position on my couch.

The only—*and I do mean the only thing*—that is stopping me from having a heart attack and making my children orphans, is that they do at least have their clothes on.

"ARE YOU OUT OF YOUR MIND?!" I shout and I watch as that little fucker jumps three feet from where he is lying on top of her, and my daughter's terrified eyes meet mine as her head snaps up.

"Sick!" SJ says, and when I glare at him, he gives me a cheeky grin. "This means I'm off the hook, right?" he adds pointing at them.

"What...what..." I close my eyes to stop myself from exploding...and to collect my thoughts. "In what world, do you think this is okay? You ditched school..."

"We got out early!" Margot's brown eyes are wide and I can see the terror and a bit of embarrassment washing over her features.

"Since when?"

"Since always?" She tilts her head as she stands up. "We had an early release today. You'd know if you checked your emails." She winces when I shoot her a warning glare. She can't possibly think this is somehow *my fault* for not knowing she got out of school early.

"So, that gives you permission to come here and do...this!?" I growl.

"Mr. Kincaid..." Her boyfriend starts, and turning my

attention to him, I glare at his disheveled shirt. I'm only slightly relieved that it doesn't appear that his jeans are unzipped.

"Are you still here?!" I shout.

He visibly shakes, and I admit, I'm happy he's intimidated by me.

"Dad!" Margot scrunches her nose at me in the same way her mother used to and I cross my arms over my chest because she is not getting off that easily.

"Say goodbye to your *friend*," I tell her. She goes to take a step toward him like she's going to kiss him goodbye and I shake my head. "Do you want to live until graduation?" I continue to glare at her boyfriend who takes a step back before giving her a look.

"I'm sorry, Mr. Kincaid," he says, without meeting my gaze as he moves toward the door before closing it behind him.

"I don't even allow you in your room with him but you think I'd allow this?"

"I..." she starts and she looks around the room like she'll find the answer before she blurts out, "We weren't doing anything!"

SJ snorts. "Lie better than *that*."

"And what are you doing here?" she says to her brother. "You couldn't have texted that you were coming home early?" Margot and Sawyer are close and I know for a fact that he's covered for her when she's done things she's not supposed to. I even have the sneaking suspicion he'll help her sneak out when the time comes. *This thought terrifies me.* I'm glad they have each other's backs, but a part of me wishes they'd just rat the other out sometimes.

"Dad took my phone, and what are you mad at me for? It's not like I knew you'd be here sucking face with your loser boyfriend."

"Both of you, ENOUGH! SJ, you have leaves to rake." I point towards the back door. "Finish your food and then I don't want to hear a peep out of you until it's done."

Peep, he mouths at me before moving towards the kitchen.

I let out a frustrated sigh and turn toward Margot. "You're grounded."

She bites her bottom lip and I see the tears forming in her eyes before she nods once. "For how long?"

"Until I say," I grunt and one of the tears falls down her face. "Don't even try it." Her lip trembles and another tear falls. "I am not falling for the tears. Go to your room."

"I have cheer practice at three." She sniffles before she starts moving toward the stairs.

"There and back and turn your location on. If you turn it off again, I'm taking your keys," I call after her.

Christ, I need a drink.

"DADDY!!!" I hear her scream, followed by the closing of the front door and then my six-year-old is busting through my office door even though she knows she should knock before entering. Luckily, I'm not on a call but I still give her a look as she skips around my desk and hops into my lap. "You forgot me at school!" Isla is six going on sixteen, unfortunately, and takes picking out her clothes very seriously and everything—*everything*—has to match the sunglasses she's wearing that day. It's somewhat of a new thing, I think, in response to her mother's death, but the therapist says it's a healthy form of personal expression and it's nothing to be concerned with *yet*. Today she's wearing light blue and white with accents of yellow and light blue sunglasses that are way too big for her face.

I pull her sunglasses off so I can see her eyes. "I did *not* forget you," I tell her before pressing a kiss to her forehead and tightening one of her loose pigtails.

"You picked Sawyer up and not me!" Her brown eyes narrow and give me a scolding look.

"Sawyer got sent home."

"Yeah, and why is that? Some hot mom at pick-up said there was a fire today. Does that have my nephew's name all over it?" My younger brother, River, comes strolling through my office door. Three times a week he picks them both up from school for me before he has to be at football practice. He is the head football coach for one of the high schools in the county, and my house just happens to be on the way there.

"A fire?" Isla's eyes widen and her mouth forms an o-shape.

"He's not going to be in school for a few days, alright?" I tell her so she knows not to panic if she's unable to find him.

Isla shakes her head and hops off my lap. "SAWYER!" she screams as she runs out of my office.

"I am this close to losing my shit," I tell River as I hold my thumb and index finger close together. "Then we get home and Margot is in the horizontal position making out on the couch with her boyfriend."

River's eyes go from shock to anger in the span of a second as he closes the door to my office. "Uhhh what?! I'll kill him. Did you already kill him? Where's the body?" he asks before sitting down on my couch. He rolls up the sleeves of his sweatshirt revealing all the tattoos he has on both of his arms. "You didn't know she was home?"

My head falls into my hands before I run one through my hair, trying my best not to pull it out. "She turned off her location and disarmed the alarm, so no."

"Shit, dude."

I drop my head into my hands. "Needless to say, they are both grounded."

"SJ's suspended?"

I nod and pinch the bridge of my nose as I think about what I'm going to do about him for the next three days. *I could bring him to the office, but that could be a disaster.* "Three days. They were considering expulsion but it was nothing fifteen grand and a recurring weekly meeting with the school shrink couldn't fix," I say sarcastically while rubbing my forehead.

He chuckles and scratches his jaw. "Fuck, and knowing him he's probably pumped to be out for three days."

"I'm giving him every chore in the world until he goes back. You want your car washed?" I ask, and he chuckles.

"Man, I've been telling you this since Bianca died; you need help." His brown eyes are sincere but a little scolding.

"I have help. I have you."

"No, you need real, live-in help. Like a nanny, bro. At least until SJ is a little older. You're doing your best, and anyone can see that, but you're not present enough and the lack of supervision is the reason behind some of this. The days I pick them up, I stay with them until five when Margot gets home from practice, and yes, she feeds them and makes sure they take baths and showers, but Isla and SJ barely see you those days because they're asleep by the time you get home. I think they would do well with more adult presence."

"A live-in nanny though? Isn't that a bit much? My kids aren't babies."

"Isla is six and SJ is ten. They are still kids and you need someone to keep an eye on Margot before you have a baby in the form of a grandchild in the mix too."

His words set in and I shift uncomfortably in my chair thinking about my baby having a baby. I still remember every second of the day she was born and sometimes it feels unfathomable that it was sixteen years ago. "How would I even go about that? How does one even find a nanny?"

"How do you think? Contact an agency, obviously. Or ask someone at that hoity-toity school you send SJ and Isles to. They probably all have nannies."

CHAPTER TWO

Elianna

THE SOUND OF A BUNCH OF BOXES HITTING THE FLOOR turns my attention down the aisle at the grocery store and I see a little girl climbing up the shelf right where there are about fifteen boxes of cookies on the ground beneath her. I blink a few times while I watch this little girl act out a scene from the cartoon *Rugrats*. I push my cart a little closer to her before darting my eyes around the empty aisle in search of her parents or anyone that might be responsible for her.

"Do you need some help?" I ask her.

She turns her head in my direction and looks at me from over the top of pink heart-shaped sunglasses. "No, I got it!" she says with a tiny strain in her voice as she climbs up another shelf in her quest for a box at the top.

"Okay, how about I grab that for you? Just so you don't fall," I tell her as I pull her down gently and set her on her feet.

"Are *you* tall enough to reach?" she says looking up at me referring to my short height, and I resist the urge to glare at her. I grab the box—*okay, while straining on my tip toes*—before handing it to her and looking at all the boxes that lay at her feet.

"Did you do this?" I point to the mess.

"Mmmm nuh-uh." She shakes her head while holding the box against her chest.

"You sure?"

"Mmmm maybe," she relents with a guilty smile before pushing her hair out of her face. She has bangs that seem like she's due for a trim but her long chocolate hair is pulled into a ponytail on top of her head. She's dressed in all pink with a little purse on her shoulder and while she is adorable as hell, I just know she has to be a handful.

"Do you want me to help you clean it up?"

She nods and we start putting the boxes back on the shelf. Just as we put away the last box, a voice comes over the loudspeaker. "Isla Kincaid, please report to the front of the store, thank you."

I look down at the cute little girl who is currently avoiding my eyes. "Is that you?"

She purses her lips. "Nope," she says popping the p.

"I don't think I believe that," I tell her. "How about we just go check, just in case?"

She huffs. "Okay."

"Are you here with your mommy?"

"No, she died." She looks up at me, and though I can't see her eyes through the pink lenses, I can see the sadness all over her.

My heart squeezes in my chest thinking about this young girl going through something I'm still going through a decade later and I kneel down so we're at eye level. "I'm really sorry to hear that. My mommy died too."

She pushes her sunglasses to the top of her head and then I

do see her eyes. Light brown and wide and lined with long lashes I'm instantly jealous of. "Really?"

I nod. "When I was older than you."

She frowns and I watch the tears form as her bottom lip wobbles a little. "It sucks." Not wanting to watch her cry, I rub her back gently. Then she wraps her arms around my neck, and though I am great with kids and they all seem to gravitate toward me, I wonder why no one has taught this particular one about *stranger danger*. She pulls away after a second and wipes her eyes before lowering her sunglasses again, like a defense mechanism I imagine she'll use for the rest of her life.

"It does suck but are you allowed to say that word?" She purses her lips again and shakes her head. I smile at her before I stand up and we move down the aisle. "I'm Elianna, but people call me Ellie. What's your name?"

"Isla," she says and I gasp in faux surprise.

"You are! So, you fibbed?" I raise an eyebrow at her and I'm surprised she looks guilty. "Are you here with your dad?"

"No, my—"

"Jesus, Isles," I hear from the front of the aisle as a man makes his way toward us. He's dressed down in a long-sleeved t-shirt with the words *Bulldogs Football* on the front, a pair of shorts, and a backward hat. He has sunglasses tucked into his collar and I'll admit he's easy on the eyes. He's obviously a coach or something, and while guys in sports don't typically do much for me *or my vagina*, he definitely has that look that tells me he cleans up *very* nicely. "I turned my head for five seconds."

"I needed cookies!" she says as she holds up the box over her head like it's a trophy.

"Tell me next time! If I go home without you, your dad is going to fucking kill me."

So, not her dad. And assumedly the person who taught her the word "sucks."

His eyes turn to me and widen before a smile pulls at his lips despite the look I'm giving him for using the word *fuck* in front of an impressionable child. "Hi, I'm sorry."

"You know you can't turn your back on a child for a second." I nod at her. My words are only meant to be a little bit scolding but I hope he senses the teasing lilt in my voice.

"She knows better." He looks at Isla before turning back to me. "I'm River, her uncle." He holds his hand out for me.

"I'm Elianna." I shake his hand before looking down at Isla. "Well, River and Isla, it was nice to meet you both."

I start to walk away when I hear a high-pitched, "Wait!"

I turn again and Isla is skipping toward me, away from her uncle who is watching us from several feet away. "I need a nanny."

"I'm sorry?"

"A nanny! Daddy says I need one."

"Isles, we can't just ask random ladies in the store," River says as he closes the distance between us, and I don't miss the way his eyes look me over appreciatively. "Unless you're interested." I blink at him a few times hearing the double meaning. "My brother is interviewing. He's going through a tough time right now. What with their mom..." He trails off and I remember vividly how hard my dad had it when my mom died.

I'm the oldest of three girls and I'd stepped into the role when she died because my dad couldn't afford the help. We did okay, but I was old enough and he worked all the time which means I didn't really have a social life until I went to college when I was nineteen. I'd only been there for a year when my middle sister, who was sixteen at the time, got pregnant and I dropped out of school to help and be there for her. I didn't go back until two years later when I was twenty-one, and now at twenty-five, I've just graduated with a degree in psychology.

River clears his throat and finishes his sentence about Isla's mother. "She passed away."

I feel for this family in this situation. I look down at Isla who reminds me so much of my youngest sister who went down a very different path than our middle sister and is currently in her first year of college at Yale. I've been an au pair three times already, spending entire summers with families in their vacation homes and I just finished my last one to come back here and start graduate school. I wasn't planning to be a nanny while I was in school. It's a significant time commitment, but I wouldn't hate the extra income either.

"I am actually...a nanny." I look back and forth between them. "I was planning to take a break because I just started school."

River's eyes widen and he takes a step back before putting his hands up. "I'm sorry, I thought you were—I mean..."

"Oh, not undergrad. I delayed a few times. I'm twenty-five."

A look of relief washes over him. "Great. Not that...it would have been bad, but the oldest is sixteen and I don't know that an eighteen-year-old would have worked for that." He laughs and my eyes widen at the thought of being a nanny to someone only nine years younger than me.

"She doesn't really need a nanny. Although she does have a boyfriend and I sometimes worry she'll get knocked up due to all the lack of supervision."

Two girls. Sounds like this guy has his hands full.

"What's knocked up?" Isla interjects while looking up at her uncle.

"Ask your dad," he says before turning back to me, and I resist the urge to chuckle.

"I bet he'll love that." I bite my bottom lip. "Just two?"

He scratches the back of his neck and gives me a nervous look. "There's a boy also. He's ten."

"Three?" I whistle and cross my arms over my chest. I don't miss the way River's eyes drop immediately toward the movement before moving back up to meet my gaze. "That is tough. He doesn't have any help?"

"Me, when I can. Our parents live in Arizona and they come up when they can, but my brother didn't want them to uproot their life." He winces. "But he's…drowning," he says before his lips form a straight line.

I think about my dad and the sacrifices he made because he didn't have any help raising us, and I think about the sixteen-year-old who is possibly being denied the chance to be a teenager because she's having to help raise her two younger siblings. Then I think about her getting pregnant because no one is around to keep her—*and more importantly, her hormones*—in check.

"Okay, I'll meet your brother."

Okay, the Kincaids do not live like I did while I was growing up. I pull up to the massive house in the gated community in Potomac, which is not only one of the nicest cities in the state but in the country. I park in the circular driveway and note a four-car garage with three cars parked out front. A Maserati, an Audi, and a BMW. Next to them is a boy, who I assume is the son, washing one of them.

I get out of my car, alerting him to my presence, and when he looks up at me he drops his sponge in the bucket before making his way over. "Here for the nanny interview?" He looks so much like the uncle it makes me wonder how much the brother and the father look alike. I notice he seems a little on the taller side for ten years old.

"I am."

He looks me over like he's silently judging me. "You don't look that old."

"Thank you," I say with a tiny curtsy.

"I just mean…the people that have been here…they've been older than my dad." His cheeks pinken a little. "You're just… younger." He trips over his words and I know this narrative well. I've dealt with boys that have had crushes on me before, but that usually passes the second they realize I'm not a pushover and I make them finish their homework before they can do anything else.

"I see." I point to my car. "You have time to do mine?"

"Sure," he shrugs, "for twenty bucks."

"For twenty bucks, I can go to an actual car wash," I respond. "How about five?"

He snorts. "How about no?"

So, a bit of smart ass then. "Hmmm." I narrow my eyes at him. "As much as I enjoy being hustled by a ten-year-old, I have to go meet with your dad." I turn to walk away before pausing and looking back at him. "Keep your fingers crossed I don't get the job. Conversations won't go quite like this if I do." I raise my eyebrows before moving up the long staircase to the front door.

I'm just about to ring the doorbell when Isla appears with a different pair of sunglasses on her face; these are yellow with star frames to match her all-yellow outfit. "Ellie!" She grabs my hand and pulls me through the door before shutting it behind me. "DADDY!" she screams *very* loudly and I briefly wonder why no one has taught her about inside voices.

"Isla Kincaid, enough with the yelling." I hear him before I see him, and then he comes around the corner, dressed in a full suit complete with a tie like he's just coming in from the office, sporting a stern look across his face directed at her.

She puts her hands on her hips and cocks her head to the side. "I wanted to make sure you could hear me!"

"I'd be able to hear you from outer space, sweetheart." His voice softens, and it's deep and rich and *hot*. Like he could narrate one of my romance audiobooks.

She ignores his comment, not grasping the sarcasm. "Daddy, this is Ellie." She points at me.

"Right, you're the woman that my brother and youngest child tricked into coming here." His eyes meet mine. They're green or maybe hazel and he gives me a dazzling smile before holding out his hand. Instantly, I know I can't take this job. I was reluctant at first with it being a single dad but a single dad that looks like *this*? *Nope. Nope. Nope.* I finally have some stability in my life after years of just the opposite. The last thing I want or need is to feel any kind of attraction to the father of the children I'm nannying. This is a recipe for disaster.

The reminder that he's recently widowed comes through my brain and I feel somewhat relieved knowing he's probably still deep in the mourning period, and thereby, not interested. So, there's no way I'd make a move, no matter how gorgeous he is.

And Rowan Kincaid is gorgeous.

"How old are you?" I blurt out, my brain clearly not working because that is not an appropriate question.

"Forty-four," Isla answers and he glares at her.

"Forty-three, thank you. Please go play."

She giggles and takes off for another room in the house.

"Sorry, I just…you're younger than I thought you'd be."

"I'd say the same but *believe me*, my brother sang your praises." He nods toward the way he came. "We can go to my office."

I follow him down a long hallway to a room at the end of the hall. He closes the door behind us and sits behind his desk. "Look, I appreciate you coming. I know my daughter can be very persuasive and if you felt backed into a corner, I apologize." I note how tired his eyes are and the solemn look he's giving me.

"No…I don't feel that way. Your daughter is lovely. Very sweet. A bit mischievous. I found her climbing the shelves in the cookie aisle. I'm not sure if she told you that."

"She did not." He sighs, running a hand through his short dark hair. "I told her to stop doing that."

"Why don't you tell me a bit about your situation? Isla mentioned that your wife passed away—"

"She said that?" he interjects, his expression confused and I nod.

"Okay, so their mother yes. She died a year ago, but we'd been divorced for about three years before that. So, my ex-wife, technically," he clarifies. "Isla doesn't talk about that much though, so I'm just surprised she told you."

"She doesn't?"

"She was only five and...I think she's still struggling with what it all means. She's also my happy-go-lucky child. Nothing bothers her. She's always smiling. She rarely cries."

My mind goes back to our interaction at the grocery store and the thought that her eyes welled up with tears in front of a perfect stranger, moments after her mom was brought up has me wondering if her father is talking to his kids about her at all or if it's that *thing* they don't talk about.

"I see...and you have two others?"

"A son, Sawyer. He's ten and my daughter, Margot, is sixteen."

"Does Margot help you with day-to-day things?"

"As much as she can, yes. I'm an attorney and there are a lot of nights I'm home late. Later than I'd like. She helps with cooking and putting them to bed at a reasonable time." *Reasonable meaning, Sawyer is probably up watching TV or on his iPad until he hears the garage door open alerting him that his father is home.*

"How will she react to having a nanny? Sometimes teenagers at that age, particularly girls, struggle with having what they deem as just a *babysitter*." I use my fingers as air quotes.

"She'll deal with it. I think part of her is happy to have some of her freedom back. She has to come home from practice most days and I know she'd rather go to her school's sporting events or do things with her friends after school. She's currently grounded, but when that's over, I know she'll be happy to not have to rush right home after her cheer practice."

"Grounded from...sneaking a boy into the house, correct?"

He winces before he leans back in his chair. "My brother told you?"

I nod. "Are you concerned about that?"

"Name a father who isn't concerned about his sixteen-year-old daughter and her boyfriend and I'll show you a liar."

I clear my throat as I attempt to broach a topic that no father wants to have. "Is she...have you talked to her about being safe?"

"God no. I'm not concerned about that per se, and I don't even want to put that thought in her head. She'd better not be having sex."

I frown not knowing if he's being naive or blatantly ignorant on purpose.

"But what if she is? She's sixteen and more than likely had the thought already." While I lost my virginity somewhat later in life because I was forced into being 'the responsible one,' sixteen was the age when a lot of my friends *and my younger sister* lost theirs.

His eyes snap to mine like I just uttered the most ridiculous sentence. "Can we not talk about this?"

"That's not *really* how it works."

His brows pinch together and I see the agitation forming on his face by the second. "Excuse me?"

"Not talking about it isn't going to magically make it not a problem. I know a lot of fathers defer to the mother about this but she doesn't have one and from what I'm gathering there is no strong adult female presence, which means this falls on you unless you want to be a grandfather in nine months."

He scoffs like I've insulted him. "My daughter isn't like that."

"It's not about being like anything." I shrug thinking about my younger sister who was the model straight-A student with all the extracurricular activities in the world and still had the time to get pregnant. "All kinds of girls get into trouble with the boys they think they're in love with. All I'm saying is having the conversation now can save you from having a very different conversation later."

"I don't need a lecture." His voice is even but still with a hint of defensiveness.

"You're right. *She* does," I tell him and he crosses his arms over his chest. "Tell me about your son. Why do you have him outside washing cars? I'm going to guess it was not his idea."

"He's suspended from school. He goes back on Monday," he says without offering more information.

I raise an eyebrow at him as if to say, *You're going to have to give me more than that.* "For...?"

"Starting a fire in a trashcan," he says without meeting my gaze.

What in God's name has been happening here?

"How did he get a lighter?"

"He's ten. He knows how to open cabinets." His eyes snap to mine, confused with a hint of annoyance.

"Was anyone hurt?"

"No."

"Did he say why he did it?"

"I'm guessing for attention?"

"Did you ask?"

A flash of annoyance crosses his handsome face. "Yes, Elianna, I asked." The way he says my name sends a tiny tremor skating through me. Almost like he's scolding *me*.

Feeling both a little turned on, but mostly irritated by his response, I push further. "And you couldn't get a straight answer?"

"He said he thought it would be fun."

"Did you stress how dangerous it could be? What if someone had gotten hurt?"

"Well, thankfully, no one did. He put it out himself with a fire extinguisher, once it got out of hand."

"He knows how to use a fire extinguisher?"

"He's too smart for his own good, unfortunately." He rolls his eyes followed by a smile that makes a flash of heat move through me.

"Have you explored the thought that maybe he's not being challenged enough and should go up a grade?"

"Thoroughly."

"And?"

He sighs again, this time in frustration like he's tired of the line of questioning. "He's not ready for middle school."

"I see." I think about how much help this family really needs and as much as I want to, I'm not sure I'm the answer. "Mr. Kincaid—"

"Rowan," he interrupts and when I meet his eyes, they look exhausted.

I remember River's comment about him drowning and I opt for a question instead. "How many people have you seen before me?"

"Twelve," he says quietly.

"In how many days?"

"Two."

Yikes. "And none of them were a good fit?"

"In their eyes, no."

"Three kids are tough." I think about all the women who probably heard this exact spiel and couldn't get out of the room fast enough.

"Yeah," he says, his eyes not meeting mine.

"Were they close with their mother?"

"I'd like to think they were equally close with us both. We had joint custody."

I'm silent for a moment as I think about how difficult this transition has probably been on all of them. "Who would you say is taking it the hardest?"

"My oldest, I think. They were close." Just my brief interaction with Isla and hearing about Sawyer's very obvious acting out makes me want to refute this immediately, but I'll reserve judgment until I spend more time with all of them.

"My mom died when I was a little younger than Margot, so I probably get her a little bit. I have two younger sisters that I helped raise. We struggled a lot and I wish I'd had help. My dad was busy working and a lot of things fell on me. He was a great dad, just...not always present." I'm already regretting the words that are preparing to leave my lips but I know I won't be able to get this family out of my head if I walk away. "I want to help you."

"You. PROMISED," my best friend, Jacqueline, says as she lifts the shot of tequila to her lips. "You said no nannying this semester so you could have a life and we could actually hang out more than once a month!" she whines as she lets her head drop to the hightop table where we are seated at our favorite bar. "This is so unfair. You're going to live there too?"

"They need a live-in nanny. It's two young kids and he works late a lot and he worries that the sixteen-year-old is on the precipice of starting to sneak out of the house and the middle child will cover for her." I haven't met the oldest yet and I couldn't quite get a read on her based on what her father told me.

"You're going to nanny for a sixteen-year-old? God, can I watch?" She snorts. "Girl or boy?"

"Girl," I say before taking a healthy sip of my spicy margarita because the thought of nannying for a girl at that age is definitely something new for me.

"Oooh, she's going to haaate you," Jacqueline sings as she tucks a sleek black strand behind her ear. "You meet her yet?"

"No, she wasn't home, but I'm going back to meet her tomorrow."

"How's the dad?" she asks with a smirk.

"Ugh, don't start." I drag a chip through the spinach dip between us.

"Is he hot? Please tell me he's hot." I push the chip into my mouth, so I don't have to answer that and avoid her gaze but she grabs my chin and turns me toward her. "No way."

I swallow nervously and wince. "Way."

"Oh my God, oh my *God!* This is gold."

I pull out of her grasp and stare at her incredulously. "Since when are you into a guy with kids? You don't even like kids! You won't even date a man who has an attachment to their niece or nephew because you don't want to go to children's birthday parties," I tell her.

"All true, but this is gold for *you* and hopefully your vagina."

"It's absolutely not like that." I shake my head not wanting to think about his eyes or his mouth or the way his hand felt wrapped around mine when he shook it. "He's going to be my boss."

"Do you have any idea how hot the single daddy nanny trope is?" she asks.

"Yes, I'm familiar," I reply sardonically.

"What's his name?" she asks as she pulls her beer to her lips.

"Rowan Kincaid."

"God, even his name sounds like sex. Besides, you rarely nanny for single dads. What's so special about this family?"

"I don't know." I shrug, knowing exactly why I agreed but not in the mood for the Jacqueline Woods inquisition and her turning me into her latest psych study. I spin my straw around my drink while I avoid her gaze and prepare to tell her the truth. "Their mom just died and…I just feel for them I guess."

"Oh, of course." She smacks her head.

I groan. "Don't start."

"Me? You're trying to rewrite the past. If you fuck the single dad, we are going to have a long talk about your daddy issues, Ellie."

"I am not going to fuck him!" I haven't had sex with anyone in almost six years and I certainly am not going to break my unofficial vow of celibacy with the father of the kids I'm nannying. I'm not avoiding sex necessarily; I just hadn't found anyone I wanted to sleep with after the horrifying experience of losing my virginity. *And the two times after that.* I've dated casually but it hasn't gone further than kissing and a couple of hand jobs that I worry I didn't even do correctly.

"Does he know that? Because you're also about to be the

gorgeous twenty-five-year-old temptation living under his roof and raising his kids."

"He was perfectly professional when we met."

"Professional, till he was jacking off before you even made it out of the driveway." She snorts before stealing a French fry off my plate.

"Ugh, shut up," I scoff while also not trying to let myself think too hard about his hand wrapped around his—*no*.

"I'm just saying…" she says putting her hands up in defense. "Look, I know you don't date *much*, but living with a hot single man…" She purses her lips and leans forward. "Things happen, you know."

"And *you* know my rule. I don't pursue anything with anyone in connection to the family. I just want to help them. I've been thinking about Isla tearing up in the grocery store when she said her mom died for three days now."

Jacqueline knows how much I give my heart to the kids I nanny and I can already hear the lecture coming about not getting attached when it's obvious I already am. "How long do you think you'll be there?"

"We are doing a sixty-day trial and then we'll reevaluate." She gives me a look from across the table and I groan. "What?"

"Well, it's just you usually have an endpoint. Usually just for a summer, which is three months. This sounds like you're potentially signing on until the youngest turns eighteen."

"No, I mean…I don't know. The money is good and I have the time. He knows I just have to go to campus once a week to meet with my advisor for an hour and Margot will be home at that time. He's also giving me two weekends off a month, so relax, we can still hang out." Her eyes light up and she does a little dance in her seat. "But I doubt I'll be there for twelve years. Besides, he may meet someone."

"Yeah," she snorts before taking a sip of her drink, "the hot nanny sleeping in his guest room."

CHAPTER THREE

"She's twenty-five? What, none of the other age-appropriate nannies would have fit?" Margot says as she leans against the doorjamb of my office with an annoyed look on her face. She's the spitting image of her mother, long sandy brown hair with strands of blonde due to the sun, brown eyes, and skin that stays tan throughout the year even in the dreary winter months.

"None of the age-appropriate nannies were willing to put up with you and your siblings' nonsense," I respond without looking up from my computer.

"Dad, you have got to be kidding me. She's young enough to be one of *your* kids."

I ignore that because I don't want to think about the eighteen years I have on her even as I feel a slight tightening in my pants at the wayward thought. "She's not even here for you. She's here for your siblings and also to give *you* a break from having to babysit all the time. You could say thank you."

"Dad, I'm fine. I don't mind helping out."

"And I love that about you, but I want you to also have time to be a teenager and I just need another adult in the house. I work late a lot and you..." I look up at her and blink rapidly, "dear daughter, have proven to me that you can't be trusted with constant access to an empty house."

"So, she *is* also for me."

"She's not here to tell you what to do. For you, she only serves as a deterrent." I smile at her.

"Ugh! Dad, this is a joke!" she says as she stomps out of my office.

I had thought about how Margot would handle it, but ultimately, she'll have to get over it. I interviewed twelve women before I saw Elianna and ten of them politely declined once I gave them the rundown. One of them, I dismissed for blatantly coming on to me and the other just wasn't experienced enough. Elianna has the experience, the credentials, a degree, and most importantly, something my children could relate to that I can't. I think about her story and how she helped her father when her mother died, and I know their story tugs at her heartstrings. I don't know all of the details, but I'll admit hers tugged on mine too.

All of this has forced me to overlook that my brother was not exaggerating in that Elianna Riley is fucking beautiful. While she's a little younger than the women I typically go for, she has a lot of the physical traits I often find myself attracted to. Long dark curly hair that hangs past her shoulders, her skin is flawless and the color of rich caramel, brown eyes, a smile that makes my heart race, and full lips I want to sink my teeth into. She's shorter than most women I date and because she's younger, her breasts sit up higher by nature and not with help. It took every ounce of restraint to keep my glances downward to a minimum.

I'm not blind to how gorgeous she is or the instant attraction I felt when I came around the corner and saw my daughter's fingers laced with hers, but she's also the first person who's come into my life in the last twelve months with any kind of plan to help. I can't fuck that up just because thinking about her makes my dick hard.

I like that she challenged me; it means she'll challenge them and I don't see her being afraid to put her foot down which is what they need. I didn't need a Mary Poppins and I'm grateful she seems like the opposite. I'm not delusional. I know my kids need structure and discipline. I just haven't known how to do that while also working eighty-hour weeks. It's been an adjustment going from having them on weekends to full time and I wish I'd had more time to prepare for it.

You could cut your hours, I think for the thousandth time since their mother died.

But I'm a partner at a major law firm, which means consistently cutting hours every week isn't exactly feasible.

So, all of the lustful feelings I may have for the woman who is moving into my house in a few days are going to be locked in a box with a lot of other things I'm currently avoiding. Engaging with my kids' nanny beyond any level other than professionally is out of the question.

I watch from the front window as she pulls into my driveway in a black SUV and I'm grateful she drives something big enough in case she ever has to drive all three of them somewhere.

"Damn, she's hotter than I remembered," I hear from next to me as she gets out of the car and my brother slaps me hard on the back.

"Why are you here?" I groan. It's Saturday, so it's not unheard of for River to show up at my house, but it's barely noon and I'm surprised he's not still hungover from last night.

"SJ told me she was meeting Margot today. I couldn't miss that," River says as he continues to stare out the window.

"Go away."

"Come on. You should be thanking me. And you should be thanking me by putting in a good word for me." He puts an arm around my neck and pulls me somewhat into a headlock. While we are roughly the same height, he's always been the rough-houser even when we were kids and I hate to admit it, but he's stronger than I am now.

"You're too old for her," I say as I pull out of his grasp.

"I am six years *younger* than you, which means I am only twelve years older than her. That's nothing."

"I know that's your preferred age you like your women and all, but you're too old."

"Oh, come on. What are you her dad too? Give me a break."

"River, no. You get mixed up with her and then inevitably fuck it up and then she wants to quit because she can't stand the sight of your face. Absolutely not. Back off and do not hit on her," I tell him quickly as I watch her walk up the stairs.

He groans. "If I knew you'd be this annoying I would have just asked her out. This is the thanks I get for looking out for you?"

"Yep." I open the door just as she approaches but not before cataloging what she's wearing. Dark denim jeans that hug her waist and her thighs but are a little looser as they go down and a plain white t-shirt tucked in. She's wearing what I think are heeled boots underneath her jeans and a short black blazer over it. She looked professional and casual and most importantly fucking stunning. Tight curls fall around her shoulders and I ignore the thought of what it would feel like to tangle my hands in them while my lips explore her neck.

"Hi," she says as her hand still hovers in the air like she had been preparing to knock. She smiles and I do my best to keep my eyes off of her lips but they're painted red and against her smile, I find myself briefly transfixed.

I clear my throat. "I saw you pull up." I nod at her. "Come on in."

"I brought over copies of all my certifications, a copy of my driver's license, and some letters of recommendation." She hands me the manila folder. I'd called two of her references, both mothers who raved about how wonderful she'd been with their children, and assured me, no matter how old my kids were, I'd hired the right woman for the job. *A modern-day Fraulein Maria*, one had said *minus all the singing*.

"Great, thank you."

"See, look at this. I knew you'd be the perfect fit," River says as he looks back and forth between us.

She looks at my brother and I hate that I notice that she doesn't look at him the way a lot of women do; like they'd be ready to fuck him in the blink of an eye. I get that too, but it's been a long time since I've been out without one of my kids in tow and they, particularly Margot, usually serve as a deterrent when it comes to women's blatant attention.

She gives him a polite smile before turning to me. "I brought over some of my stuff as well."

"Oh great. River can help with that." I look at him and nod toward the door. "SJ!" I call, wondering if he's even awake because I haven't seen him since breakfast and he's known to go back to sleep after that.

"I saw him in the pool when I came in. Looking really *grounded*," River snorts.

"You have a pool?" Elianna blinks her wide eyes at me. "And he's out there…without supervision?"

"Oh, all of my kids can swim." She stares at me almost dumbfounded, and again, I hate feeling like the world's worst parent. "Isla knows not to go out there without Margot."

"Margot was out there too," River adds and I wonder if she really was or if he just sensed my embarrassment over not being more present while my ten-year-old is in the pool. *Or even knowing he was out there for that matter.*

"And is this how it's going to be?" I ask her. "You just constantly making me feel like I don't know what I'm doing?"

She furrows her brow but doesn't appear to even be the slightest bit contrite. "No, but more than half of the drownings that occur each year are in home pools, and while yes, they are typically younger than your children, there is a large number of those between the ages of five and nine."

"Good thing my son is ten and on a swim team, I might add." I watch as her warm brown cheeks grow a tinge red.

"As much as I am living for the love fest already, I'll go get your stuff." River holds his hand out. "Keys?" She hands them to him and he's out the door without another word but shoots a look from behind her while he mouths the word, *RELAX.*

I begin to walk away from her, hoping she'll follow when I feel a hand on my arm and a gentle squeeze stopping me in my tracks. "I'm sorry, I wasn't trying to make you feel any type of way," she says once the door closes. "I've just seen accidents with kids and pools and while it's been nothing fatal, I'm just very cautious." I look down at where she's holding me and try to ignore the way her warm palm feels against my skin or the way my pulse skitters a little. When she slides her hand away, I hate the way I notice the absence of her touch.

"It's not you, Elianna. I'm just a little defensive, but I appreciate your apology." And I suppose I shouldn't be considering I hired her because I need help.

She bites her bottom lip and my eyes immediately move to her mouth again. *Fuck, eyes up.* "Are you ever going to call me Ellie? That's what people call me."

I raise an eyebrow at her. "Well, you didn't tell me I could." Even though my daughter called her that when she introduced us, I don't believe in calling people by their nicknames until they express permission.

"Well, you can..." She trails off.

"Noted, but Elianna is a very nice name, it would be a shame not to use it." She averts her eyes even as a smile pulls at her lips.

SJ saunters in from the back door, very clearly having been in the pool and I give him a look. "What part of 'grounded' makes you think you're entitled to a pool day?" I ask him as he pulls some chips out of the pantry. He has a towel wrapped around his shoulders that he pulls over his head like it's a hood.

"You said I had to clean the pool today, you didn't specify that I couldn't clean it while swimming," he says as he opens a bag of Doritos. He lifts his chin at Elianna. "Oh, I can't wait for this. YO, MARGOT!"

"Sawyer," I warn him. "If you don't want to be grounded *through* Halloween, I suggest you not instigate," I threaten, knowing my son loves Halloween and more importantly, all the candy he eats for the weeks following.

"Dad, me and my friends already have a costume planned."

"And you'll be staring at it while it sits in your closet on October thirty-first if you don't behave for the next six weeks."

"Fine," he grumbles as he leans on the counter and continues stuffing his face with chips.

Margot comes walking into the room and her eyes meet mine first before dropping to the woman standing next to me who I just noticed has an amused expression on her face like she found my interaction with my son humorous. I also notice that Margot appears from a different part of the house making me believe that she was definitely not outside with Sawyer like River suggested.

"Hi," she says, and while my daughter isn't shy, she is sometimes a little uneasy around new people, so I'm not surprised when she comes to stand between me and her brother.

"Hi, Margot," Elianna says with a warm smile, and then before anyone can say anything she speaks up again. "Do you think you and I can talk for just a second? Without these two?" She nods her head toward me and SJ and Margot's eyes widen. She shoots me a look and Elianna lets out a laugh. "I'm not going to bite, but I figure you'll give me the most honest interpretation of what actually happens around here."

I watch as Margot visibly relaxes and the tension leaves her shoulders. "Okay, sure." She nods and I note Sawyer giving her a look that I can imagine says, *do not tell her anything.*

"Well, that was boring," Sawyer says as they leave the room.

"You, go see if your uncle needs help bringing her things in." He pouts before moving toward the door. "SJ," I call after him, and when he turns around, I nod toward the pool. "Be careful when you're swimming out there by yourself, yeah?"

"I am!"

"No back flips off the side."

His eyes widen because that's never been a rule. "EVER!?"

"No, just…not when you're alone," I tell him, knowing that one of my son's favorite things to do is to make up tricks to do off the diving board.

"Jeez, the nanny has been here five minutes!" he grumbles as he leaves the room.

CHAPTER FOUR

Elianna

"So, what do you want to know?" Margot asks as she plays with the pillow she placed in her lap. She offered to give me a quick tour of the upstairs and we ended up in her room which is practically spotless. Not at all how I kept my room when I was sixteen which was like a tornado had ripped through it at all times. I get the feeling that Margot may be more mature than the average sixteen-year-old, and I wonder how she got this way.

"Well, first, I want you to know that I realize that you're older and may not need the same level of supervision," I tell her. "I also know that you've been doing a lot to help your dad with your siblings and I want you to know in case he hasn't told you, that it doesn't go unnoticed." She nods and I continue. "I lost my mom when I was fifteen as well, so…I get some of the things you may be going through." I clear my throat in preparation for her protest. "Or maybe I don't, but I'm available to talk about that… if you want."

"I'm sorry to hear that, but I don't need another shrink."

"And I'm not licensed to be one. At least not yet," I tell her as I shake my head. "But in case you wanted to talk to someone who also went through her most important teen years without their mother, I can commiserate."

"Is this the spiel where you tell me you want to be friends?" she asks and it's the first glimpse of that signature sixteen-year-old girl attitude.

"No, I'm too old to be your friend, and I'm going to assume you are in no shortage of them." I narrow my eyes at her. "You strike me as the popular type." Genetics have been good to her. Naturally tan with a dusting of freckles and gorgeous glossy hair with natural highlights that women spend thousands of dollars trying to obtain.

A smile pulls at her lips. "So, what are you then…if not my nanny or my friend."

My eyes meet hers and I can see the guard she has up. I wonder how hard it'll be for her to let me in. "I don't know yet. I'm going to let you decide the kind of relationship you want us to have."

"Me?"

"Sure." I shrug. The biggest pressing concern I think there is with Margot is the boyfriend and the possibility of her sneaking out, but if I'm living here, my presence will fix that on its own. I don't *need* to explicitly tell her I serve as her personal warden.

"Okay…" she says reluctantly, like she's not exactly sure of my angle.

"So, your dad says that you're a cheerleader and have practices every day after school?" She nods. "And until now, you've been coming home after school to relieve your uncle who picks up your siblings?"

"Right."

"So, given that I'm here now and you aren't forced to come straight home, what will you do with that free time?" I ask her.

Her eyebrows pinch together like she's contemplating the answer. "I don't know. I...like spending time with Isla and helping her with her little bit of homework."

"Oh, well...that's lovely. I'm sure she enjoys that time with you."

"She does."

"Are you close with your siblings?"

She nods. "We have to be. We're all we've got."

"Well, you have your dad."

She chuckles. "Sure, but you're here because a lot of the time our dad is not. Yes, we've got him in the general sense but not always for day-to-day stuff. I forge his signature on half of all of our things for school." She clears her throat. "I mean, he knows," she clarifies. "I tell him when I do. It's just easier."

"Probably a lot on you though."

She shrugs. "It's okay." And a part of me wonders if she really thinks that or if she's just trying to make things easier on everyone else.

"Do you know why your brother is acting out?"

She snorts. "No. I told him to stop, and no offense, if I can't get him to, no one can."

"Fair, but you have to have some idea?"

"Isn't the obvious answer that he wants attention from our dad and misses our mom?" She shrugs and her lips form a straight line.

"Of course, I just wasn't sure if there was more to it. Maybe something at school that your dad isn't privy to."

"No, school is where the Kincaid kids thrive." She laughs. "We all excel and have friends. SJ acting out is a new thing but he's still the smartest in his grade. They are practically begging my dad to move him up a year but that would move him to middle school and I honestly think my dad just hasn't been ready to have us at three different schools yet." I detect a hint of resentment in her voice and I wonder if she's among the people begging him to move her brother up.

Our conversation is cut short when Isla comes bounding into the room excitedly and hops on the bed between me and Margot. She's wearing an orange short-sleeved sundress with an orange hat backward and two low bun pigtails sticking out beneath it. I'm surprised not to see sunglasses but I suppose the hat serves as her accessory today. "Hi, Ellie! When did you get here?"

"Not long ago. I was just getting to know Margot a little."

"Do you want to have a tea party?" she asks swinging her feet.

"Well, I'm not staying for much longer today, but how about on Monday when you get home from school?" I ask her, not wanting to blatantly tell her no while also giving her something to look forward to.

"You'll be here?" she asks enthusiastically.

"I will be here." I nod.

"Daddy says you're going to live here now. Does that mean we can have sleepovers?"

Margot chuckles and tugs on one of her buns. "She's not here for play. She's here to help, Isles."

She gives me a little pout and just as I'm about to tell her that *sometimes* we can have sleepovers, their father appears in the doorway.

"Daddy!" Isla hops off the bed and runs straight at him. He scoops her up and presses a kiss to her cheek.

"Hi, Princess. Listen, I have to run to the office to grab a brief, but I should be back in an hour or so."

Isla immediately frowns and begins to kick her feet. "But you said we could get ice cream!"

He sets her down and kneels in front of her. "And we still can..." My heart squeezes in my chest over the fact that he looks just as disappointed as she does.

"Nuh uh, last time you said that, you weren't back to tuck

me in!" Remembering he called her the *happy-go-lucky* child, I'm wondering what exactly constitutes that in his eyes.

"I won't be that late, I promise."

She huffs and puts her hands on her hips. Instantly, I watch him remove them, keeping her hands encased in his. *Okay, so he keeps the sass in check. That's good.* "I have to go, Angel. I'm sorry."

"Can Margot take me?"

He looks up at his eldest daughter and she nods; I'm guessing this is how a lot of these conversations go. "Sure, honey." He stands up and looks at Margot.

"There's a football game tonight, so I'm cheering," Margot explains.

"What time?"

"Eight," Margot says and he sighs.

I'm guessing even he thinks he could be gone a little longer than the hour he promised.

"I can…stay a little longer," I tell them. "Just in case Margot has to go before you're back."

His eyes meet mine and I can see the relief in his eyes from just that one sentence. Like he's not used to things ever being that easy. "Let's talk for a minute before I leave," he says waving me toward the door.

"Do you want to come get ice cream?" Isla grabs my hand and squeezes.

I turn toward her and her sister. "No, I think I better stay here with your brother. Kids that are grounded don't get ice cream," I tell her as I follow their dad out the door. I see he's changed since I got here, making me think that he probably just received a call requiring him to leave. He's not in a suit, but he's definitely in business casual with black slacks and a gray polo.

"I'm sorry. I was not expecting this and I'd ask River to stay but…"

"It's absolutely not a problem. I'll be here in two days anyway," I tell him as we make our way down the stairs and toward his office. The house isn't obscenely large but just big enough that I may get lost the first few times I go exploring.

He closes the door behind me and instantly hands me a key and a folder of his own. "Just codes for things and details about the kids. Isla has a nut allergy and while I think she's growing out of it, she does get a stomach ache or a little itchy and uncomfortable if she comes into contact with it."

"Does she have an EpiPen?"

"She used to but we've never needed it. Her mother was very good about...all of that." I shift nervously in my seat and I wonder if he's confused by my response because he continues speaking. "Margot and SJ are both really good about paying attention as well and even Isla knows certain things to stay away from or to ask if she's not sure. You won't have to—"

"No, that's not it. My last family had a child with a severe nut allergy to the point that I carried one of his EpiPens. I just...you said their mother was good and that Margot and SJ are but you didn't say you are." I blink at him. "And now I'm thinking you're going to be offended that I asked."

He clears his throat. "We've had two instances since she moved in. Both times it was just me and her, so she's not thinking to ask because I'm her dad and why would I not know what I'm feeding her? I wasn't even thinking." He swallows and I can see the guilt all over his face. I feel like shit for bringing it up and making him feel bad for something I know he beats himself up for. "I have antihistamines and she's very good about telling you if something doesn't feel right."

"I see." I nod. "Any other allergies?" I ask while I flip through the papers inside. Most of the information is things like their favorite foods and snacks, information on their after-school activities, bedtimes for SJ and Isla, and how long SJ can be on any kind of gaming console per day.

"No."

"Mr. Kincaid—"

"Rowan," he corrects for the second time.

"I think I'll stick to Mr. Kincaid if you're going to keep calling me Elianna," I tell him with a small smile. Not to mention, I've never called any of the parents by their first names. It kept a line of professionalism I didn't want to cross.

"Fine. You were saying?"

"I think you're doing a great job. I don't know exactly what it's like to be a single parent, but I was raised by one for a while and I know it's tough, and sometimes you feel like you aren't doing anything right. You don't ever have a second to breathe or I don't know…have one hour to do something for yourself. I hope having me here helps you breathe a little easier." I give him a small smile. "Even when you think I'm giving you a hard time."

The smile reaches his eyes and while I'm happy to see him at ease, I wish the sight didn't make my heart flutter. "I appreciate that," he says.

I nod before standing up and then I'm out the door.

Hours later, Margot has left for the football game and their father still hasn't returned from the office much to Isla's annoyance. While the ice cream she got with Margot lessened the burn slightly, I could see the disappointment all over her face when it was time for her to go to bed and her father still wasn't home. He FaceTimed her to say goodnight and apologized, promising they could do something the next day. She was more than thrilled that I was willing to read her two books before she went to sleep.

It's now nearing eight-thirty and Sawyer is sitting in the kitchen while I put the leftovers from dinner in Tupperware dishes. I learned that *none* of the Kincaid children are picky when it comes to food and I was shocked that all three of them loved the four-cheese rigatoni I made. Margot even managed to eat a few bites before she left and threatened SJ not to eat it all before she got home.

For the other kids I took care of, I was used to making an emergency grilled cheese or chicken tenders if one of them wasn't into what I made. I didn't believe in being a short-order cook, but I don't believe in sending kids to bed hungry if they honestly try what I make and genuinely don't like it.

"So, what's your story?" Sawyer asks as he takes a bite of ice cream. While I didn't let him go with the girls to get ice cream earlier, Margot conveniently didn't finish the majority of hers and offered it to her brother. I can't deny that it makes me smile how sweet the three of them are with each other. I've nannied for more than a few families whose kids were at the age where they wouldn't spit on the other if they were on fire, so it's refreshing to see their dynamic.

"What do you mean?" I ask as I wipe the counters down.

"Where are you from? Did you go to college? Siblings? You got a boyfriend?"

I shoot him a look at his invasive last question. "Are you always so nosy?"

"Yes." He nods as he taps his spoon against the ceramic bowl like he's waiting for my answer.

"I'm from Ohio. I moved here for college and I went to the University of Maryland where I studied psychology. I'm in graduate school now to be a child psychologist. I have two younger sisters. One still lives in Ohio with her husband and daughter and my youngest sister is in her first year at Yale," I tell him.

"Yale?" His eyes light up. "So, she's really smart? Does she like it?"

"She does. Why do you ask, are you thinking about going there?"

He shrugs non-committedly. "My dad wants us looking at all the Ivy's."

"Is that what you want?"

"I'm ten. I don't know what I want yet."

"With the intelligence of what...a sixteen-year-old?" He shrugs again and I narrow my eyes at him. "Okay, boy genius."

"You didn't answer my last question."

"Do you think that's your business?" I ask while raising an eyebrow.

"Ummm, yes? Especially if he shows up here to take you out or something. That would be a problem for my uncle who wants to ask you out," he says before taking another bite of ice cream.

I blink at him in surprise. "Did he put you up to this? Because you have no chill."

"No, but I'm sure he'll be curious."

"Well, I am currently unattached," I tell him. "It's hard when I'm nannying anyway. Do *you* have a girlfriend? Or are girls still gross?"

"Not gross. There is a girl...in my class."

"Oh?"

"She's cool," he says while not meeting my gaze and I resist the urge to giggle at his flamed cheeks.

"Is she the reason you're acting out at school? For *her* attention?"

"Don't shrink me," he scoffs.

"Don't avoid the question."

The sound of the garage door opening stops our conversation and just before we hear the door open, Sawyer shakes his head at me as if to say not to say anything in front of his dad.

"This conversation is not over," I say as I point at him and he rolls his eyes dramatically.

"I'm sorry I'm so late," Rowan says as he makes his way through the door carrying a stack of files under his arm that he did not leave with.

"Isla's pissed," SJ says through another bite of ice cream and I frown at him just in time for Rowan to respond.

"Don't say 'pissed.'"

"Well, she is!" He slides the bowl across the counter to me and I look at it and then back at him and then back at the bowl before raising an eyebrow at him. He sighs, reading my look before getting up and grabbing the bowl to rinse it himself.

"She was fine. We read a few books and she went down easily. No tears." I smile at Rowan. "But you probably do need to make it up to her tomorrow."

He nods and makes his way around the island in the center of the massive kitchen to open the refrigerator. "Thank you and thank you for staying." He pulls his eyes away from the Tupperware and looks at me in question. "You cooked?"

"Yeah, and it was great," Sawyer chimes in from the sink before he puts his dish in the dishwasher. "She said she's going to make tacos next week."

Rowan looks at me. "So, you've learned the way to my kids' hearts is through their stomachs then?" He looks impressed.

"I am not that easy," Sawyer says before he heads out of the kitchen. "I'm going to my room. Night, Dad. Night, Elles," he says and I smile at the nickname he's already created for me.

"I'll be up in a bit to say goodnight," Rowan calls after him.

After a few moments, Rowan peeks his head out of the kitchen toward the stairs, presumably to make sure Sawyer isn't within earshot. "How did it go?"

"Oh! So smooth," I tell him. "You have great kids, Mr. Kincaid. I know it's only day one but believe it or not, I've found that the most important dynamic for kids is the one between their siblings. If things are good between them, everything else will fall into place. Margot said that they are all each other has." I study Rowan's reaction, wondering how he'll take that and he doesn't seem to flinch.

"That's good. I'm glad they've had each other. My brother

and I have always been close and I'm glad they have that." He puts the bowl in the microwave.

"Do you have any other siblings?"

"No, just us."

"He's younger?"

"Yeah. He looks it, huh?" He chuckles and I shake my head. *Yes, he does look younger and has fewer gray hairs and may be a bit more in shape due to the differences in their jobs, but Rowan looks distinguished and gorgeous and way more my type. He looks like a man who might moonlight as a model between his long nights at the office.*

"Not necessarily, I can just tell from the one interaction I saw earlier." I smile. "Perks of the job, I guess."

He pulls his food out of the microwave and sits on one of the stools. "Did Margot say when she'd be home?"

"She didn't, but I assume she has a curfew?"

"I mean she usually comes in before twelve," he answers easily and without looking at me like it's the most normal thing in the world for a sixteen-year-old girl not to have a curfew.

I furrow my brows curiously. "But she doesn't have an explicit time to be home?"

"She usually just texts me if she's going to be late, but once it gets to a certain hour, she usually just sleeps wherever she is."

"Do you always know where she is?"

"I have her location and she knows better than to be somewhere late at night that I don't know. I've thoroughly vetted all of her friends' parents," he says with a chuckle.

"Well, that's good, but what if they're out of town?" His fork hovers near his mouth and he looks at me like the thought never crossed his mind.

"Huh, I hadn't thought of that." He rubs his forehead.

"Remember what kids were doing when we were young?" I clear my throat. "Well, when *you* were young. I wasn't even thought of, but you get what I mean."

He gives me a look followed by a fake laugh. "Thanks."

"If your system works, I won't rock the boat for now, but there is going to come a time when she tries to come in the house at a ridiculous hour because, '*I didn't know when my curfew was,*'" I say as I mimic Margot. "Teenagers will take a mile if you give them this much," I add holding my thumb and index finger less than an inch apart.

"Noted."

"Especially if she's given all this free time since I'm here. You didn't worry about that as much I assume because she had to be home to help. All I'm saying is I'm keeping my eye on her." I cross my arms over my chest.

"I appreciate that," he says. "A lot." He clears his throat. "You've been here less than a day and I already feel like things are…easier."

"That's what I'm here for." I smile and watch as his eyes drop to my lips instantly before he drops his gaze to his food.

I let out a breath, trying to ignore the tingly feeling shooting through me from just that look. "I should probably head out."

"Right. Let me walk you out," he says as he gets up from his stool.

"Oh, no, please eat. I'm fine. I don't think any trouble will come from here to my car in this fancy neighborhood." I giggle and he doesn't move to sit back down.

"It's dark," he counters.

"It's barely nine o'clock," I argue back.

"God, you're worse than SJ. Can you not argue with me?" He groans and the gravelly sound of his voice makes my nipples tighten in my shirt.

I have got to get this under control.

I roll my eyes and grab my jacket and my purse off the chair. "Fiiine," I say as I walk toward the door.

I hear him behind me and before I can reach the front door,

I see his hand dart out to open it for me. I wish on top of everything else this man wasn't chivalrous. We walk down the stairs slowly in silence, only the sounds of nature surrounding us when his voice cuts through the air.

"I spoke with some of your references by the way."

"Oh?" I say just as we hit the bottom step.

We are a few steps from my car when he speaks up again. "You got rave reviews. Everyone said that I'm lucky to have you."

CHAPTER FIVE

Eliana

"Why are you up so early?" I hear from the entrance to the kitchen when Margot comes padding into the room. It's early, almost seven in the morning, that Monday and I know she's about to leave for school.

"It's not that early," I tell her.

I notice she's not dressed in a uniform, but a long skirt with a t-shirt tucked into it, and it suddenly dawns on me that, unlike Isla and SJ, Margot doesn't go to private school and I wonder why that is.

"SJ and Isla's school doesn't start until eight-thirty and good luck waking either of them up a second before seven-thirty." She rubs her index finger in a jar of lip balm and glides it over her lips.

"Right, but I knew you would be leaving."

"You're up for...me?" She tilts her head to the side, and at this moment I wonder if she's not used to anyone being concerned about *just* her.

"Sure. You should eat in the morning."

"Oh, I usually stop for a bagel on the way." She shrugs.

I narrow my eyes at her before looking at my imaginary watch and then back at her. "Don't you have to be in first period at seven-ten?"

She shrugs before she slides her denim jacket on and pulls her wavy hair out of the neckline. "Okay, I might leave between first and second period to get breakfast." I blink at her a few times, wondering why she feels so comfortable revealing that information to me. "Oh, I decided we could be friends." She smiles and I shake my head at her because I do not intend to be the kind of friend that will keep *those* kinds of secrets. "Oh, come on, my second period is a joke. My teacher doesn't care if I'm a little late."

I narrow my eyes curiously. "What class is it?"

"AP bio?" she says with an innocent look.

"Margot! That doesn't sound like a joke."

"Whaaat?" she whines. "My teacher doesn't care, as long as I bring him back something!"

"Well, I made you a breakfast sandwich."

"What's in it?"

"Just eggs and cheese on a whole wheat bagel. I know what you like," I tell her, having spent the majority of my first night here studying their files.

"Fine," she says, grabbing the sandwich I wrapped in aluminum foil. "I won't go for breakfast *today*."

"You shouldn't be going at all. What if you're missing information in that first half when you're ditching?"

"My bio teacher is friends with Uncle River. I can assure you, I'm getting an A by default, I'll see you later," she says with a chuckle as she glides out of the room.

"That's not doing you any favors for the AP test!" I call after her.

"When's her AP test?" I hear Mr. Kincaid's voice from around the corner and then I see him completely dressed in a charcoal gray suit, a crisp white shirt, and a powder blue and white striped tie. He moves through the kitchen and past me toward the Keurig and his scent wafts around me. *God, he smells and looks good. Spicy and sexy as fuck.*

"I'm…not sure. I'm guessing May?" I answer. I decide to keep the information about her perpetual absences from the first half of her biology class to myself for now and change the subject. "The notes you gave me didn't give me any idea what you like in the mornings, but I made eggs and bacon. If you don't have time to eat here, I can make you something to take," I say holding up Tupperware.

"Oh, you don't have to make breakfast for me."

"I know…but I'm making it for the kids anyway."

He looks toward the large bowl that has pancake batter. "You're making pancakes?"

I nod. "Breakfast is the most important meal of the day at this age and Sawyer and Isla like pancakes."

"True, but they don't expect it during the week." He takes his travel mug from the coffee maker and pulls it to his lips. "So, SJ goes back today and he has to meet with the counselor after school, so you'll only be picking up Isla at three."

"I saw it in the notes, I remember," I tell him while I flip a pancake. "I was thinking we would go to the grocery store and then swing back after to get Sawyer. Is there anything you want or need me to get?" I say like one run-on sentence. I've been told that I need to take a break or at least a breath between thoughts and I inwardly cringe at the thought that I was talking too fast.

He doesn't respond and I glance up at him to find him studying me. "I rarely meet people that aren't lawyers whose minds work as fast as mine." He chuckles and I turn back to the stove, hoping that he can't see the slight embarrassment on my face. "Whatever you get is fine. Believe me, if you take Isla, she'll have a list all her own before you even make it through the door," he says as he grabs his bag. "Call me if you have any problems. You have my direct number at the office."

"Yes, and your cell and your email and your…fax?" I wrinkle my nose and shake my head. "Not sure what I'd need that for but I appreciate that you have all the bases covered."

"Right, well…"

"Go!" I tell him as I put a hand up and begin to wave him out of the kitchen. "I know what I'm doing. Your kids will all be alive when you get home."

"It's not them I'm worried about," he grumbles before he's out the door.

"So, you're going to take us to school every day now?" Isla asks from the backseat.

We only had one meltdown this morning because she spilled syrup all over her lime green outfit, forcing her to change which meant her clothes no longer matched the sunglasses she wanted to wear. I normally advise children to wait and get dressed until after they eat for this exact reason, but Isla came downstairs fully dressed and I'll admit I was impressed that she's able to get herself ready in the morning with minimal assistance.

"I sure am," I say as I look at her through the rearview mirror. "I'll pick you up too."

"Oh yay! Uncle River sometimes takes us to get a snack after school. Can we do that?" Isla asks.

"What kind of snack?"

"Ice cream or donuts!"

"So just pure sugar then?" I ask, starting to better understand why Isla seems to be in a permanent state of bouncing off the walls. "I think we can do that if sometimes we do something a little healthier too?" I look over my shoulder toward the surly ten-year-old who's been in a mood ever since he came downstairs.

"Are you ready to talk about whatever is bothering you?" I ask him.

"He's grumpy!" Isla adds and Sawyer turns to look at her.

"Santa isn't real." He deadpans.

"SAWYER!" I squeal and he turns to look at me with a grin despite the scowl on my face.

"She knows! I spoiled that for her ON ACCIDENT, last Christmas."

Luckily, we are approaching a light, so I turn to look at Isla whose lip I can see trembling a little and I turn further to glare at Sawyer. *Fix it!* I mouth at him and he rolls his eyes and sighs.

"I'm sorry, Isles." I hear a sniffle and when I look at her, she nods and holds her hand out for him. He takes it and then I see her slip her other hand under her sunglasses and wipe her eyes. I wonder if she's really unpacked how she feels about that yet. We pull up to the school and Isla's already halfway out of the car before I am.

"Wait, Isla!" I call after her.

"Sabrina and Cori!" she says before shutting the door and I see her take off for two girls standing not too far from the drop-off area.

"Those are her best friends. She's fine," Sawyer says as I get out of the car, my eyes trained on the three girls as they start jumping up and down.

"Do you need me to go in with you or anything?"

Sawyer gives me a look as if to say, *are you kidding me?* and shakes his head. "No, and you don't need to take Isla in either. She usually meets up with her friends there or I'll walk in with her."

I nod, my eyes still not leaving the excited trio even as they skip their way toward the stairs. "Santa's not real?" I snap my eyes to his just as they make it inside and I cross my arms over my chest.

"Sorry!"

I narrow my gaze at him. "You're already on thin ice, Sawyer Jack!"

"If you're going to call me that, you might as well call me SJ." He rolls his eyes as he hoists his backpack on his shoulder. "I have to meet with the counselor after school. So, see you at four?" And now I'm wondering if that was the cause for his sour mood.

"I'll be here."

He's gone without another look toward me and I watch as he high-fives a few kids on the way inside.

The day goes by pretty quickly as I spend most of it cleaning and doing the laundry that had been piling up in the laundry room. Even though the house is fairly clean, due to a housekeeper that Mr. Kincaid hires to come in once a week, I took it upon myself to do some deep cleaning. I also spent a good amount of time putting my things away in my room which happens to be directly across the hall from Mr. Kincaid's office.

I'm just finishing vacuuming the hallway when I cast a glance toward his office. The door is open and though it would make sense for me to clean this room like the rest on this floor, part of me is hesitant to go in without him present. I cross the threshold reluctantly, deciding that a quick spin around the room is harmless. His office is mostly dark with a large shiny mahogany desk currently littered with papers, but in that way it almost looks organized. A cognac-colored leather chair sits behind the desk that matches an L-shaped couch in the corner. There's a fireplace in the corner as well and just above it is a television mounted on the wall that sits between two floor-to-ceiling bookshelves with hundreds of books. I walk toward them and drag my eyes over the casebooks, encyclopedias, and assumedly other law books all organized alphabetically and then by size.

There's a door that leads outside to a small terrace with two chairs and a small table where I also spot an ashtray with the remnants of a cigar. Next to it, there's a hammock and I wonder how many nights in the past year he's gone out there just to take a breather. I turn on the vacuum to finish up when something on his desk catches my attention. He doesn't have a ton of pictures on his desk, just four solo pictures of each of the kids, but the one that catches my attention has all of them including their mother.

It must have been when Isla was born because their mom is holding a pink bundle in her arms while Sawyer presses a kiss to Isla's forehead. They are all staring down at her with bright beaming smiles and even though she's not staring at the camera, I can tell how beautiful their mother was. Margot is the spitting image of her. Golden skin and luscious curls that were somewhere between blonde and brown. I know that she and Mr. Kincaid were divorced at the time of her death, but a part of me is now curious about the circumstances around their divorce.

Did he still have feelings for her? Are those feelings even stronger now that she's gone and he's dealing with not only his but his children's grief?

I shake my head and turn away from the picture, refusing to let myself go down this road of questioning when it really should not matter.

It doesn't. I'm just curious. I try to argue with myself while also trying not to cast another glance at the picture that Mr. Kincaid inevitably looks at several times a day.

Before I know it, it's three and I'm back at Isla and Sawyer's school. Isla comes running down the stairs toward me, her clothes slightly disheveled and her pigtails more than slightly lopsided.

"Hi, Ellie!" She twirls in a circle before launching herself toward me, wrapping her arms around me, and giving me a squeeze.

Remembering that she hugged me after only knowing me for a few minutes makes me wonder if she's naturally affectionate or just trying to fill the void of a woman's hugs. I kneel in front of her and tighten her pigtails.

"Hi! How was school?" I ask her while I pull her backpack from her and begin motioning her toward the car.

She's already talking a mile a minute when I hear a woman's voice cut through the conversation. "Excuse me?" I turn my head toward a woman wearing leggings and an oversized crewneck sweatshirt staring at me from over the top of her sunglasses. Her hair is a glossy chestnut brown with bouncy waves falling below her shoulders that can only be a product of a fresh blowout. She pans her gaze downward at Isla. "Isla, sweetheart, do you know this woman?"

"She's my new nanny!" Isla cheers proudly and I give her a smile.

"Hi, yes. I'm Elianna Riley. Today is actually my first day, so you'll be seeing much more of me." I hold my hand out for her to shake and she gives me a smile in return that I am sure is fake before sliding her hand into mine.

"I see. I'm Abigail Covington, head of the parent-teacher administration. I...didn't realize that Rowan was looking for a nanny. We have all been so worried about him." She blinks at me a few times before looking me over, no doubt cataloging everything about me. "You're a little young, no?"

"I...guess I met his age requirement?" I say with a small shrug, trying my best to keep the sarcasm out of my voice, but I hear hints of it.

"You can't be much older than Margaret." She narrows her gaze.

"I think you mean Margot?" I correct.

She paints on another fake smile and tilts her head to the side. "Of course. Well, Elianna it was lovely to meet you and I look forward to getting to know you. Please let me know if you need help with anything."

"Great." I nod. "I'll be sure to let you know." I open the door for Isla to climb into her seat. I typically nanny during the summer and only for families, so I'm not used to the single—or *not-so*-single—mom who sees the new nanny as a threat in her quest for the single dad. My eyes find her again, now standing with a group of other women all staring toward my car. I turn away from them and back toward Isla. "You ready to go?" She gives me a toothy smile and a thumbs up. "Great, now tell me about your day."

CHAPTER SIX

Rowan

It's nearing ten-thirty when I pull into my driveway that night. I was in court for the majority of the day foregoing lunch, so not only am I exhausted, but starving and in a foul mood. The reminder that my nanny is also a built-in chef does manage to lift my spirits slightly when I walk through the door and can smell whatever she cooked. The house is mostly quiet but I do hear the low sounds of the television in the living room making me wonder who is in there.

I swear to God it better not be SJ.

I set my briefcase down and move through the kitchen toward my living room to see Elianna on the couch watching what looks like a true crime documentary. "Hey," I say.

She jumps and presses her hand to her chest as her eyes dart to mine, wide and unblinking before she lets out a deep breath. "Oh my God, hi."

"Sorry, I figured you heard me come in."

"No," she points at the television, "and these always make me a little jumpy." She looks back at what she's watching and then up at me and I notice that her face is completely void of makeup making her look even younger than usual. *And still gorgeous as hell.* She's underneath a blanket so I can't exactly make out what she's wearing, besides a loose t-shirt that hides her curves and I find myself thinking about what's beneath it. I chastise myself for *not the first time today*, for thinking about Elianna that way.

"I like to be in a central place until a parent gets home, just so I don't miss anything. I also find that kids feel a little intimidated in the beginning looking for me in my bedroom…" she rambles.

I shake my head to stop her and also stop myself from ogling her further. "You don't have to explain to me why you're watching television out here instead of in your room. You can do whatever you want, Elianna. Don't let me interrupt you either. I'm just going to heat up whatever you cooked. Smells great by the way."

"Oh, great. I hope you like it. The kids certainly did. I think everyone is asleep, even Margot. She was exhausted when she got home from practice."

"How was SJ's first day with the school shrink? Did he say anything?" I ask her and I watch as she pauses her show and pulls out her phone.

"We, quote, 'spent most of the time talking about my feelings about Mom. How I'm handling it and if I am talking about her and my feelings enough. They understand I am going through a tough time blah blah blah. Nothing I haven't heard before.'" She looks up at me. "End quote."

I can't stop the smile from pulling at my lips from her making detailed notes on SJ's response. "Sounds like my son."

"He seemed okay though. Maybe a little annoyed? But since

it was his first day, I did take him and Isla for donuts after I picked him up and he perked up a bit after that."

"Before dinner?" I respond jokingly, shocked that she doesn't have a strict 'no sweets before dinner' policy.

She winces guiltily. "Well—"

I chuckle, realizing that she did not pick up on my humor, and shake my head at her, to stop her from explaining herself. "Elianna, I'm kidding. I'm sure there have been days when my kids have had a mountain of sugar for dinner."

"I told them it wouldn't be an everyday thing, but everyone had a good day and those should be celebrated sometimes."

I nod, feeling grateful for what feels like the tenth time today that I have some help with Isla and SJ, and head toward the kitchen when I hear her footsteps behind me. "Isla asked about a sleepover this weekend with Sabrina? I told her I would talk to you."

"That's fine with me..." I turn to look at her as I pull what I think was meant to be a plate for me out of the refrigerator. I point at it and she nods with a smile. "Are you okay with having another child here?"

"Oh yes, definitely, but...she wants to go *to* Sabrina's house," she says and I wonder why she suddenly appears nervous. "I just...I wasn't sure if you let her stay over at other children's houses yet?" I pull off the cellophane and put the plate in the microwave.

"Oh, well if it's just to Sabrina's house then yes, they live right down the street and I know her parents well. Her mom was Bianca's best friend." Realizing she may not know who exactly that is, I clarify, "Bianca was their mom."

"Right. Okay, good to know. Does Sawyer have any houses that he's automatically allowed to go to? It's just easier for me if I know these things ahead of time."

"Any of his close friends are fine, but they all typically want to come here because of the pool and the game room in the basement." I pour myself a glass of wine from the bottle I opened a few days ago. "Do you want a glass?"

"No, thanks." She shakes her head.

"Okay, don't feel like you can't. I trust you know your limits and the kids are asleep."

"Well, thank you, but I'm also not a big wine drinker. I much prefer beer or...tequila," she jokes.

"Ah, I remember that age."

"Can you?" she asks with a cheeky grin and I narrow my eyes at her.

"The cracks on my age are not well received, Elianna. I am not that old." I pin her with a scolding glare and I'm grateful that she can sense my humor this time because a giggle escapes her lips.

I hope she doesn't think I'm that old.

"My apologies," she says.

I wish I didn't notice the sound of that breathy laugh or how it sends a surge of blood south and a lustful flash across my mind of her on her knees in front of me. Not only is she beautiful and smart with a hint of fire but she is fucking sweet and it's a dangerous combination that makes my dick hard. I have been on auto-pilot, operating on survival mode since Bianca died, and for the first time in a year, my dick, which had been previously comatose, seems to be coming to life at the thought of my kids' nanny's pouty lips wrapped around it.

I try to keep my eyes off of her mouth, but the smile pulling at her lips drags my gaze to them. I haven't slept with another woman in over a year and suddenly I am hyper-aware of that fact.

No, I told River that she was off-limits. That means she has to be off-limits to me as well.

"Are you alright?" she asks, breaking me from my thoughts. "You're staring and your food is ready." Sure enough, the microwave is beeping and my eyes are still trained on her.

I shake my head and turn away. "Sorry, I'm just thinking about something I meant to do before I left work for the day." I grab the food from the microwave. "I didn't mean to interrupt what you were watching. You're welcome to go back to your show."

She nods before disappearing, leaving me alone to eat like I do most nights. I don't hate it, but part of me wishes she'd taken a seat and talked to me about how the rest of the day went just to fill the silence. It doesn't take long before I'm finished eating and moving back toward the living room to find her engrossed in her show again.

"Dinner was great. Thank you. How'd you learn to cook like...that?" I narrow my eyes at her because, from two dishes alone, I can tell that she didn't learn from only a cookbook. It was the kind of cooking that came more from instinct than words on paper.

"My mom and grandma were *and are* both great cooks. They both kind of taught me and when my mom got sick, she would walk me through a lot of dishes so I could learn how to do it. She could have written them down, but that wasn't how she learned and she used to say cooking was all about feeling. After she died, I still had my grandma who taught me a lot and I'll still call her if I'm stuck." She smiles but then her smile falls slightly. "Sorry, I guess that was kind of the long way to say family." She giggles and I only allow myself a minute to fixate on how she glows when she talks about her family.

"I'm happy to hear the long way. Does your grandma still live in Ohio?"

"She does, strong as a bull. Fairly certain she'll outlive me."

I smile at her joke though I see through her attempt at humor tailing after her comment about her mother's death. "I'm sorry about your mom. I don't think I said that when you first mentioned it in your interview, but I am...sorry."

"Oh." Her eyes widen and she averts her gaze back to the

television. I notice that she blinks her eyes a few times before turning back to me. "It was a long time ago."

"Doesn't make it any less sad or me any less sorry."

I don't stay in the living room for long. I didn't want to encroach on Elianna's private time and I did still have some work to do. So, after changing out of my clothes and checking on the kids, I'm sitting in my office when Elianna walks by on the way to her room.

"Did you...clean in here?" I ask her, having noticed the vacuum lines and the faint smells of Lysol and Windex. She hadn't touched anything on my desk but I did notice the shiny glass of my sliding glass door and the mirror in the corner. Not to mention the shininess of my mahogany coffee table.

"Oh yes, would you prefer I not come in here? The door was open and I was vacuuming..." she winces. "I'm sorry, I should have asked."

"Please don't apologize," I tell her, wishing she'd stop explaining herself for everything. "Thank you." I look down at my desk. "And for not moving anything around on my desk. If there's ever a time I don't want anyone in here, the door will be locked."

"Got it."

"Should I even bother keeping my housekeeper twice a week?" I ask her.

She takes a tentative step inside my office. "Well, it's just, with everyone in school..." She lets out a breath and puts her hands on her hips. "I've never nannied full-time during the school year. It's always been during the summer when the kids are always around so I always had something to keep me busy. I didn't...really have anything to do after I prepared for dinner."

"Don't you have homework? For your class?"

"I already did that," she tells me, and although I shouldn't be surprised based on what I know about her, I am shocked at her ability to balance so many things with ease.

"Are you always so on top of everything? All the time?"

Her lips form a straight line and she nods. "Yeah, kinda." She shrugs, "I've always had to be. Just with my sisters and my dad and…everything. Then when I started taking care of other people's children…it just stuck."

"What do you do to relax? Do you know how to relax?" I chuckle and she crosses her arms over her chest.

"Don't you work like eighty hours a week?" she retorts.

I chuckle at the fact that she doesn't exactly have a filter and says whatever is on her mind.

"Not when I was twenty-five." I snort. "No, when I was twenty-five…" I trail off, trying to remember what I was doing at her age. "Well, I was about to be a father, but Bianca and I had fun before that. Probably too much of it."

"I have fun," she counters. "I go out with my friends sometimes, but it's hard to do that when you're a full-time nanny."

"You can have time off for yourself, Elianna. I don't expect you to be on call twenty-four hours a day seven days a week."

"I know. You've given me two weekends off a month and every Wednesday evening when I have to go to campus. Trust me, that's more than I usually get."

"You can have more than that if you need it. Trust *me*, you're already helping me out a lot."

She shakes her head as if the idea is ridiculous. "It's my job."

"I know," I tell her. "I can still appreciate it."

She chuckles and rolls her eyes. "You really are a first-timer with the whole nanny thing. Talk to me the next time you hire one. I bet you'll be much tougher."

"Next time? Planning your exit already?" I ask, my eyes wide and a bit terrified that she's already thinking of leaving.

"No!" She shakes her head. "I just mean…" she starts and then bites her lip.

"I hope you know you can't leave until Isla is eighteen," I say with a hint of humor though part of me hopes she'll just agree to that and we can end this whole conversation.

"Eighteen!" she says. "You will not need me until she's eighteen. Isla is..." She hesitates and I see something fleeting pass over her eyes, but I don't know her well enough to know what that's about. "She's going to be fine." She clears her throat. "I meant, you know, you might meet someone. I will always be willing to help out, but I may not need to live here full-time, you know? Also, that's twelve years from now and I'd like to think maybe I'd be married or something by then and maybe I would have kids of my own and not still be doing this?" She shrugs. "Who knows?"

"That's fair," I tell her. In twelve years she'll be thirty-seven and the expectation that she'd devote the next decade of her life to my children might be unreasonable. "Not about me meeting someone necessarily, but the other things you mentioned."

"You could meet someone if you got out more. I hope you'll take advantage of having me here and maybe go out some. With your brother or maybe friends? A lady friend?" She raises her eyebrows up and down and I can't help but laugh at her animation.

"You sound like River. I don't have time for that." I've dated some in the past year but nothing past a first date and no one-night stands. I'm not unfamiliar with the concept, but the way River goes through them, it seems like they've just gotten more complicated since I've gotten older.

"Make time." Her brows pinch together like she's preparing to scold me. "Come on, you're getting on me about relaxing."

I steeple my hands beneath my chin. "Which by the way, you still have not told me what relaxing activities you do."

She huffs. "I like to read, and I go for runs sometimes, and I get massages. I also like to shop." She lists them off on her fingers.

"Oh, Margot will love that." I groan thinking about the last time I let Margot loose in a mall with my credit card without giving her a budget. I had four missed calls from American Express in the span of one hearing.

"Yes, I assume that is how we'll really bond." She smiles, though from what I heard this morning, it seems as if they've already sort of bonded and I can't believe it only took my kids two days to accept her. I didn't expect anything less from Isla, and SJ is always fifty-fifty on whether he'll like someone, but Margot is usually wary about new people. "What do you do to relax?"

"Have twenty minutes of peace and quiet," I tell her. "Sleep when I have time." She looks at me horrified and I chuckle. "I do like to read. Thrillers mostly." I point to the patio on the other side of the glass door. "I go out there and have a cigar every once in a while, and just…take a breather, I guess."

"What did you do before you had them full-time?" she asks me.

"I'd golf with River. Sometimes we'd go fishing. And yes, we would go out sometimes, but then I made partner and started working more, and then Bianca died and…I had so little free time that whatever time I did have, I spent with them. And even still it's not nearly enough."

"I get that," she whispers. "My dad didn't do much outside of raising us either."

"He's still in Ohio?"

"Yes," she answers. "I really worry about him. He lives by himself and I just…I wish he'd dated more when I was younger. Now, he's older and he rarely goes out and I just feel like he's lonely with all of us out of the house. He devoted so much of his life to us and now…" She trails off. "I feel like he gave us the best years of his life and now he's older and too tired to do anything else." She snaps her eyes to me and her eyes widen like maybe she hadn't meant to say all of that.

"I'll bet he doesn't feel like that at all. I'll bet he thinks it was the best years of his life *because* he had you three."

Her eyes soften and I watch as her eyebrows pinch slightly

before she continues. "My sister, Emily, checks in on him a lot. I'm glad she's still there."

"Elianna and Emily…" I ask her, thinking about my parents who had a plan to give all of their children R names before a complicated second pregnancy made it so only two was an option. "Any chance there's a third E name?"

"Eden. My youngest sister."

"She's in college…at Yale, right?"

She purses her lips and tilts her head to the side. "So, Sawyer's nosy line of questioning was really for you?"

"No, but SJ is chatty and wants to know everything. Mostly for leverage." I lean back in my chair, my work completely forgotten as I talk to her. I haven't felt this relaxed in ages and I don't know if it's from having another adult around or if it's *her*. "He mentioned that if you ever went to visit her, maybe we could go with you to look around."

"So, he *is* interested. He said you want him looking at all the Ivy League schools."

"I do, but mostly I want him to be happy. I don't want to force him into anything like my parents did to me." She frowns at my choice of words and though I don't have the energy to go down this road, I opt to give her the cliff notes. "My dad is a lawyer; I was the oldest son…" I wave my hand. "You know the story."

"Yeah, I'm familiar." She nods. "River didn't want to do the same?"

"Hell no, and River wasn't expected to do anything except be the baby." I snort. "I love him to death but he didn't have half the pressure."

"Does that bother you?"

"It used to, but no." I shake my head. "And to be honest, if River was a lawyer too, I'd truly be fucked. The flexibility of his schedule has saved my life." I chuckle before continuing. "And even when it did bother me, I never blamed him for the differences in what was expected of us. He's been my built-in best friend since he was born."

She puts a hand over her heart. "That's so sweet!"

"Don't tell him that though. He's still a pain in my ass."

"I imagine."

"Are you close with your sisters?"

She rubs her forehead before she takes a seat in the chair in front of my desk. "It's complicated." I don't say anything while I wait for her to continue. "My younger sister Emily…" She twists her mouth. "She thinks I try to be her mom." She swallows. "And maybe I did. Obviously not now, but when she was sixteen and pregnant and I dropped out of college to help her, I probably did." She shrugs. "But she was scared and we didn't have a mom and I only knew one way to take care of Emily and Eden and it probably was too motherly. Maybe a part of me resented her because I thought they were going to be fine when I left and then as soon as I did everything fell apart. I figured she'd do for Eden what I'd done for them both and I was disappointed that she didn't." She leans back in her chair and looks up at me. "I probably pushed too hard and now our relationship is…fine, but it's not what it could be." She fidgets with her fingers in her lap and gives me a shy smile. "We're getting deep here."

"I don't hate it."

Her big brown eyes meet mine before she looks toward my computer and then the papers all over my desk.

"I should leave you. I know you're busy and I didn't mean to interrupt." She gets up from the chair.

"You didn't," I tell her, wishing that she didn't feel the sudden urge to leave. I want to learn more about her and something tells me she doesn't talk about her relationship with her sister much. "I'm here if you ever want to talk more…about that."

She hesitates before nodding and leaving my office.

CHAPTER SEVEN

Elianna

Before I know it, it's been three weeks since I started working for the Kincaids. There haven't been any serious meltdowns or tantrums and I was hoping that this wasn't the calm before the storm. The time when a nanny first starts and children behave like angels before they turn into hellions. I had high hopes it wouldn't be like that, but I was prepared for anything. I haven't really talked to *Mr. Kincaid* since that night in his office. He's been coming home even later each night since and holes up in his office until after I'm asleep, I imagine. I can see the fatigue all over his face each morning when he leaves for work.

If I'm even awake by the time he leaves.

Margot has already left for school when Mr. Kincaid pads through the kitchen, very clearly not dressed for work. He looks as if he's just woken up, his hair slightly disheveled, his clothes wrinkled from sleep and it's the first time I've seen him like this.

Still so strikingly handsome even first thing in the morning.

He yawns, mumbling a quiet *good morning*, before making his way to the coffee maker. I try my best not to pay attention to how the sweatpants cling to him or the t-shirt that shows off his toned arms. It's loose across his torso, so I can't make out a ton of definition but I do see a hint of a happy trail when his shirt rides up slightly. I avert my gaze not wanting to think about the hair there or what lies just beneath it.

"Long night?" I ask as I start cutting up some fruit for Isla and SJ's lunches.

"I think I slept an hour," he says while pulling a mug out from the cabinet.

I frown, seeing the exhaustion all over his face and thinking about how he has another long day ahead of him. "Oh, can I make you some breakfast?"

"No, I—" he starts before he leans against the counter. "Actually yeah, whatever you're making the kids is fine."

"I was just doing eggs and fruit today, but I can make you an omelet if you like. You just have to tell me what you like in it. When are you leaving, so I can make sure it's ready?"

"I'm working from home today," he tells me and the slight tremor that moves through me in response tells me I'm very aware of the fact that it means we'll be alone here all day.

So? You've been in the house alone with dads before.

When, exactly?

"Oh. That's good. You've been working really hard and...you look tired."

"Thanks," he replies sardonically before he takes a sip of his coffee.

"I mean you look good—" I freeze, realizing what I said. "I'm just glad you're taking a day for yourself to rest," I correct.

"I wouldn't call it a day for myself," he says, "I'll still be working. But...I think I'll take the kids to school. I feel like I've barely seen them all week." He takes another sip, but his eyes stay trained on mine over the mug.

"They'll love that," I tell him as I zip up Isla's lunchbox. Right on cue, she comes running into the kitchen still in her pajamas. "Ellie, Ellie!" She hops up on one of the bar stools. "Hi, Daddy!" she adds with a wave before turning back to me. "Can you French braid?"

"I sure can." I nod. "Do you want me to do them for you?"

"Yes, pleeease!" she says with her hands steepled under her chin before putting a hand on each side of her head. "Two."

"Okay," I tell her as I begin scrambling her eggs.

"Isles, how do you feel about Daddy taking you to school today?" Mr. Kincaid asks her.

Isla looks at her Dad before turning to me, confused. "You're not taking us?" I know it's only been three weeks, but children thrive under structure and a schedule so I'm not surprised that she's confused when she expects me to take her and pick her up every day. "Are you leaving?"

"No no, of course not!" I shake my head as I plate her eggs along with her fruit and a piece of toast. "Your Daddy just wants to take you today."

"Okay." She shrugs before plucking a blueberry off of her plate. "Are you going to pick us up from school too?"

I glance at Mr. Kincaid to allow him to answer that question. "Either me or Elianna."

"Okay...but please don't be late. I don't like being the last kid there." She gives him her best side-eye and I resist the urge to laugh at her attempt to lecture her father.

"That happened one time, Isla, and you weren't the last kid there. Sawyer was with you."

"Two times," she says holding up two fingers.

He nods at her before he presses a kiss to the top of her head. "I won't be late, Isla," he tells her before he leaves the room, and I admit, I stare after him a little too long. I'm grateful it's just Isla in the room who doesn't notice.

I have to stop, I chastise myself. *I do not have a crush on Mr. Kincaid.*

Well, that's been shot to hell now.

I look up from where I'm chopping an onion for the lasagna soup I'm making for dinner when I hear the basement door open and out of the corner of my eye, I see Mr. Kincaid walking up the stairs from the basement, shirtless and dripping sweat. I only catch a quick glimpse but it's enough to see his chest and toned back glistening before he makes it to his bedroom. I set the knife down on the cutting board so I don't accidentally sever a finger while I'm in the trance brought on by seeing the v-cut of my gorgeous employer.

Employer, Ellie. Absolutely not.

I wipe my hands and pull out my phone immediately.

> **Me: SOS**

> **Jacqueline: Present!**

> **Me: I think I have a crush.**

> **Jacqueline: Oh! who who who??**

> **Me: Who do you think?! Rowan, obviously!**

> **Jacqueline: I KNEW IT! OMG what happened**

Me: Nothing! And nothing is going to happen

Jacqueline: Why not!? Fuck Hot Daddy Rowan ASAP and tell me everything!

Me: Can you not?

Jacqueline: I've been your best friend for almost six years. You knew this was what you were getting when you texted me. Be serious. Now, when are you getting waxed?

Me: Not helping!

Jacqueline: Okay, I can make the appointment for you? Does that help?

Me: BYE

Jacqueline: Okay but before you go, can I ask why nothing can happen?

Me: Because it'll make things very messy and so many things could go wrong.

Jacqueline: Maybe. But how about you don't focus on that? You always overthink everything. What if you just did what you wanted to do and didn't obsess over what could possibly happen next?

> **Me:** Because this is bigger than just me!

> **Jacqueline:** Look, you've put everyone first your entire life. You never do anything just for you.

> **Me:** It's called being considerate of other people and their feelings.

> **Jacqueline:** What about your feelings? More specifically the warm and tingly ones you get when you look at Hot Daddy Rowan?

> **Me:** Can you stop calling him that?!

> **Jacqueline:** Why? It's foreshadowing of what you'll be calling him in a few weeks.

"What are you making?" I'm typing out my reply when his words cut through the silence and my head snaps up to look at him. He's still sweaty from his workout but he's at least put on a shirt and I find myself simultaneously grateful and disappointed for that. He walks by me to the refrigerator and I try not to breathe when he passes me but I still get a whiff of that masculine sweaty scent.

"Ummm..." I pause, having momentarily forgotten what I'm making while I was trying not to ogle him. "Lasagna soup."

"Sounds good." He takes a long sip of water. "I have a call that got moved to two-thirty now, so I will need you to pick up SJ and Isla...if you can." He adds as an afterthought, like it would be an inconvenience for me to do my literal job.

"Yes, of course." Neither one of us says anything for a second, and I feel the heat starting to creep up my neck toward my cheeks. "Was there something else?" I ask.

"No...ummm..." He looks off to the side like he's searching for something to say. "Isla really loved her hair. She talked about it the whole way to school. Thank you for...doing that. I'm terrible at it and Margot is usually gone by the time Isla wakes up." He trails off. "Her mom was always the one to do it and I know that's just one of the many things she misses. I'm glad that this is maybe one less thing she doesn't have to miss." He smiles before giving me a curt nod and then he's out of the kitchen and heading back toward his room.

I am so screwed.

I don't see him for the rest of the day—*something I'm slightly disappointed about*—and I still hear him on his call when I'm preparing to go pick them up from school so I send him a text.

> Me: Leaving now to go pick up Sawyer and Isla! Is there anything you need me to do on the way home?

I'm barely out of the front door before he responds.

> Mr. Kincaid: No, thanks. See you in a bit.

I'm at the school ten minutes before school lets out just like always. Hearing Isla tell her dad not to be late sent a feeling of disappointing nostalgia through me. It wasn't often, but I remember being one of the last kids left at school before my younger sister, Emily, started. On both occasions, my parents thought the other was picking me up and I was left at school thirty minutes after the next to last kid was picked up. I remember feeling embarrassed and also like a burden to the teachers who had to wait with me.

The worst.

I rarely have had to pick kids up from school but I always vowed to make sure I was on time or early if I ever did.

I'm reading a book on my phone while I wait when I notice a woman walking toward my car. It's not the same woman that introduced herself last week...*Abigail something?* But she is one who was in that group of women who were undoubtedly sizing me up. I roll my window down as she approaches and give her a smile. "Hi."

"Oh, I wasn't expecting you today since Rowan dropped them off." She blinks her shimmering blue eyes at me which probably have most men in a daze.

Do they have a tracker on this man or something?

"Oh, well. I'm here." I giggle nervously, trying my best to keep the conversation lighthearted.

She tucks a dark strand behind her ear. "We just didn't get a chance to finish talking and...I wanted him to have this." She hands me a neatly folded piece of paper. "This is...kind of embarrassing, having you be the middleman and all. It's like high school all over again." She shoots me a dazzling smile revealing perfectly straight teeth and I can't quite tell if it's genuine.

I look down at the paper in my hand and try to ignore the tiny pang of annoyance shooting through me. "I'll make sure he gets it."

"This might be totally inappropriate but...woman to woman... you've been there a couple of weeks now, and I'm just curious, do you know if he's seeing anyone?"

"Oh...uhh I have no idea." *And even if I did, I certainly wouldn't tell you so it could be the topic of gossip amongst all of the mothers in the parent-teacher administration.*

"I see. Well, if you could just give him that and tell him Corinne says hi." She raises a hand to wave and when I turn in the direction she's looking, I notice the kids have started to file out of the building. "Thanks again, sweetie," she says before she walks toward a little girl who is walking toward us. I try not to let her words feel like a condescending dig but irritation flares through me.

I get out of the car when I see Isla walking toward the car and

I'm impressed that her braids are still intact. "They didn't fall out!" she says and I nod, grateful that her hair is thicker and also that I'd used a little bit of hairspray. "It looks so pretty!" She holds up her hand and I give her a high-five.

"Sure does!" I tell her as I help her into the car.

"I thought Dad was picking us up?" I hear Sawyer's voice from behind me and then he's moving around to the other side of the car. I follow behind him after making sure Isla is buckled in and climb into the driver's seat.

"He had a call, but you'll see him at home."

"Do you know if he's in a good mood?" he asks.

I look at him through the rearview mirror and narrow my eyes at him warily. "Why..."

He turns his head to look out the window, avoiding my gaze. "Well...I may have gotten into a liiittle...back and forth."

"Sawyer..." I warn.

"It was nothing!"

"It sounds like *something* if you have to gauge your father's mood before you tell him whatever it is."

He rolls his eyes. "I'm not suspended again!"

"Well, thank...goodness?" I tell him as I slowly move through the pick-up line.

Isla looks over at him. "Don't make Daddy mad!"

"I'm not! I didn't do anything," he snaps.

"Do you want to do a trial run on me?" I ask him and he shakes his head.

"Nope. I'll take my chances."

We make our way out of the parking lot and I find myself interested in whatever it is that he did that he doesn't want to tell me. Sawyer is quiet most of the way home while Isla, as usual, is talking a mile a minute, filling us in on all of the latest first-grade gossip. When we make it home, Isla immediately takes off for Mr. Kincaid's office and Sawyer moves upstairs without another word or even a glance my way. I thought Sawyer and I were in a good place, and I'll admit I'm a little disappointed that he felt he couldn't share whatever it is that got him in trouble.

I make my way down the hallway toward my room to put away my bag and grab my slippers when I hear Isla talking to her dad. I look in his office and I see her sitting in his lap scribbling on a piece of paper while she tells him about her day. Mr. Kincaid, who seems to be listening intently, looks up at me with a smile briefly before it falls.

"Wait, what did you say?" He grabs the pen from Isla's hand and turns her little face toward him.

"Sawyer's not suspended," she says and I realize Isla really did give him the rundown of everything that happened today.

"Why would he be—" He looks at Isla, knowing she probably doesn't have the full scope of the story, and turns to me. "Do you know anything about this?"

"It's true, he did say he's not suspended, but I don't know what happened." I wince.

"Christ." He groans before getting up and putting Isla on her feet. "SAWYER KINKAID, MY OFFICE NOW!" he yells.

"Oooh." Isla giggles before holding a hand over her mouth.

"Go with Elianna," he says as he ushers Isla out of his office while pointing at me and I see Sawyer coming down the hall.

His annoyed eyes dart between me and Isla. "I've been home for five whole minutes." He deadpans while looking at me.

"I told him you weren't suspended!" Isla says proudly, like she thought she was helping.

He sighs before shaking his head. "I will remember this when you start screwing up."

"Sawyer..." I say in a scolding tone and he rolls his eyes before walking into his dad's office.

CHAPTER EIGHT

Rowan

"Start talking," I tell him before he's barely across the threshold to my office. It's been less than a month since I got a call from their school regarding Sawyer's behavior and I knew I shouldn't have gotten so comfortable. "Dad, it's not a big deal." He sits in the chair in front of my desk.

I cross my arms over my chest. "Oh? Then why are you *'not suspended?'*"

He looks at me innocently. "Well, I *sorta* got into a fight with a guy at school."

I feel the anger rising but until I get the full story, I find myself wanting to know who the hell put their hands on my son. "A fight!? Sawyer…"

"Not physical, relax. I did push him though."

I feel the anger leaving my body only to be replaced by annoyance. "I will certainly not relax. What happened?"

"He was…talking about Ellie, alright?"

My eyes widen, because of all the things he could have said, I was not expecting him to say that. "Elianna?"

He holds his hands out. "Do we know another Ellie?" he asks, giving me a look that says *duh*.

"You are about one smart comment away from being grounded."

"He was talking about my 'hot nanny.' I guess he overheard his dad talking about her."

Irritation spikes in my veins thinking about some ten-year-old repeating whatever vile comments he may have heard his father say, and I remember that Ellie said she didn't know what happened. "And you didn't tell Ellie?"

He shrugs. "I didn't know what to say."

Fair. I imagine it would probably be an awkward conversation for anyone to have with her let alone a ten-year-old. "What did this kid say?"

"Just that she's hot and that his dad wishes he'd thought of hiring her first." *Asshole.*

I run a hand over my jaw and eye him pensively. "How much trouble are you in?"

"I have detention for two days next week."

"Did you tell your teacher why you were fighting?"

He nods. "I did. The other guy got five days. As much as I don't like snitching, he was being an ass."

I groan. "Don't say ass."

"Well, he was!"

I scratch my forehead, not wanting to condone him getting in an altercation but proud of him for not letting anyone talk any shit. "Alright. Get out of here," I tell him and he jumps up.

"Sweet, I'm not in trouble?"

"No. You let me know if that kid says anything else." I haven't completely ruled out going straight to that kid's father myself.

"You got it, boss." He salutes before he's out of the door without another word, probably thinking I might change my mind about him being in trouble if he lingers too long.

"And keep your hands to yourself!" I call after him.

A few moments later, Elianna appears in the doorway with a frown. "He was fighting?"

"He just pushed a kid…"

"*Just?*" I can tell she wants to ask more questions but she looks down at the small piece of paper in her hands. "Before I forget, I was supposed to give you this." She walks into my office. "And to tell you that Corinne says hi." She nods, holding it out for me to take.

"Who?" I ask as I take the piece of paper and Elianna tilts her head to the side.

"Really?" she snorts. "Shoulder-length dark hair, blue eyes, really pretty. She's a mom at the school. She said she talked to you this morning."

Memories of more than a few moms surrounding me at my car while I was trying to say goodbye to Isla come flooding back and I internally grimace. "Right, thanks."

"She seemed nice. Maybe you could ask her out? Remember the whole trying to get out more thing?" She points at the piece of paper in my hands. "I did peek. It's her phone number. She wants you to call her."

I open the paper and sure enough, I see the ten numbers printed neatly underneath her name. "I never said I wanted to get out more. Besides, I don't think so."

"How come?"

"Because I'm not interested?" I look up at her before tossing the piece of paper to the side. "And why did you peek anyway?" Maybe it's wishful thinking but I wonder if she is feeling a little jealous.

A hint of pink coats her cheeks. "Curiosity? You seem to be very popular with the moms at Rosewood. She's not the first to mention you," she says with a wink.

"I'm sorry if they're bothering you."

She waves me off. "No, it's fine."

"I'm not interested in any of the moms at their school," I tell her, and I hope she believes that but I try not to fixate on why that is.

"Okay, well, I did my job," she says and it seems like she's about to leave when she stops. "Wait, what happened with Sawyer?"

I rub a hand behind my neck and let out a disgruntled sigh. "Shut the door."

She does as I ask, but her eyes look nervous. "Is everything okay?"

"Maybe? It seems that Sawyer heard some kid talking about his…nanny."

Her hand freezes while she's tucking a curl behind her ear and I can see the embarrassment all over her face. "Me?"

"Mmmhmm. I'm not even mad at how he handled it. If I'd heard some man talking about you, I would have probably done worse."

"Oh." She swallows and I wonder if I've made her nervous. She crosses her arms over her chest. "What did he say?"

"I believe the word *hot* was used?"

A hand covers her mouth. "Oh my gosh. I am so sor–"

I stare at her dumbfounded. "You can't be serious. You're not actually going to apologize, are you?"

She fidgets with her hands and avoids my gaze. "I just…don't know what else to say. He got in trouble over it and…do you want me to talk to Sawyer?"

"No…he's fine. Everything's okay. Do not apologize either." Her eyes meet mine, sparkling and gorgeous and the words are out of my mouth before I can stop them. "Can't say I blame that kid to be honest."

Later that night, I'm sitting on my patio having a cigar when the sound of the glass door opening gets my attention. SJ and Isla are asleep and it's a Friday night, so Margot probably won't be coming in a minute before her newly set midnight curfew. As I expected, she is enjoying having more freedom and not having to come home right after school. I check her location again and see her icon hovering over the movie theatre where she told me she'd be tonight. She's never blatantly lied about her whereabouts before but I also know it only takes one instance of mischief for something to happen or for it to become a habit. So, when I turn my head toward the source of the noise, I'm not surprised to see Elianna poking her head through the opening. "Hey, I don't mean to bother you, but I just want to make sure you aren't planning to eat anything else before I put the food away."

"No, I'm good and you're not bothering me." I've noticed that this is the second time she's said something along these lines and it makes me wonder about the people that she's nannied for who may have made her feel like she was a burden. "I wish you'd stop thinking you were," I add as an afterthought, probably brought on by the glass of scotch I'm nursing.

She shifts her feet and I briefly wonder if my comment has made her uncomfortable. "Well, you say you come out here to have twenty minutes of peace and quiet, if I recall," she says as she leans against the door jam.

I lean forward in the chair, resting my arms on my thighs while I fidget with the glass in my hand. "Right."

She doesn't say anything for a few moments but I can feel her gaze on the side of my face. "Are you okay?"

I don't respond at first because I don't want to unleash this on her. I don't want to talk about what today was or what it meant that I felt this strange wave of sadness that I still don't understand. "I didn't think I would struggle with the grief this much," I tell her when I realize she probably won't believe me if I tell her I'm fine. She takes a slow step outside, sliding the glass door behind her, and sitting in the chair next to me. "We were divorced, you know? I guess I'm surprised that her absence and the grief that follows still have the power to catch me so off guard." I take another sip, wishing the burn would erase the one caused by my words.

"Grief is one of those things that really can't be explained. There's no real reason as to why it sneaks up on you and I don't think you're ever really *through* it."

"I mean I guess I shouldn't be surprised why it did today. It was our wedding anniversary," I tell her. "Fourteen years and three kids and now she's just...gone." I sigh, feeling the weight of my words pressing down on me. "I guess a part of me feels guilty. We were married and then we got divorced and she met this other guy. He was pretty decent. He was crazy about my kids. He loved her better than I did, and...she barely had any time with him." I feel the emotion in my throat.

"Life sometimes can just be really unfair," she says softly with understanding eyes.

"It's different but I feel similarly about Isla. She barely had any time with her mom and now she has to live the rest of her life without her." Memories of having to explain death to my very confused five-year-old flashes through my mind and my stomach turns.

The faint sounds of the trees rustling are the only sounds to be heard before Elianna cuts through the silence. "I can't speak for your kids but I will say that my youngest sister, Eden, was a little younger than Isla when our mom died, and...it was not easier...by any means, but *different* than it was for me and Emily. Eden misses the idea of having a mom because her memories aren't as clear and the ones she does have are when my mom was at her sickest. Her memories have faded so much over the years that she'll tell you that sometimes she forgets the sound of her voice whereas Emily and I can still hear it clearly. I used to be jealous of her when we were younger. I thought that if some of my memories would just fade, it wouldn't hurt as much. Of course, Eden wishes she had more memories. It just sucks all around for everyone involved because everyone has their own journey with grief. Their own pain." She gives me a forlorn smile. "Even you. Even though you weren't married or the love had faded. You're probably mourning your marriage all over again through a different lens. Like you're mourning the love of a *past* life."

I look over at her, but she's not looking at me. Instead, she's looking out at my backyard. "You said your mom was sick?"

"Yeah, she had cancer. It was…tough." She shivers and I realize she's only wearing a thin long-sleeved shirt and sweatpants. It's slowly inching below fifty degrees but I'm wondering if it's her memories causing the sudden tremor and not the weather. She doesn't say anything more and I take that to mean she won't be elaborating.

"I'm so sorry." I rest a hand over hers and give it a brief squeeze. "Their mom died in a car accident." I swallow. "It was raining and she was on her way to pick up SJ from school. Isla wasn't in school yet, but she wasn't with her. She was with Bianca's mother." I hear the sharp intake next to me and I can already hear her thoughts because it's the same most people have. *SJ blames himself for what happened.* I lean back in my chair. "He doesn't know." I rub the back of my neck. "I mean he's a smart kid, so he might know that the reason she'd be in the car at that time is because she was going to pick him up, but I've never explicitly said it. My brother went to pick him up and he never thought anything of it. He just assumed it was the plan all along and River was just a little late." My eyes shut as the memories of that day come flooding back. "I've never driven that fast in my life. I didn't even have enough sense at the moment to realize that if I had gotten in an accident, they could have potentially lost both of their parents in one day."

"I'm really sorry, Rowan," she says. "For you and them."

"Thanks." I down the rest of my drink and reach next to me

to grab the bottle of scotch. "I assume you won't join me," I say to her as I pour myself another drink.

She bites her bottom lip and looks behind her toward the door and I wonder if she's going to agree. "Maybe later? I just... Margot isn't home yet and in case for whatever reason someone needs to go get her, I'd rather be safe. But I'll sit here with you."

I chuckle darkly. "The fact that you even thought of that and I didn't...I hate feeling like a shitty dad. Like the person who was better at parenting died."

"No. That's...you're not a shitty dad, Rowan. And if this is the road you're trying to go down tonight, I'm taking that from you," she says looking at the glass in my hand.

"This is only my second drink. I'm not drunk. Far from it. I feel this way while I'm sober, trust me."

"And alcohol can aggravate those feelings." She gives me a hard look. "Do I need to take that?" She points at my glass.

"No."

"Now, say you're a good dad."

"Elianna, I'm fine."

"Say it, or I'm taking it."

I side-eye her briefly before looking down at my drink. "I'm a good dad."

"Say it again."

I grit my teeth. "You're being ridiculous."

"Well, that makes two of us then."

I snap my eyes to hers and she's giving me a look that's almost scolding.

"I'm a good dad."

"They are lucky to have you, Rowan. They are crazy about you. Any annoyance you may feel from them is normal child growing pains. They miss their mom, of course, but they would be just as distraught had it been you in that car."

I rarely talk about Bianca and my feelings surrounding her death to anyone but my therapist and I haven't talked to her in months. Every once in a while, I'll talk to River but I've never even gotten this deep with him so I'm shocked that I've unloaded all of this on Elianna. "Thank you for listening by the way."

She nods. "Is this why you worked from home today?"

"Maybe? I actually didn't realize it until I was on my first call of the day, but maybe subconsciously I knew it was today and my mind just made me believe I needed the day due to exhaustion."

"I'm glad you stayed home. You should take more days."

"I wish it were that easy." My phone lights up on the table in front of us. I lean forward and I see a text from Margot telling me she's on her way home. "Margot's on her way." Elianna nods but she doesn't say anything. She just tucks her feet under her and continues to stare out into the night. "Do they tell you that?" I ask her and she turns her head to me, tilting it to the side in question. "The kids...do they tell you that they wish I was home more?"

"They haven't specifically said that, no, but I know they wouldn't hate spending more time with you." She gives me a soft smile and leans forward again. "They're going to be okay, Rowan. You will all be okay."

"This is just not how I saw this going, you know. Even after we divorced...I still always saw her in the picture. Their graduations and I don't know sitting next to her when they got married. She was a really good mom."

"Life rarely goes the way we think it will."

"How did you think yours would go? You're still so young. You can still take your life any way you want to go."

She chuckles. "I think my life is kind of set now too. I feel as if I'm so conditioned to take care of everyone else and their needs that I don't even know what it is *I* want. Something that's just for me. I'm here for school but I'll probably go back to Ohio when I graduate."

"Is that what you want?"

"I don't know. I like Maryland but being away from my dad can be tough."

"Are you guys close?"

"Yeah." She winces. "Probably another sore subject with my younger sister because she says I'm the favorite." She rolls her eyes. "Which is such BS by the way. Eden is the favorite. I was just…the only one who could help and it took a lot off of my dad. So our bond is different. He trusts me with everything. A lot of things are in my name. I'm his power of attorney…" She waves her hand as if to say et cetera. "Normal oldest sibling things plus some. You get it, I'm sure."

I knew the pressures of being an older sibling well. "Of course."

"Not to mention, my dad was pretty pissed when she got pregnant."

The fact that her sister was the same age Margot is now, sends a wave of anxiety through me and it worries me that I don't know for sure if her and Gabe are doing…well *that*. "I'm shocked he didn't kill whoever the dad is." I chuckle, thinking about what I'd do in that situation and I'm pretty sure it involves having to pull some strings to avoid jail time.

"Oh, believe me, the only reason he didn't when he found out was because the father wasn't eighteen yet and he didn't want to go to jail for endangering a minor. By the time he turned eighteen, my niece was two and my father was in love with being a grandfather. My sister married him and they're happy, but sometimes I think my father is just waiting for him to step a toe out of line, so he can beat the hell out of him for it all."

Sometime later, we're still sitting outside in relative silence when Margot slides the glass door open. "Hi?" Her eyes ping-pong back and forth between us and Elianna gives her a warm smile.

"Hey, are you hungry?" she asks as she stands up.

"No, I ate at the movies," she says while staring at me with a look I'd never seen before.

"Well, I'm going to put the food away then," Elianna says before sliding past Margot, rubbing her shoulder as she passes. "I like this lip color." She points and then closes the door behind her.

Margot stares after her before turning her annoyed eyes—that at the moment remind me of her mother—to me. "You're drinking with the nanny now?" She raises an eyebrow at me and I narrow my gaze at her.

"No? Just me. You see? Only one glass." I hold it up. She crosses her arms over her chest. "Yes?"

"And how would you feel if Gabe and I were sitting outside in the dark like this." It's not exactly dark with the lanterns I have lining the terrace but it definitely gives it a sensual glow.

"Pretty angry because you're not old enough to drink," I tell her, not liking where this conversation is headed.

"You know what I'm saying."

"Actually, Margot, I don't."

I can feel the tension between us but she doesn't press it further. "Whatever. I'm going to my room." She doesn't wait for a reply before she's back inside, and just like that all of those earlier feelings are back.

CHAPTER NINE

Elianna

The following day is Saturday and my first weekend off since I started. Mr. Kincaid tried to give me last weekend off but not only did I not have any plans, he ended up needing to be at his office in D.C. for most of the weekend. I had no problem staying home.

But tonight, Jacqueline is all but forcing me out for one of the city's fall bar crawls. My plan is to stay the night at her apartment in case I do get a little drunk. I don't want any of the Kincaids seeing me like that. *Even if something tells me Rowan would be proud that I finally did something besides worrying about everyone else.*

"Now you're sure you don't need me to stay? I can cancel," I say to Mr. Kincaid who's sitting on the couch, dressed down and looking deliciously relaxed, with Isla who has one of her dolls in her lap while she brushes her hair. I giggle as I listen to her talking to her doll and telling her to *stop moving so much.*

"No, you go and enjoy yourself. We'll be fine." He lifts his arm and stretches it along the back of the couch, a move that is so simple, and yet it makes the complicated feelings I have for this man go haywire.

"Where are you going?" Isla asks without looking up at me.

"Just out with one of my friends."

"Is she your best friend?" She gathers the doll's hair into a ponytail before letting it fall in cute frustration.

"Yes, I would say so."

"Like me and Sabrina? Oh! Daddy, can Sabrina come over?" She looks up at him and purses her lips before she stands up on the couch and kisses him on the cheek. "Please please please."

"Honey..." He shakes his head and she strikes while he hesitates, kissing him on the cheek again. *She's got him*, I think to myself. "I'll call her mom in a bit."

"Yay!" She plops back down and continues brushing her doll's hair.

"I can stay if Sabrina is coming," I tell him, resisting the urge to tell him he's such a sucker.

"No, I will be fine. I've done it before." He gives me an annoyed look followed by a smile. He seems to be in much better spirits than he was last night and I hope it isn't all an act so that I don't cancel my plans. "Besides, it's a rare night that Margot isn't going out, so I have backup." He waves me off and I head back to my room to pack for the night. I'm almost finished getting ready when there's a light knock on my open door and I see Margot standing in the doorway.

"Hey!" I smile cheerily as I slide my curling iron into my overnight bag and she cocks her head to the side.

She tucks one of her long tresses behind her ear before pulling it all to one side. "Dad said you're going out tonight."

"Yeah, against my will, I think." I roll my eyes.

She plays with the ends of her hair, twirling it around her finger. "With a guy?"

"No," I snort. "With my best friend."

"Oh…well, you look hot," she tells me. I look down at the short black leather skirt, knee-high boots, and white strapless top I'm wearing.

I beam because getting approval from a teenager is the highest compliment. "Thank you."

"Any chance I can borrow that?" She waves her index finger up and down indicating she means my entire outfit.

"Maybe in two years?" I smile at her and she rolls her eyes.

"So, you're not coming back tonight?" She nods toward my bag.

"I just thought we might be out late, and I don't want to come in late and risk waking anyone up."

"Any chance there may be a guy you're interested in that might be showing up?" She probes and I'm wondering what she's getting at.

"Not…that I know of?"

"You just look really good. Wasn't sure if it was for a guy."

I look down and then back at her wishing she was at the age that she'd understand that getting dressed for yourself will always be more fulfilling than doing it for a man. "No, Margot. I did this for me."

"Okay…well, have fun, but not too much, and be safe." She giggles as she gets up and calls over her shoulder. "Make good choices!"

I make my way into the foyer and see Isla still sitting on the couch but her dad is nowhere in sight. "Where's your dad?"

She peeks her head over the couch and shrugs. "Oooh, you look pretty!"

"Thank you!"

"DADDY, ELLIE'S LEAVING!" she calls and I wince at the volume of her scream.

"Isla...I could have texted him."

Mr. Kincaid comes in from the dining room and I can't help the warm feeling that washes over me when I see the look in his eyes. He drags them slowly from my feet all the way to my eyes and then back down. I watch as his nostrils flare every time they pass over my legs, and the way his teeth dig into his bottom lip when he drags them across my chest makes my knees weak.

"Wow." He blurts out and I can't stop the smirk that pulls at my lips. "I mean..." He closes his eyes and rubs his jaw and when he opens them, I can see the lust all over his face. "No, I meant wow." He closes the space between us. "You're not coming back tonight?" he asks when he notices the bag at my feet.

"It just might be late and I don't want to worry about waking anyone up. I also don't like to take an Uber late at night by myself."

He looks down at the bag again and then back at me. "It makes me feel better that you don't do that, but I can come get you. It doesn't matter if it's late," he offers and I'm fairly certain I am not ready to be around him when I've been drinking.

At least not until I get over this crush I have on him.

"Also, Jacqueline and I can get a little...crazy," I whisper. "I know..." I put up two hands. "Try to contain your shock. I just don't want to come home like *that*. Margot's impressionable!"

He gives me a look of derision. "I can assure you, she's seen an intoxicated person before."

"That's not the point. I am supposed to be a good example."

"You are, Elianna."

Feeling the pressure, I add, "If you are asking me to come back tonight, I can..."

He shakes his head. "That's not it. I just don't want you to feel like you can't. Or that you don't have a safe way to get home. I will come get you, that's all." I make a mental note to figure out how I feel about him referring to his house as *home*.

"I appreciate that, but I'll be fine. Besides, I haven't seen Jacqueline in a while. If I don't go, she might show up here and I don't know that I'm ready to introduce her yet."

"I'd love to meet your friends. Any of them are welcome here." His voice is soft and smooth and heats me all over despite the words not being particularly sexy.

"Thanks." I lick my bottom lip and I swear I hear a groan not quite disguised by the sound of him clearing his throat as he takes a step back. My phone vibrates and it breaks through whatever tension is crackling between us right now. I see a text from Jacqueline asking for my ETA and I turn toward the door. "I'm going to go."

"Okay." He nods. "Just…be safe."

"I will." He reaches past me to open the door for me and when I turn around after walking a few steps outside, I see his eyes at least a foot down, making me fairly certain he was just staring at my ass.

"I am *so* glad you could come out tonight!" Jacqueline squeals as she orders us a shot each at the first bar. "I need to hear everything about hot Daddy by the way."

"There's nothing to tell." I hesitate before taking a long sip of my tequila soda while I avoid her excited gaze.

"You're lying." She narrows her eyes at me as she hands me the lemon drop shot that I'm already regretting.

"No…I…I don't know. He was kind of intense when I was leaving tonight. He offered to pick me up later…"

Her eyes widen as we grab an empty hightop table. "He did? Oh, that's so hot. The whole responsible and overprotective man thing?" She waves her hand over her face like she's fanning herself before letting out a giggle.

"I think he was just worried about me getting home."

She adjusts the corset she's wearing that has stopped practically every man in his tracks all night. "Exactly!"

"He also said 'wow' when he saw me. But...maybe that doesn't mean anything?" I ask, while secretly hoping it does.

"Oh, I think he's into you." She swirls her straw around her drink.

"You don't even know him."

"First of all, who wouldn't be into you? Second, maybe I don't know *him*, but I know men." She taps my nose with her index finger.

"He's different and he's older. He's a dad, remember? He's not like any guy that either of us has dated."

"Which means far less bullshit for you to decipher! No having to read the signs or wade through fuckboy signals. Ah, he just keeps getting better and better." She shimmies.

"I don't even know why we're having this conversation because—"

"Because you've had two shots and a mixed drink and you've never been able to contain your thoughts when you're drinking," she interrupts and I glare at her.

"*Because* I am not going to do anything. It's just a crush. He's still my boss. He's off limits."

"Ugh." She scoffs and pulls out her phone to reapply her burgundy lipstick. "I wish I had sexual tension with someone that was off limits." She grins at me before holding her phone between us. "Let's take a pic!"

A few bars, a few hours, and more than a few drinks later, it's almost two in the morning. Most of the bars are about to close, but when Jacqueline and I are together we are known to be out until last call. We are in the line for the bathroom when my phone vibrates with a text and I almost drop my phone when I see who it's from.

> **Mr. Kincaid:** I don't know if you're back at your friend's apartment yet, but I just want to make sure you're okay.

"Shut the fuck up! He's waiting up for you?" Jacqueline squeals as she reads over my shoulder.

"He's probably just working," I say but my heart flutters at the thought that he might be waiting to make sure I get back to Jacqueline's safely.

"Tell him to come get us!"

"What? Jacqueline, no."

"Why!? I want to meet him." She giggles. "And it's so annoying to get an Uber to whip us by Taco Bell."

Remembering that he said he wanted to meet her or any of my friends, I roll my eyes. "Let's just get pizza before we get in the Uber."

"Or have Daddy pick us up!"

"I'm not making him drive thirty-five minutes at two in the morning to pick us up just so you can get late-night food."

"I am suuuure he won't mind and I'm even more sure you can find a way to thank him for his service." She nods at my phone. "What are you going to say?"

"I don't know! And I'm drunk but don't want to sound drunk and you're drunk so neither of us is reliable right now!"

"Just say we're leaving the bar soon."

I'm trying to type what she said but I've already forgotten what exactly that was. "Wait, what do I say?"

"God, Ellie this is not hard. Okay, listen. Say, 'hey comma. We are heading back soon.' Feel free to use an exclamation point. That's a personal preference," she explains like she's teaching a class on drunk texting. "Then add, when can I suck your dick?" she says as we move up in the line.

"When…can…I—" I start typing before I glare at her. "Jacqueline!" She chuckles before pulling her beer bottle to her lips and finishing it. "Okay, sent."

And that's the last thing I remember before I blacked out.

The sounds of my phone ringing breaks me out of the last few minutes of sleep and I moan at the shrill noise that pierces the air.

"Jesus Christ, why is your phone on sound?" Jacqueline whines from next to me. "Turn it off!"

"It's a phone call." I groan, already feeling that special kind of annoyance that only comes with a hangover. "Who is calling me?" I open one eye slowly before both fly open when I see Mr. Kincaid's name across the screen. "Fuck. It's Rowan."

"Isn't it your weekend off? How did they survive before they met you?" she says as she gets up and trudges into her bathroom.

"Yes, which is why it could be important!" I clear my throat and get off the bed. Despite the hangover that I feel creeping into all of my senses, adrenaline kicks in and I run into Jacqueline's kitchen to pour myself a glass of water. I down half of it and clear my throat in hopes it'll make my voice sound presentable and not like I had multiple tequila shots last night.

I press the button to call him back and he answers on the first ring. "Well, good morning, sunshine. How are you feeling?" His voice is light and so incredibly sexy for… I look at my phone to see what time it is. *Eight-thirty in the morning.*

"Hi. Sorry I missed your call, is everything okay?"

"Yes, of course."

"Okay…" I trail off as if to say *then is there a reason that you're calling me at eight-thirty on my Sunday off?*

"You told me to call you at eight-thirty to make sure you were up."

I freeze. "What?" *When did I say that?*

"When we talked last night..." He trails off. "How drunk were you?" He chuckles with a bit of an edge to his voice and I wonder if I was super embarrassing and annoying. *Oh, my fucking God.*

"Oh, uh...I just forgot."

"Do you remember talking to me?"

SURE DON'T!

"Kind of?" I say as I pull my phone away from my ear and put him on speakerphone to pull up my text messages.

"I see. Well...I will let you go and I will see you whenever you get back today."

I can hear a hint of what sounds like disappointment in his voice and while I want to make sure he isn't, I need to see what it is I said to him last night. "Okay, I'm probably going to head out soon. So, I'll be there in a bit."

"Don't feel like you have to rush. I'm taking the kids to breakfast in a little while."

"Oh, that sounds fun!"

"I'll see you later, Elianna." His tone is vastly different from how he answered the phone just a few minutes ago.

"Bye," I whisper and immediately go to my call log and mentally thank drunk Ellie that I don't see a phone call which means at least I'll know exactly what was said. *God only knows what I could have said if we spoke on the phone last night.*

I remember him asking me if I was back at Jacqueline's and then the rest is a blur.

> Me: Hey, we are heading back soon!

> Mr. Kincaid: Did you have fun?

> Me: Yes! But I'm drunk.

> Mr. Kincaid: Is your friend?

> Me: Yes, way more than me haha

> Mr. Kincaid: Are you guys okay to get back? You're worrying me a little.

> Me: Don't be. I have been of legal drinking age for four years you know!

> Mr. Kincaid: I'm aware.

> Me: Is there a reason you're so worried about me? I mean you did offer to pick me up from the bar.

FUCK. *Ellie, no!* I rub my forehead wishing these next text messages were just figments of my imagination.

> Mr. Kincaid: Do you think there's a reason?

> Me: Jacqueline does!

> Mr. Kincaid: Who's Jacqueline?

> Me: My best friend, obviously!

> Mr. Kincaid: Well, you never said her name. But what does she think?

> Me: She thinks that you may be into me.

OH MY GOD. I stare at my phone. "JACQUELINE WOODS, I SWEAR TO GOD!" I shout before I stomp back into her room to find her face down on the bed with her pillow over her head.

She moves the pillow and raises her head slightly, her eyes half open and hazy. "What!? And my head is pounding, bring it down several decibels, damn."

"Did you know I was texting Rowan last night?"

"Yeah, but you wouldn't let me see!"

"You encouraged this behavior!" I exclaim before dropping to her bed and continuing to read.

Mr. Kincaid: And what do you think?

Me: You didn't deny it!

Mr. Kincaid: Correct, I did not.

Me: omg.

OH MY GOD.

Mr. Kincaid: Let's talk about this tomorrow when you're sober.

Me: Okay. Call me at 8:30 please to make sure I'm awake.

Mr. Kincaid: You got it, sunshine.

Later that afternoon, after having brunch with Jacqueline, where we went over every possible scenario that could happen between me and Rowan that day, I head home. The house is quiet when I get there and I wonder where everyone is. I didn't see Margot's car in the driveway, so I assume she may be out. I put my bag in my room and surprisingly I don't see Rowan in his office. I head down the hall and up the stairs to the second floor and I hear talking coming out of Isla's room. When I walk in, I see her sitting on the floor playing with her dolls.

"Ellie!" she cheers, hopping up and running to me. I drop to one knee and she lunges into my arms, squeezing me tight.

"Hi!"

"Will you play with me?" she asks, handing me one of her dolls.

"Okay, but where is everyone?"

"Margot left. SJ is playing video games in the basement and Daddy is taking a nap."

"Are *you* supposed to be taking a nap?" I ask her.

She gives me her most innocent look and giggles. "I'm not tired!"

"Well, I could use a nap," I tell her, feeling the fatigue of my hangover catching up with me. "Do you want to come watch a movie in my room?"

She nods enthusiastically before scooping up her dolls and grabbing a tiny blanket from her bed. She follows me down the stairs and before I realize what she's doing I see her knocking on her dad's door. "Daddy, Ellie's home! I'm going to watch a movie in her room, okay? Okay." She scurries down the hall toward me and just as she enters my room, I see Rowan open the door and his eyes lock with mine.

"Hey." I wave and a sexy smile that makes my knees weak finds his face before he returns my wave.

"Hey, sunshine."

"Ellie, what movie!" Isla calls and I look at her sitting on my bed.

"One sec, Isla," I tell her as I move down the hall and out of her line of sight toward her father. "Can we talk later about last night?"

He nods. "I think we need to."

"I'm so sorry..." I whisper.

"For what you said or not remembering you said it?" He raises an eyebrow at me but a smile pulls at his lips.

"Both?" I offer weakly. "I don't want to make things uncomfortable or awkward."

"You didn't do either of those things. I think I did that."

I shake my head. "No! I asked."

He leans against the wall in the hallway. "I didn't have to answer."

"Was it the truth?"

"Do you think I'd lie about that?" I shake my head slowly. "Can I ask you a question?"

"Sure."

"Why did you ask me in the first place? Your question about why I worry about you?"

I look to my open door where I know Isla is sitting on my bed waiting to watch a movie with me. This isn't the time or place for this conversation but the last thing I want is for Rowan to feel unsettled when he'd been honest with me. "Because I wanted to know if you were into me...*too*."

CHAPTER TEN

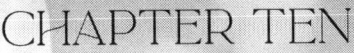
Rowan

I BARELY SLEPT LAST NIGHT THINKING ABOUT THE conversation I had with Elianna. I don't know what possessed me to tell her that I was into her. I was completely sober, unlike her, and yet I was the one having the drunken confessional. I suspected she felt similarly and I'm glad I was right and didn't completely fuck everything up.

I hear Isla and Elianna giggling in her room just as SJ comes up from the basement.

"Is Ellie back yet? I'm starving. What are we having for dinner?"

"She is, but she's resting so I'm thinking about ordering in. It's still her day off. And how are you starving? We just got back from lunch an hour ago." It was supposed to be breakfast but naturally, getting three kids out of the house at one specific time is always a challenge.

"Works for me. What are we getting?" He pulls his hood up over his head and moves toward the refrigerator. I'm surprised when he pulls out the bowl of mixed fruit Elianna put together instead of going to the pantry for chips like he usually does and it's just a reminder of all of the little things Elianna has changed since working here.

"Chinese food?" I ask him and his eyes light up.

"Sweet. You know what I like."

A squeal comes from Elianna's room and SJ looks at me before biting into a strawberry. "I thought you said she was resting?"

"Isla is in there with her watching a movie."

He glances again toward the sound before he walks to Elianna's room with the bowl of fruit tucked under his arm. Twenty minutes later, when he doesn't return, I peek my head in her room and see Isla curled up next to Ellie on her bed and SJ lying on the couch in the corner, equally engrossed in the movie.

"You're watching a Disney movie?" I tease my son. "I thought you said they were for babies."

"Lion King doesn't count," he says through a mouthful of fruit.

Elianna looks over at him and gapes at him in shock. "You watched Beauty and the Beast with us last weekend."

"That is a secret!" SJ groans.

"I can't hear!" Isla looks at SJ before turning back to the TV mounted on the wall. Elianna and I share a smile before I leave them to finish their movie.

One movie turned into three and then there was dinner and bath time and Isla wanted to read a book, so it's almost nine before I have a moment alone with Elianna again. SJ and Margot are both in their rooms, though I assume neither of them is asleep so I know we have to keep our voices down. I'm standing next to

Elianna while she washes the dishes from dinner, trying my best to help her but she keeps waving me off.

"You know we have a dishwasher, right?" I tell her.

"It's called a pre-wash! God, my mother would be turning over in her grave, if I just put dishes directly in there." She scrunches her nose before handing me what looks like a squeaky clean plate.

I shake my head as I put the plate in the dishwasher. "Did you have fun last night?"

"I did."

"I'm kind of surprised you're a little party animal under there," I joke. "For some reason, I saw you only nursing one drink the whole night."

"It's called being professional while at work! But yes, the Ellie that isn't working has a bit of a different vibe."

"Is that so?"

She nods as she rinses another plate. "Yep. I can let loose!"

"Glad to hear it."

I inch closer to her, letting my shoulder brush against hers and I watch as the gentle touch affects her. She glances up at me before turning back to the dishes. "Mr. Kincaid."

"I think you can call me Rowan."

"That's what I was going to say…" She trails off and I don't think I like where this is going. "I don't make it a habit to get involved with…" She swallows. "Anyone in the family I nanny for… let alone the father." She bites her bottom lip and I sense the nervousness all over her. "I do like you, but…I think this has the potential to get really messy and quickly." She blinks up at me. "And I'm sorry I kind of set all of this in motion last night and my intention was absolutely not to jerk you around and…"

"Hey." I stop her because I can already see her spiraling. I know that she hadn't intended to do that at all. Elianna is kind and cares about everyone's feelings, and I know even at this moment, she's thinking about everyone else's but hers. "I didn't think you were."

"You hired me to focus on them," she says. "And...I can't if I'm focused on...well, *you*."

I turn so that the back of me is against the counter and I can look at her straight on. "I respect that, Elianna."

She looks up at me. "I'm sorry."

"Stop apologizing." I reach for her hand and give it a squeeze hoping it doesn't make her uncomfortable.

Her brown eyes find mine and I can see the sadness lurking behind them, which I've only seen once when we talked the other night about her mother and Bianca. There's always so much light in her eyes, it's a bit jarring to see it extinguished. "Maybe whenever you leave us." I smile at her and her eyes immediately leave mine to turn back to her dishes.

"Maybe."

"I should get some work done," I tell her and she nods without looking at me. "Elianna..." I start because I feel like she's about to break down on me, but she shakes her head.

"I'm fine. I just don't do well with any kind of confrontation."

"This isn't confrontation, Elianna. Look at me." She does briefly before casting her gaze downward, but even in that brief look, I saw the tears swimming in her eyes. "We're good, alright?" She nods again. "Can I see a smile?" She gives me one that looks a little forced but I'll take it for now. A part of me wants to hug her but I don't want to push her, so I just nod and head to my office.

The next few days I barely see Elianna. I was already planning to have a very busy week, and maybe I'm now using that as an excuse to stay out of the house and allow Elianna and I to get back to how things were. I didn't want there to be any awkwardness between us and I got the feeling that she needed some time to get back to normal.

My thoughts are interrupted by the sound of my phone ringing and I see it's my brother.

"I feel like I haven't seen you in months. Wasn't hiring a nanny supposed to give you some free time?" he says before I can even utter a greeting.

"Work has been kicking my ass. What's up?"

"Nothing, I just hadn't talked to you. I wanted to see how things were." It was true; I usually talked to him more, especially on the days when he picked the kids up from school. Now that he isn't doing that anymore, there isn't a specific need for us to be constantly talking, but hearing his voice reminds me that I've missed it.

"Sorry, man. That's on me."

"I'm not crying over it. I'm fine." He chuckles. "But you're good?"

"Yeah." Part of me wants to tell him about what happened with Elianna but then I remember *nothing actually happened.*

"Well, now that we've gotten the pleasantries out of the way, what are you doing tonight?"

I lean back in my chair, already regretting the curiosity moving through me. "Why?"

"Come on. We haven't been out in ages."

"It's a Thursday."

"And? You used to love going out for Thursday Night Football and Washington's actually good this year."

"Why do I feel like there's more to this story?"

"Okay, and maybe because there's this new bartender at The Dugout." *And there it is.*

"Since when can't you go to a bar by yourself? You work better without a wingman anyway." I chuckle because while we were both no stranger to women's attention, I'm usually more reserved and River entertains everyone unashamedly. *At all times.*

"Well, I do also want to hang out with my big brother. Sue me," he says sarcastically. "Come on, just a drink…" I hesitate and he speaks again. "Or four."

"One drink, River," I tell him and I can't tell if he claps or slaps whatever's in front of him before he lets out a cheer.

"Let's gooo. Alright, I'll pick you up around eight?"

Knowing that getting River to leave a bar a second before he's ready *or before he's decided who he's going home with later* is nearly impossible. I shake my head. "Nice try. I'll meet you there."

"Well, I wanted to see the kids too, but you know what, that's even better, you can drive."

"I'm not staying all night with you."

"That's fine. I can Uber later."

"Fine." I rub my temples, trying to stave off the headache I feel forming behind my eyes. "See you at eight."

When I get home that night, Elianna is in the kitchen while Isla is sitting at the table coloring and I'm starting to notice that wherever Elianna is, Isla is never more than a few steps away. "Daddy!" Isla gets off the chair and I lean down to give her a hug.

"Hi, sweetheart. How was your day?" I set my briefcase and laptop bag on one of the chairs.

"Great! Art day is next week." She holds up a picture she's drawing. "See! That's our house. There's you, and me, and Margot, and SJ, and Ellie!" She points at each of the stick people and Elianna looks over at us with a smile.

"I'm in your picture?"

"You live here!"

She smiles before going back to seasoning the chicken breasts in front of her.

"What's that?" I ask, pointing to a small brown thing with ears in the corner of the paper, but I already know what it is.

"A doggie!" she says giving me her best puppy dog eyes. Isla has been begging me for a dog since the day they moved in to live here full time but I've been hesitant because I didn't think she was old enough. Now, she's enlisted SJ and Margot in her campaign and I know it's only a matter of time before she convinces Elianna too.

"That's a beautiful picture, honey." I press a kiss to her forehead before I stand up and make my way to Elianna.

"Hi."

"Hi," she responds and while things don't feel awkward, I can still feel the tension between us.

God, I fucking wanted her and I'm pretty sure she still wants me too.

She looks so pretty tonight. Her hair is pulled up on top of her head, except for a few curly tendrils framing her face. Her lips are pink and glossy and I want to taste them to see if the gloss is flavored. I realize I'm blatantly staring at her and haven't said anything. "Ummm, I'm going to get a drink with River in a bit. I probably won't leave until after Isla is asleep…"

"Oh!" She claps. "That's good. I was wondering if you were ever going to capitalize on having me here and actually go out sometime." She laughs. "Do you have time to eat before? Dinner should be ready by seven."

Obviously. One of my favorite things about coming home is figuring out what Elianna has made for dinner that night. "Yeah, I'll eat. It smells great."

"SJ is outside practicing for his game Saturday and Margot is sitting out there with him."

I nod and make my way through the house toward the back where I see SJ practicing his shots on the small soccer goal River got him. Margot is sitting at the table on the patio doing her homework, heckling him between missed shots.

"Booo!" Margot yells when he misses and he shoots her his middle finger.

"Uh uh, SAWYER JACK!" I yell at him and when his scared eyes snap to mine he pales slightly.

"When did you get home?" he asks nervously as he runs after the missed ball.

"I don't want to see that. You know better," I tell him. Margot snickers from behind me and I turn and glare at her. "From you either."

She scoffs. "Excuse me! Did you see me do it?"

"I'm just warning you." I loosen my tie and look at all of the books littering the space in front of her. "Test tomorrow?"

"Next week," she tells me as she continues to take notes on her flashcards.

"Sucks not to be as smart as me and barely need to study, doesn't it?" Margot scowls at SJ as he jogs over and gives me a high-five. "Hey, Dad."

"How was school?" I ask him.

"Fine." He shrugs before taking a sip from his water bottle on the table.

"Just letting you guys know, I'm going out for a little tonight with Uncle River."

"Oh sweet, for the game? Can I come?" SJ asks.

"Nice try." I chuckle. "And you need to be in bed at halftime."

"Daaad, come on," he groans.

"Sawyer," I warn.

I sense movement in my periphery and when I turn, I see Margot making a face at him telling him to *relax*. I narrow my eyes at her. "I don't want him up until eleven-thirty when he has school tomorrow."

"One day won't kill him!" Margot says.

I roll my eyes, very used to being ganged up on by my two oldest children. "If you stay up, I don't want to hear a word about you being tired tomorrow." I point at him.

"Oh bet!"

"Not. one. word." I point at him and he cheers before going back to his soccer ball.

"You're annoying," I tell her and she gives me a grin.

"You love me!"

I press a kiss to her forehead. "The most," I tell her like I have ever since she was a kid.

"Love you the most," she responds before she turns her head back to SJ. "Let's go fourteen, even I could have made that shot!" She giggles and I snap my eyes to SJ and he looks at me innocently before making an obvious show of shooting her his index finger.

⁓⁓⁓

"You good, Row? You're kind of quiet," River asks me and I shake my head before taking a sip of my beer.

"Yeah, just a long day. Long week, really."

"I hear you." He smiles at the bartender who he's been flirting with ever since we sat down, and she shoots him another coy grin.

"River Kincaid," she says as she stands in front of us, "this is the second time this week. Are you in love with me?" Her blonde hair is pulled back into a sleek ponytail and her blue eyes are so striking even I do a doubletake. Her lips are painted bright red and all it does is make me think of Elianna's lips and my recent obsession with wanting to taste them.

"Is it that obvious?" He leans forward and bites his bottom lip as he drags his eyes up and down over her salaciously. "What time are you off tonight?"

"I close tonight but I have an early class tomorrow." She tears off a piece of receipt paper before writing something on it. "Maybe this weekend? I'm not working Saturday." She giggles before sliding it to him.

"I'll text you." He smirks and she nods before walking away and I give him a look.

"An early class? How old is she?"

"She's a senior, relax." He shrugs still staring after where she disappeared.

My eyebrows practically shoot to my hairline. "A WHAT?"

He turns to look at me and groans. "In college…calm down!"

I put a hand over my heart because while eighteen is a little young even for my brother, I really can't be too sure. "You're going to kill me."

"Speaking of younger women..." He blinks at me.

"Yes?"

"Ellie?"

"What about her?"

"Oh, come on. I saw the way she was looking at you when we left."

"How was she..." I ask nonchalantly because I have been trying my best to keep my eyes off of her in mixed company.

"With stars in her eyes, dude. I think she likes you."

"No, I don't think so," I tell him. "She's just comfortable around me, that's all."

"If you say so." He shrugs. "I swear she gets more gorgeous every time I see her, I respect the restraint you have because I wouldn't have lasted a day."

"Believe me, I know," I say sarcastically, just as I feel something pressed up against my other side and a hand on my bicep.

"Shit!" the voice murmurs and when I turn toward whoever is touching me, I see a woman I've never met before. "I'm sorry! I dropped my purse." It seems like she was just walking by but once our eyes meet, I see hers widen and she hesitates for a moment before she takes a seat on the barstool next to me.

"You're fine, no problem," I tell her, and her eyes immediately drop to my hands. I can guess she's looking to see if I'm wearing a wedding ring.

"I come here all the time and I've never seen you here." She nods at River. "I see him often." She adjusts the glasses that sit in front of her charcoal eyes and bats them a few times at me.

"Because I have a life unlike my big bro here," he says before slinging an arm around me and using his other hand to squeeze my cheeks obnoxiously.

"I have a life, thank you." I shoot him a fake smile. "I'm just very busy," I tell her.

"He's allergic to fun," he says through a bite of his burger.

She giggles and leans her elbow on the bar so she's completely facing me. "What's your name?" she asks.

"Rowan."

"Well, Rowan, I'm Lydia, and…it was really nice to meet you," she says with a smile and then she's off the stool and gone without another word.

River slowly blinks at me in shock and shakes his head in disappointment. "Have you just completely forgotten how to talk to women? She was cute and into you! Did you join the priesthood without telling me?"

I glare at him. "I don't have time for—"

"Make time," he interrupts. "You can still date, you know. Single fathers do it all the time. Don't tell me you want to wait until Isla's eighteen because you'll be…shit," he whistles, "I don't even want to think about it because that'll force me to think about how old *I'll* be in twelve years." He groans and presses a hand over his heart dramatically. "All I'm saying is don't shut yourself off from the possibility of having some fun, going on dates, and getting to know someone. I'm not suggesting marriage or even trying to get laid—which you *should* be thinking about by the way—but some companionship wouldn't hurt."

"I know," I say, thinking about the woman at home that I started to get to know and it hits me that she's the only woman I want to go on a date with.

I stayed out longer than I planned, getting home a little after eleven to find Elianna on the couch just like always. River actually left with me, much to my surprise, and dropped next to Ellie on the couch as soon as we got in.

"Are you staying?" I ask him, wondering if he doesn't feel like taking an Uber home and is planning to crash in my other guestroom.

"I'm leaving. I didn't really get a chance to talk to Ellie when I was here earlier." He turns his gaze to Elianna. "Ellie, we have to work on my brother."

Her eyes snap to mine in question, and I frown wondering where he's going with this.

"Oh?" she asks.

"Yes, oh?" I sit on the adjacent loveseat and shoot him a warning glare that I hope he heeds.

"He never gets out and then when he does, he's practically repelling women," he explains. "This very attractive woman tried to talk to him tonight and he was having none of it."

She looks over at me before turning back to River. "Well, maybe he wasn't attracted to her?"

"He said like four words to her, one of which was his name. He didn't even give her a chance."

"Well—" Elianna starts before River interrupts, pointing at me.

"And tell her *why*, Row."

"River..." I glare at him before I look at Elianna who seems to be waiting for an answer. "I just...wasn't interested."

"You're never interested! There has to be someone that catches your eye, *sometime*." He nudges Elianna. "Tell him to stop being old," he whispers loudly and I scoff in response. "Alright, my Uber should be here in a sec. I'm leaving my car here; I'll swing by in the morning if I have time," he says before he waves at me and then he's out the door.

Elianna stares after my brother before she turns back to face the television. "Did you think she was attractive?" she asks without looking at me and I'm surprised by her question.

"Why do you ask?"

"I just mean maybe he's right and you should give her a chance. If there's an attraction."

"There wasn't," I tell her.

"Are you sure?"

"Trust me, I know when I'm attracted to someone." I give her a look I hope she can read before I stand up, not wanting to go any further down this road and risk being right back where we were on Sunday. "Goodnight, Elianna."

CHAPTER ELEVEN

Elianna

After I dropped SJ and Isla off at school, I found my mind drifting to Rowan. I know I told him I wasn't sure if we could go down this road, but can I just ignore whatever I'm feeling for him, *forever*?

I'm putting a load of laundry in the washing machine when my phone rings and my mood is instantly lifted when I see who is calling. "Hey, Dad!"

"I figured I should call you since I haven't heard from you in a month," he says with a hint of humor though I know he's mostly serious.

I roll my eyes at the guilt trip I'm used to ever since I moved to Maryland. "It's been like a week."

"Same difference! I just wanted to check on you. How are you?"

"I'm good! What are you up to today?"

"Same old. It's a nice day, so I'm about to go hit a bucket of balls with Jeff," he says in reference to his neighbor.

"Sounds like fun. How's my niece?" I ask because my father doesn't go longer than a day without seeing his granddaughter, Eloise. *Who my dad refers to as Little Ellie, and I love it.*

"She's good, but you haven't talked to your sister?"

"Not for a couple of weeks," I tell him.

He lets out a disappointed grunt and I steel myself for the incoming lecture. "What's wrong this time?"

"Nothing?"

"You're not in a fight?"

"No?" I respond, like the tension between me and my sister is something that could be reduced to something as simple as one fight. *And my dad knows that.*

"I hate when you two aren't talking. You should call her."

"Phone works both ways, Dad."

"You're the oldest, El."

"That argument is so tired! She's twenty-two! At what point does being three years younger than me stop absolving her from any responsibility?"

He huffs and I already know what's coming next. *More about how the rift is somehow my fault.* "Don't start, Ellie."

"Did she put you up to this?"

"No? But I saw her and Trent last night and she mentioned that she hadn't talked to you. She didn't even know you had a new nanny job."

"Pretty sure I told her." *Definitely told her.*

"You sure you didn't just tell Edie?" he asks, referring to my youngest sister.

"I told them both. Per usual, Em doesn't listen to me."

"Yes. She does, Elianna. You need to stop shutting her out over whatever tension has been between you from when you were younger."

I pinch the bridge of my nose, feeling the tension building from unresolved childhood conflict. "Is this why you called?"

"No," he says with a bit of edge to his voice. "I was calling because I wanted to see what day I should expect you to fly in for Thanksgiving."

I freeze, unsure of what to say because I hadn't given it much thought. "Oh…"

"I can't imagine you'll need to work that weekend. They can give you the time off?"

I hadn't exactly told my father that I'm nannying for a single dad. I just told him I got a new job and when he assumed it was a family complete with a mother that also lived in the house, I just didn't correct him.

"Yeah, I'm sure," I tell him as I rub my forehead. I already know Rowan would give me time off for Thanksgiving in a heartbeat but I feel a little ache in my chest at the thought of not spending the day with them.

And who would cook for them?

I guess I could prepare everything before I left?

"Can I let you know? It's not even Halloween yet."

"Well, you know prices are just going to keep going up for flights. They are already expensive."

"Worst case, I'll drive again." I make my way into the kitchen and take a seat at the table.

"Alright, well keep me posted. I think we are going to Emily's this year."

"We aren't having it at our house?" My dad still lives in the house he raised us in, the house that once upon a time he lived in with my mother, and that's where we typically go for all the major holidays.

"No, we decided we're going to go to hers this year."

"We? I don't recall voting on that. We've always done it at our house." I try to ignore the tears building in my throat that we are changing a twenty-five-year tradition like it's nothing.

"And we're switching it up this year. Don't make this into a whole thing, Elianna," he scolds.

"Grandma's on board too?" I ask, referring to my mom's mom who is a creature of habit and typically hates any kind of change.

"She wants to be anywhere her only great-granddaughter is, of course."

"Okay, well...yeah, I'll let you know as we get closer."

"Fine. Call your sister, Elianna. I'm not kidding."

"Did you give her this same lecture and tell her to call me?" I try to keep the edge out of my voice, but I hear it and I'm sure he does too.

"What did I say?" he says and a scowl finds my face, once again feeling like I'm a teenager and I'm just expected to always understand my sister's feelings because I'm the oldest.

But who understands mine?

Ever.

"Okay, Dad," I say, quietly. "I'll call her later."

"Good. I love you, Ellie. You know I do and I'm always on your side."

Are you?

"I know. Love you too." I nod.

"Talk to you later."

I end the call and before I can stop myself, I'm pressing the phone to my ear to call Rowan. I know I shouldn't make this call when I'm still feeling emotional about the phone call with my father, but *fuck it*. I'm tired of putting everyone else first. For once, I want to do what I want.

"Hey," he answers and just the sound of his voice calms my heart which I didn't even realize was pounding. I bite my bottom lip, not sure of what to say now that my emotions are coming down. "Elianna?"

"Are you busy?" I ask.

"What's going on? Is everything okay?" I notice he doesn't answer my question because *of course he's busy, Ellie.*

"Yes, the kids are fine. They're all at school. I'm sorry. I shouldn't have called."

"We have to work on how much you apologize. Talk to me and tell me what's going on." His voice is soothing and calms my nerves.

"It's not about the kids," I admit.

"That's okay. Tell me what's wrong, Elianna." And those simple words have a direct line to my heart.

"Do you have plans for Thanksgiving?" I blurt out. "Like do you go to your parents' in Florida? Or somewhere else?"

"No, not usually? Last year was pretty lowkey because it was right after Bianca passed. We ordered takeout from a restaurant that had a Thanksgiving menu. It was not great." He chuckles. "Is that what has you upset?"

"It's just my dad wants to know when I'm coming home and…I wasn't sure if you needed me."

"Oh, no Elianna, I would never keep you from your family. You can have any time off that you need." I don't respond because I'm struggling to find the words. "Is *that* why you're upset? I hope you know I wouldn't demand that you stay here."

"I know you wouldn't." I play with the ends of my hair nervously. "I…I'm not sure I want to go home though."

He's silent for a second. "Elianna, you're more than welcome to stay. I didn't think I needed to say that. You saw Isla's picture, right? I'm sorry to tell you, you're officially family."

A quiet gasp escapes me. "Thank you…" I trail off before adding, "Besides, who would cook?"

A knock on my bedroom door pulls me away from my phone and I see Rowan standing in the entrance to my room. I try not to notice how handsome he looks in sweatpants and a t-shirt but my eyes aren't on board with that idea because I can't stop ogling him.

"You busy?" he asks and I shake my head. "Come have a drink

with me." I eye him warily and he gives me a boyish grin. "I know you don't like whiskey. I'll make you a margarita." He waves me out of bed before he leaves my room.

It doesn't take much convincing and soon we are sitting in the living room with a margarita each. I'm sitting on the couch and he's in a lounge chair and I'm glad we have this space between us to hopefully keep the temptation at bay.

"So, tell me why you don't want to go home?"

"You figured there's a reason, huh?" He raises his eyebrows at me before taking a sip of his drink. "It's so silly."

"I'll bet it's not."

"We always have it at my dad's. I guess you could technically call it my house since it's the last place I lived in Ohio. This year, apparently the plan is to go to my sister's house and nobody even talked to me about it. We've only ever had Thanksgiving at one place. It was the last place we had Thanksgiving with my mom, and it just…feels weird not to do it there." I sigh. "Plus, as soon as my dad got on the phone, he was on me about not talking to my sister more. Like it's all my fault. Somehow, it's always all my fault." I feel tears springing to my eyes and the last thing I want is to have a breakdown about my family drama in front of my boss. *Or whatever he is.* "Sometimes, I just feel like no one hears me."

"I get that," he murmurs. "If it's any consolation, I hear you." I look away from the glass I'm holding in my lap to meet his eyes which are full of understanding. "You've had to be strong for people your entire life. Who's strong for you?"

A shiver moves through me and I rub my arm to try and warm my chilled skin. "Me? I guess." I know my family loves me but they haven't always been my strongest support system. Sometimes I feel like I love them the way they need to be loved but they don't do the same for me. And that is a tough pill to swallow.

"Stay," he says. "For Thanksgiving and…Christmas if you want. The kids will want you here."

I tilt my head to the side, already knowing that we are headed in a dangerous direction but not wanting to stop. "Just them?"

He takes a sip of his drink and licks a stray drop from his bottom lip. My sex pulses instantly. "You already know I want you here."

Butterflies begin flapping their wings in my stomach and move to my chest making my heart race. "Rowan…"

"Sunshine."

"Why do you call me that?"

He hesitates for a second and gives me a sweet smile. "Because you have become one of the bright spots in what has felt like a very dark year," he answers.

"That's so sweet," I whisper.

"*You* are so sweet," he responds instantly.

I look down at the space next to me before raising my eyes slowly to his and then back to the couch and I'm pleased he understands what I'm asking without having to say it. He gets up from his chair and sits next to me.

"I like it."

"Good."

I turn toward the television which is playing an old Law and Order: SVU rerun that is loud enough to drown out the sound of us talking to anyone upstairs but quiet enough that we can still hear each other clearly. I set the glass on the coffee table in front of us before tucking my feet under me and fidgeting with my hands in my lap. "I can't stop thinking about you…and that scares me a little."

"Tell me why."

"I told you why," I say quietly. "I…" I whisper. "This could turn out horribly." Even if I wasn't his children's nanny, I've never known a situation with a man to end up any way other than awful or awkward and I'm struggling to figure out why this would be different even though *he* is so very different from any man I've ever met in my life. "This…I can't…you're my boss, and…" I'm rarely at a loss for words and suddenly I can't get them out, but I feel his hand wrapping gently around my wrist effectively stopping me from trying.

"Not right now, I'm not." His hand is warm and sends tingles up my arm and through my body as he tugs me closer to him and before I realize what's happening, I'm straddling his lap and all the reasons as to why we *shouldn't* fly out of my brain.

I feel him growing beneath me and I bite my bottom lip to prevent myself from whimpering at the feeling of what I believe to be a hard, atypically large dick pressing upwards against me. "Elianna, forget about all of that. Forget who I am for a minute. Forget why you're here and who we are to each other. Tell me what you want." His voice is low and husky and a shiver moves through me at his words. Not to mention, I can't remember the last time someone asked me what I wanted. "You said you haven't always been able to take what you want because you're always worried about everyone else. I'm asking you to take what you want. Don't worry about anyone else but you."

My eyes drop to his mouth. Lush, full lips that I've been dying to know the taste of and how they feel against mine. I can feel his eyes still tracing my face even while my eyes are trained on his mouth. My hands move up his chest and when they cover his heart, I feel it pounding under my palms. I wonder if he's as nervous as I am. I inadvertently shift in his lap, momentarily forgetting where I am and *more importantly what I'm sitting on* and the groan that leaves his lips is so sexy and feral, I can't even stop myself from wanting to know how it would feel vibrating through me.

I lean forward and press my lips to his, and the sound transforms into a growl as his tongue snakes into my mouth without missing a beat.

Finally. Oh. my. God.

He tastes like tequila, lime, and a hint of salt, and *fuck his lips are soft.* The sound of his beard scraping against my skin sends a shiver through me and I can't help but think about the sound it would make if it were to ever drag along my inner thigh.

I moan in response when his dick presses even harder against me and I grind downwards trying my best to stimulate my clit through our clothes. Then I feel his hands on my hips holding me in place. He pulls his lips from mine and they're instantly at my ear before he bites down gently. "Elianna," he says and I hear a hint of scolding in his voice.

"You said to take what I want and I've never…I've never done this before. I wanted to feel it." My words are quiet, but I know he heard it because he loosens his grip on my hips and I shift again, pressing myself harder against him.

He lets out a shaky breath as he pulls back to look at me, his eyes full of hunger. "What… exactly?"

"Ummm this?" I squeak, looking down at where I'm sitting. "Through our clothes." He raises an eyebrow at me like he's amused and I feel heat rush to my cheeks in embarrassment before swallowing hard. "Dry humping." His dick jumps beneath me and I gasp at the feeling. I'm guessing he likes my choice of words.

"Elianna, I need to ask you something and I need you to be honest with me." His eyes are shining greener than usual, like the color of fresh-cut grass and I feel myself getting lost in them so I blink to break the trance. "Are you a virgin?" His hands move from my hips to my forearms, and he wraps his hands gently around them. His thumbs begin drawing circles on the backs of my arms and I want to melt even further into him at the feeling.

"No," I whisper, shaking my head. Although I don't have many sexual experiences and none of them were what I'd call *good*, I have had sex before. I think he's struggling with what to ask next so I expound. "But it's been a while."

"What's a while?"

I hesitate for a moment before answering. "Six years?"

His eyes widen and his mouth drops open before he lets out a breath. "Fuck, Elianna. I am so—" He starts and I can feel him trying to move me off his lap when I squeeze my thighs to try and keep him from moving me. Or at the very least give him a sign that I don't want to be moved.

"Don't apologize. I want this."

"But you said…"

"I know," I whisper while hovering an inch above his mouth.

"I don't want you to feel pressured. I didn't realize…" I hear him struggling but I hear the underlying words. *I didn't realize how innocent you are.*

"Would you prefer I wear a sign?" I raise an eyebrow at him and I watch as the tension leaves his face. "I haven't had particularly great experiences the few times I've had sex so I decided to wait until I met someone I thought I'd actually enjoy it with."

Just as quickly as it disappeared, the tension is back and I feel his entire body go rigid. His grip on my hips loosens and moves up slowly, dragging lightly up my spine. "Please tell me someone didn't hurt you."

"No." I shake my head. "Not like that."

I watch the relief flood him and he visibly relaxes. He rubs his jaw and leans his head back against the couch. "Thank fuck. Being a father to two girls, that is my biggest fear. Having one of them come to me…" He trails off as he lifts his head and I can tell he's staring off into space even though his eyes are trained on my hands that he's holding in his. They dart up to me. "I would destroy anyone for laying a finger on them."

Even though he's a lawyer, I'm not entirely sure which way he means 'destroy' and now really isn't the time to unpack that. "As I've said many times before, you're a good dad, Rowan."

He seems like he's breaking himself of the hellish thoughts brought on by this conversation and has something else on his mind because a smile pulls at his lips. "Even though I can't stop thinking about my kids' nanny?" He brings my hands to his mouth, dropping a kiss to a few of my fingers.

I let my hands slide down his torso. "Kiss me again," I whisper against his lips before brushing them against his. My tongue darts out and I drag it gently along his bottom lip before sucking it into my mouth and nibbling gently and then letting him go.

His lips are on mine instantly as he sits up and pulls my hips, forcing me downward on his dick as he hardens again. I wrap my arms around his neck and play with the hair at his nape, letting the silky dark brown strands slip through my fingers every few moments. I can feel his hands moving me the way he wants me which is coincidentally the way I want also and soon we find a perfect rhythm that sends electricity shooting through my body as I grind against him.

Oh my God. Oh my God. Oh my God.

I'm wearing a fitted long-sleeved shirt but I can feel the goosebumps underneath, my entire body tingling brought on by the fire building between my legs. My hips roll against him, doing my best to drag against his shaft. "Rowan," I moan quietly against his lips.

"God, I fucking love the way you say my name." His voice is hoarse and gravelly and I feel my nipples begin to tingle in time with the heartbeat thumping between my legs.

"Do you?" I whimper when his lips find my neck. "Better than when I call you Mr. Kincaid?" I giggle when his dick twitches again. "I guess you like that too."

He grips my hips to stop me from moving and chuckles into my neck. "Don't train my dick to react when you call me that. It's already hard enough to keep it in check when we're in the same room."

My hands move between us and reach under the t-shirt he's wearing and then they're on the drawstring of his pants. I don't undo them, but I tangle them in my fingers long enough that he knows what I want. "You want them off?" He gives me a cocky grin before darting his gaze to where my hands are between us.

"I want...to see."

"*Just* see?" he responds with a hint of teasing in his voice.

"Maybe...touch?" I smirk and I don't know where this sudden

boldness is coming from. Maybe it's because I've never felt this way before and I'm being driven by my hormones for the first time in my life. My mind is only focused on one thing at this moment and it's how I can keep feeling this way. "Can I?" I ask and his nostrils flare.

"Whatever you want," he says and his voice sounds strained. I drag a finger over the top of his sweatpants and I'm surprised that I don't feel an ounce of nerves.

I guess being horny outweighs any nervousness.

I pull the drawstring slowly, my eyes not leaving his, and just as I reach my hand inside preparing to wrap around him, I hear a voice from the top of the stairs and then again like the voice is moving...*closer.*

"Daddy! Daddy!"

I'm off his lap in an instant, moving to the other end of the couch like he's on fire and I watch as he stands up and adjusts himself. I try not to pay attention to the way he reaches inside his sweats to move his dick so it's not sticking straight out. I lick my lips and I don't miss the growl that leaves his lips. "We are not done," he says as he moves to the entryway of the living room just as Isla comes bounding into the room, a stuffed bunny in one hand and a teddy bear in the other.

"Daddy!"

"Honey, what's wrong? Why aren't you asleep?" he asks as he kneels in front of her, pushing her disheveled hair from her face.

"I had a bad dream," she whimpers before she lunges into his arms and rests her head on his shoulder. Only then does she see me and her head perks up instantly. "Ellie!" she exclaims.

"Hi, honey." I smile at her. "I'm sorry you had a bad dream." She pulls away from her dad and moves toward me before climbing on the couch to sit next to me.

"Uh uh, back to bed," Rowan says, crossing his arms over his chest.

"Ellie, can I stay with you?" she asks as she rests her cheek on my arm and while I usually hate when a kid tries to use me to get out of doing what a parent tells them, I'm tempted to say yes before Rowan interrupts.

"No," Rowan says and I frown at him, wishing he wasn't being so tough on her just because he's irritated that she interrupted us.

"But—" she starts.

"Isla Jude," he says and she looks up at him. "I'll take you back to bed. You're not going to rope Elianna into letting you stay up."

Her warm chocolate eyes flit up to mine and she crooks a finger at me so I'll lean closer. Then she covers her mouth, presses her hand against my cheek, and whispers in my ear, "Will you take me?"

An unfamiliar feeling washes over me that she'd rather me take her back to bed instead of her father because I'm not used to that. Usually the kids that I nanny for are dying for more attention from their parents, especially the little girls when it comes to their fathers. I look up at Rowan and then down at Isla. "I can take her."

Realizing that's more than likely what she whispered, he nods and I get off the couch, Isla's hand already encased in mine as we make our way to the stairs. "G'night, Daddy!"

"Night, honey," he says, and when I turn to look over my shoulder, I meet his hungry eyes as they practically undress me.

CHAPTER TWELVE

I'M STANDING OUTSIDE OF ISLA'S ROOM WITH MY HAND hovering over the handle as I prepare to go inside. It's been almost thirty minutes since Ellie brought Isla upstairs and I've almost worn a hole in the living room floor pacing back and forth while I wait for her to come back. I've never known Isla to want anyone to take her back to bed besides me. There were even a few times their mother called me in the middle of the night because Isla was inconsolable and kept asking for me. She is growing out of the fear of monsters under her bed thanks to Sawyer telling her that basically nothing is real.

The only good thing to come out of him spilling the beans about Santa Claus, the Tooth Fairy, and the Easter Bunny, I guess.

But she still felt more settled when I was the one to take her over anyone else, so asking Ellie sent an unfamiliar feeling through me. It felt like a combination of happiness that she is connecting with someone and concern that she is connecting with her in a way that will make it extremely difficult for her when Ellie inevitably leaves.

And now I'm thinking about her leaving.
Fuck. She can't leave. Not after…

"Can I?" I hear her soft voice in my head asking if she could touch my dick while she was sitting in my lap. I'm fairly certain that's a scene that's going to play on a loop in my head for the rest of my fucking life. Her face, her voice, the softness of her curves under my hands while she ground herself against me.

A feeling of pride shoots through me when I remember that I'm the first man she's ever done that with. The only man she's ever rubbed her sexy little body against and I'm instantly curious if I can make her come that way.

I finally push through Isla's door quietly, hoping that Isla is asleep and Ellie is on her way out of the room. What I do not expect when I enter Isla's room is both of them asleep on Isla's full-sized princess bed. Isla is pressed against Ellie's side but what strikes me the most is that her hand is still encased in Ellie's. I stare at them for a moment before I move closer and press a kiss to Isla's forehead and then to Elianna's. She stirs slightly but doesn't wake up, and despite the fact that I want her to so she's not sleeping in here for the rest of the night, I know it's mostly because I want to pick up where we left off before Isla interrupted. Before I can talk myself into waking her up, I'm out of Isla's room.

The next day is Saturday, *thank God*, because it took me at least another hour—half of which I spent with my hand wrapped around my dick while I pictured Elianna's cunt wrapped around it—to fall asleep which meant it was almost five in the morning before my eyes closed for the night. Now, it's ten in the morning and the only reason I'm awake is because I hear Isla screaming Sawyer's name followed by, "*Look what you did!!*" And, "*Shhhh! Dad's still sleeping,*" from Margot.

Definitely one of the cons of having my room on the main floor instead of upstairs.

I briefly wonder if Ellie ever came back downstairs or if she slept the whole night in Isla's room. I reach for my phone and I'm pleasantly surprised to see a text from her.

Surprised and fucking giddy like a teenage boy getting a message from the girl he likes.

> **Elianna Riley (Nanny):** Did not mean to fall asleep on you. Isla's bed is surprisingly comfortable.

A smile finds my lips and before I can tell myself that she may not be under the same carnal haze that we were in last night or that she may be freaking out about what we did, I type out a response.

> **Me:** Not as comfortable as mine.

My heart momentarily stops knowing that she's probably in the kitchen with my kids cooking and if Margot or SJ happen to see her phone light up with a message from me, they may question it, or worse, open it.

And what if she has text message previews enabled?

Shit. Does she have a passcode on her phone?

Of course, everyone has a passcode on their phone.

But they still may be curious as to why I'm texting her instead of just coming out and saying whatever I need to tell her.

I'm out of bed and moving into the bathroom quickly before I let myself spiral any further and convince myself that my kids are currently interrogating her about why I'm telling her how comfortable my bed is.

A few moments later, I'm walking through the kitchen to find all of my kids fully dressed and eating French toast. Ellie's eyes meet mine from her seat at the table over her cup of coffee and I don't see her phone anywhere in sight. She gives me a shy smile before her eyes move to Isla.

"Hi, Daddy!" she says waving her hand and patting the seat next to her for me to sit.

"You slept late," Margot says without looking up from her phone.

"Yeah, I was uh...up late." I try not to let my eyes drift to the gorgeous reason I was up late sitting on the other side of the table next to SJ. "Why are you guys all dressed?" I say as I make a cup of coffee.

"I'm going to the away soccer game and we are all meeting at the school at noon." Margot looks up from her phone. "And then I'm sleeping over at Mel's."

"I want to talk about that before you leave." I don't miss the eye roll before she gets up from the table in a skirt that seems a little too short for a soccer game in October despite her tights underneath.

"Fine. Leaving in thirty!" She tells me.

"Thanks for coming to *my* soccer game!" SJ calls after her and Margot peeks her head back in.

"Since when do you care?"

He puts a hand over his chest. "I always care. I am hurt," he says with his usual sarcasm.

"You'll get over it. Good luck though." She blows him a kiss before she disappears.

Isla hops up from her chair and moves to the corner of the kitchen to grab something sitting on the floor. When she comes back, she holds up a sign that's almost as tall as her. The sign says '*Go Sawyer! #14*' written in bright blue paint. "Look what Ellie and I made!"

SJ wrinkles his nose. "You are not bringing that," he says as he looks at his little sister.

"Yes huh! Ellie said we could," Isla responds instantly.

"Can we not? That's so embarrassing," he retorts.

"Oh, come on, I think it's cute!" Ellie says. "She even used your favorite color. She worked hard on it, SJ."

"No one else is going to have a sign." SJ looks to me, I assume to be of some help but I shake my head.

"Your sister cared enough to make you this sign. Sounds like no one else has anyone that cares about them coming to their games," I interject, and Ellie glares at me.

"Not true! But Isla's still bringing it."

SJ groans. "Fine."

"What time are you guys leaving?" I ask, knowing that I should know this but I don't always make his soccer games. I think I've only made one of the five so far this season. I usually use this day to work with no interruptions because Isla either goes to the game too or goes to Sabrina's for the day.

"Maybe thirty minutes?" Ellie tells me.

"Okay, I'm just going to shower, and I'll leave with you," I tell them and SJ's eyes immediately widen.

"No way. You're coming?" SJ asks, and I hate the way the shock is so evident in his tone.

"Yeah...if that's okay?"

His face lights up and seeing him so excited warms my heart. "Hell yeah."

"Hell yeah!" Isla repeats and I glare at Sawyer and then at Isla all the while I see Ellie trying to hide a smile behind her hand.

"You both know better."

"He said it first!" Isla giggles before she holds up her sign over her head as best she can. "Go Sawyer, hell yeah!" she repeats and I look at her.

"Isla Jude, you have one more before you're in trouble."

She looks at Ellie and giggles before she skips around the table and climbs into her lap. "Sorry, Daddy!"

"Do you want some breakfast? I can make more French toast?" Ellie asks and I shake my head.

"No, I'm good, thanks. I'm going to go talk to Margot and

then shower. Do you know anything else about what she's doing tonight?"

"Gabe is out of town if that's what you're asking," SJ interjects before he gets up, puts his plate in the sink, and heads out of the kitchen.

"Well...that does answer one of my questions," I say, grateful that SJ somehow seems to know everything about what goes on in this house.

The thought kind of terrifies me after what happened last night with Ellie though.

"Isla, are you going to Sabrina's after the game?" I ask her, wondering if there's a chance the house would be empty tonight except for Ellie.

"No, she's coming here."

"Is she sleeping over?"

"Yes! Ellie said she could!"

I nod, knowing that at least that will keep Isla preoccupied for the majority of the night. Plus, Margot will be out...and usually Sawyer has friends over after the game. That might mean Ellie and I can have five minutes alone tonight. My eyes drift to hers hoping she can see the ideas of everything I plan to do to her if we have any alone time later.

"Isla, you ready to go?" I ask her.

"I just need my sunglasses!"

"What color?"

"Blue, for SJ's team."

"Okay, go get them and your coat," I tell her and she nods before hopping off the chair and running out of the room. I'm acutely aware of her footsteps going up the stairs and then I don't hear anything, leaving Ellie and I alone in the kitchen.

"Hey," I say with a smile and when she returns it, I can feel my heart start to pick up speed.

"Hi," she says and I immediately start counting backward from ten in hopes it'll keep my dick from rising in response to the pink spreading across her bronzed skin. *She is so fucking beautiful.* "I saw your text...I just couldn't respond at the time."

"I didn't even think about the fact that you weren't alone when I sent it. Sorry."

"It's okay. I have a passcode on my phone and I put your messages on mute after I texted you so if you responded it wouldn't just pop up on my screen."

"That's smart." I let out a sigh of relief that she'd had the foresight to do that. I take a few steps, closing the distance between us and she shakes her head.

"Not now," she whispers and I swallow realizing how close all of my children are and though their voices all enter a room at least ten seconds before they do, I don't want to risk it.

"Tonight," I tell her. I'd meant for it to be a question but I hear how it comes out. Direct with a hint of dominance, and her eyes widen like that one word transports her back to last night and everything we did.

She nods rapidly. "Okay."

"I mean...if that's something you want...to continue what we started." The last thing I want is for this very inexperienced woman almost twenty years younger than me to feel like I coerced her into something.

"I do. I know what I said before but...I have to stop ignoring what I want. And...I really want you," she whispers before she walks by, barely brushing against me. Her scent surrounds me and I want nothing more than to submerge my face in her neck to keep it on me.

"Elianna," I grunt and spin around just in time to watch her disappear around the corner without another look back.

CHAPTER THIRTEEN

W E ARE WALKING TO THE SOCCER FIELDS, AND JUST before Sawyer takes off, he bumps his fist against Ellie's.

"Good luck!" She calls after him.

"GO SJ!" Isla cheers while still holding Ellie's hand and dragging the sign behind her. "Oh, there's Sabrina, byeeee!" she says before she takes off running toward her best friend who is already sitting on the sideline in a pink chair that matches my daughter's that I'm still holding. She's pretty fast for a six-year-old. Even her physical education teacher has sent a note home asking me to consider enrolling her in soccer, but Isla isn't having any of it.

Not only does she seem to hate wearing any kind of tennis shoe, but she prefers to be in a dress at all times and is terrified of getting hit in the face with a soccer ball after seeing it happen during SJ's games.

"Do you want your chair?" I call after her and she turns around and nods and waves me toward her.

"Yes please!" We continue walking toward them and just when I approach them, Sabrina's mother, Daphne looks at me like she's seen a ghost.

"Well well well, look who it is!" Daphne and I have the best kind of relationship one can have with someone who was best friends with your ex who eventually died. After the divorce, she wasn't my biggest fan, but after Bianca passed, she put her grievances aside for Isla and Sabrina's friendship. When Bianca and I were married, we went out with her and her husband often, and while her husband—Rob—isn't who I would call a close friend, he is tolerable when he isn't being a total dick. I spot him next to the coach with a few of the other dads probably trying to tell the coach how to do his job.

"Always nice to see you, Daph." I nod at her with a hint of sarcasm.

"I was not expecting you. The office must be on fire without you." She gives me a fake smile before giving a real one to Ellie and raising her sunglasses back over her eyes. "Hey, Ellie."

I look at Elianna who responds with a wave and a smile before I roll my eyes and nod my head away from them. She follows me until we are out of earshot of her and most of the parents.

"You guys are friendly," she observes.

"I think I mentioned that she was their mother's best friend, so...she has a lot of thoughts about *everything* when it comes to me." I pause but Elianna doesn't say anything so I continue. "She thinks I work too much." I chuckle. "Like I haven't heard that before," I add sardonically.

She hesitates for a moment before she speaks. "I know Sawyer is really glad you're here and that's all that matters."

"I should be here more..." I shake my head.

"You've been doing the best you can," she says and when I look down at her, she's staring at the field watching the teams warm up. If there weren't so many people around, I'd slide an arm around her waist or over her shoulder. She looks up at me, "I'm glad you're here too."

She bumps her shoulder against my arm playfully before we both turn our gazes back to the field where I see them getting in formation to start the game. Sawyer looks over at the sidelines and I watch him scan it, probably looking for me and when he sees me, he nods before turning back toward the ball. I suddenly feel a pang of guilt as I think about all the times he probably looked for me when I wasn't here.

"I can't stop thinking about last night," she whispers, and I watch as her eyes look around to make sure no one is paying us any attention.

I turn to her, surprised that she's choosing to bring this up now. "You want to talk about that now?"

She looks up at me and her mouth falls open slightly and I watch as her tongue darts out to lick her bottom lip before her teeth scrape over it. "We're alone."

A smirk pulls at my lips and I slide my hands into the pockets of my jacket. "I haven't stopped thinking about it either, but I haven't stopped thinking about *you* all week."

She looks up at me with those innocent eyes that I'm beginning to think may not be so innocent just as the whistle blows and I watch as all of the kids scatter.

I'm about to tell her my plans for the next time we're alone when I feel a hand on my shoulder and a squeeze followed by, "I know SJ has to be hyped that you're here." River appears next to me, dressed in jeans and a Bulldogs football hooded sweatshirt under a denim jacket. "Let's go fourteen!" He cheers and Sawyer's head immediately looks toward us and smiles. River comes to Sawyer's games more than I do, but he's missed the last few due to the football team he coaches having afternoon games, so I know Sawyer is excited to see him too.

Isla's head snaps toward us when she hears my brother from where she's sitting and she jumps up to run to us. "Uncle River!"

"Isles!" He drops to his knee before he picks her up. "I've missed you, pipsqueak."

"Me too. Ellie doesn't always let us get donuts after school," she whispers loudly and River looks over at her with a grin.

"She doesn't? Well, maybe I was giving you a little too much sugar." He kisses her cheek and squeezes her.

"A little?!" Ellie chimes in.

"Oh, what was that?! Ref! That was out!" He shouts before shaking his head. "Pay attention!"

"Yeah!" Isla yells with a giggle before River sets her back on her feet and she goes back to where she was sitting with Sabrina.

"Ignore him. He takes every sport way too seriously, even when they're children," I tell Ellie with a groan. "What are you doing here anyway? You didn't tell me you were coming, I figured you had a game today?"

"The game was last night and we crushed them. My quarterback is insane, I think he has a chance to be All-American if he would just focus and stop trying to fuck every girl in a three-mile radius."

"Sounds like someone else I know," I say with a knowing look thinking about how my younger brother was in high school when it came to girls and focusing on anything else but them.

"Jealous?" he jokes and I roll my eyes just as a man I don't recognize approaches the three of us.

"River, what's up man." He nods, shaking his hand, before looking at me. "Sawyer's father, right?"

"Rowan," I tell him and he shakes my hand before looking at Ellie.

"Hey, Ellie." He smiles wide, revealing his teeth, and I'm instantly on the defense, irritated that this guy might be trying to flirt with her.

"Hi, Paul." She smiles politely and I'm grateful I don't see the look in her eyes she had last night when she was looking at me. Or any time she's looked at me for that matter.

"I was hoping I'd see you today. I wanted to say thank you for the tip about the chicken piccata, it was—" I'm interrupted from listening to their conversation by River ushering me away closer to the sideline.

I turn back to look at them even as we're walking away before I turn my gaze to River in question. "Why are we moving?"

"Give them some space, jeez." He doesn't take his eyes off the game before he continues. "Would you want some dudes hanging around when you're trying to flirt with someone?"

"And why is he flirting with my nanny?" I ask, not even trying to hide the irritation in my voice.

"I guess, you won't accept the obvious answer which is *because she's hot?*" he jokes, smacking my arm.

I clench my jaw and turn my head again to see them talking, and although she's smiling, she meets my eyes briefly before turning back to him. "He's not married?"

"Recently divorced. He seems like a pretty decent guy. I've talked to him a few times—good defense!" He claps before turning to me. "What's crawled up your ass?"

"Nothing." I shake my head before running a hand through my hair as I try to calm my frustrations. I look down the sideline and manage to catch the look of a few men staring behind me. Some of them are hiding it better than others but a few of them are obvious in the fact that Ellie has their attention. "Why are they acting like they've never seen a woman before?"

He follows my gaze and chuckles before turning back to me. "Because twenty-five-year-old women that look like *that* rarely come to a ten-year-old's soccer game, and if they do, they are rarely single."

"Well, she shouldn't have to deal with that."

"Deal with what? I can assure you that Ellie is no stranger to male attention."

Her comments last night come rushing back to me and feelings of protectiveness bloom in my chest. "You don't know that."

"Let's see, she's gorgeous and smart and charming and great with kids. No, you're right, men *never* notice her. You're being real fuckin' weird. Like—" He pauses and moves to stand in front of me so he can look me in the eye. He turns his baseball hat he's wearing backward to really study me before his brown eyes narrow. "No shit! I fucking *knew* it," he whispers before punching me softly on my arm. "I should kick your ass, you hypocrite." He points at me as a wolfish grin pulls at his lips. "You said *I* was too old for her, but what you really meant was, 'no, River, *you* can't stick your dick in her because *I* want to!?'"

"Lower your voice," I grit out. Glancing behind me, I notice that Paul or Pat or whatever the fuck his name is still talking to her, so I'm sure they can't hear us, but I still guide my brother even further away from them. "And don't talk about her like that," I snap.

"Did you guys hook up?!" He claps his hands together once. "Oh, we are getting a drink later tonight. How? When? I need to know everything," he says excitedly and I'm sure he's probably the only person as excited about this revelation as I am.

"I'm not telling you anything."

He snorts. "If you don't, I'll go over there and ask Ellie myself."

"You won't."

He raises one eyebrow at me and I'm not even sure why I said that because I know for a fact that River absolutely would. "Watch me." He starts back toward her when I grab him by the arm to stop him from moving.

"You're such a fucking pain, you know that?"

"Did you guys fuck?!" he asks excitedly as he joins me back at my side.

"No," I tell him, trying to focus on the game and not the way Elianna felt in my arms when she ground her cunt against my dick.

"But…" He looks at me as if to say, *I know there's more to this.*

"Well, not yet."

"Oh shit. So, you're going to?"

I sigh, knowing that I'd probably end up telling him eventually. "We probably would have last night, but Isla woke up."

He groans. "I swear that's why I don't have kids. Always cock-blocking. What were you doing?"

"Kissing on the couch. That's it." I swallow. "Well, she was in my lap."

He whistles and slaps my back. "Well, fuck, man, I'm proud of you. It has been a long time. Like a year?"

"Yeah." I clear my throat, suddenly very aware that it's been a long time since I've slept with a woman. I've never had any complaints in that department, but the thought that I won't last longer than thirty seconds with Ellie sends a wave of unease through me. "I like her."

"You like her? Or the thought of being inside of your nanny?" He nudges me as a smirk pulls at his lips.

"Her." I scratch my jaw. "Trust me, I wish she was anyone else *but* my nanny. She's so easy to talk to. I've told her things. Things I've only said out loud to my therapist. Things only you know. Stuff about our childhood and Bianca and the kids…last night wasn't exactly the first time anything happened between us." I sigh, and give him the rundown from last weekend and how we both admitted we liked each other before Elianna stopped us from going further.

"I *knew* I noticed something the other night before we went out. That was one of the reasons I came in when we got home and brought up the girl at the bar. If there's one thing I know, it's jealousy can make two people figure out their feelings for each other really fuckin' quick."

"You're joking."

"Well, it clearly worked." He crosses his arms over his chest and gives me a look. *I guess he's not wrong.* I recall her asking me if I was attracted to her and I'm fairly certain I noticed a jealous glint in her eye.

"She's worried about how this will affect everything and…I get that. Part of me is worried I'm making a mistake but a bigger part is more worried that it's not going to stop me." I swallow hard. "No one has turned my head in almost a year and now the one woman that should be off limits has all my fucking attention."

"Well, I don't think it's necessarily a mistake. You're both adults and you both understand the risks. If you're attracted to each other, what's the problem?"

"The problem is my six-year-old is very attached to her. So is my ten year old for that matter though he pretends he's not. If things end badly between us—"

"Okay," he interrupts, "let's come back from the edge, how about you cross that bridge when and if you get there? Have you even talked about what all of this means? What if she just wants sex? You guys could be like…boss and employee with benefits."

"Yeah, because that always works out so well." I roll my eyes. "And I don't think that's what she wants. I don't think that's what I want either…"

"All I'm saying is if you guys communicate what you want honestly like adults, then there really shouldn't be a scenario in which this ends *badly*."

I stare at my brother incredulously. "Well, this is rich coming from a guy whose way of communicating with women is by changing his number."

"I only did that *twice* and both times were because ghosting wasn't working. And I communicate. It is not my fault that I say one thing and women hear something completely different." He clears his throat. "For instance, I tell a woman that I don't want a relationship and *this is just sex* and the next morning, she asks if I want to come to brunch to meet her parents. Mind you, I was three hours from here for an away game." He throws his hands up in exasperation before letting them fall. "What do you want from me?"

"Well, maybe stop sleeping with women with the emotional maturity of a napkin."

Read: women in their early twenties.

"Their tits sit higher and their inhibitions are lower, sue me. But let's get back to you, I assume you are planning to keep all of this from the kids."

"Yes, definitely," I say remembering the night Margot came home and seemed to be suspicious of why we were out on the patio alone. "Margot might suspect something but it might be all in my head."

"Well, given that she's older, you do have to be more careful when she's home, but unless she's caught you doing something, just assume she doesn't know anything," he says. "Are you going to have any alone time tonight? You want me to take SJ and Isla for the night?" As much of a pain as my brother can be, I'm reminded that he'd do anything for me and my family so I'm not surprised he asks. He's gone above and beyond to help me the past year however he could.

"No, Isla is having Sabrina over."

He nods. "Cute kid. Too bad she's the spawn of Satan."

"Daphne isn't Satan." I roll my eyes even though I know my brother isn't loyal to anyone above me so I'm not surprised that this is his take.

"I'm not talking about Daphne; I'm talking about her husband."

"Oh." Well, that's surprising. My brother is the extroverted one who gets along with everyone. "I'm not a huge fan of him either, but what's your problem with him?"

"He's just a tool *and* I was at a bar across town a few weeks ago and he was looking *really* chummy with some woman that was *not* Daphne."

My eyes widen in shock. "What? Are you sure? You know what? I don't want to know anything because I don't want to get involved." I shake my head, thoroughly annoyed by this knowledge already. "God, you're such a gossip."

"I'm a high school teacher and football coach, of course I am.

What else you want to know?" He chuckles. "Oh, Jake cheated on Mikayla with Adrianna last weekend at Steve's party."

My eyes dart to all the parents on the sidelines trying to see if any of those names ring a bell. "Who the hell are they?"

"I don't know. I think they're juniors." He shrugs. "You know who talks more shit than the girls in my third-period biology class? My entire football team in the locker room. It's like I'm constantly listening to a fucking soap opera—"

"Thanks for ditching me!" Ellie's voice interrupts our conversation and she appears next to me sporting a scowl with a hint of a smile beneath her full lips. She narrows her eyes at us before turning back to the game.

"I'm sorry," I tell her, wishing River wasn't here so I could tell her how much I *did not* want to leave her alone with another guy. "We thought maybe you'd like some space and we didn't want to interrupt."

"Yeah, that was my bad," River interjects. "Thought you may be interested and we didn't want to be in the way."

Ellie looks up at me and then at my brother before turning back to the game. "No, I'm not interested."

CHAPTER FOURTEEN

Rowan

I'VE BEEN IN MY OFFICE SINCE WE GOT BACK FROM SJ'S GAME, so it isn't until later that night that Ellie and I finally have a moment alone.

Despite Isla having her best friend over, she wanted to include Ellie in all of their activities including a very long tea party and the first two Toy Story movies. *SJ says she's not ready for the third one yet.* SJ and two of his friends from his soccer team have only emerged from the basement twice to get more snacks and I don't think we'll see them again for the rest of the night. Now, Isla and Sabrina are upstairs in Margot's room watching a movie and I know it's only a matter of time before they're asleep.

"Hi." I hear Ellie's soft voice from the entrance to my office and when I look up, she's leaning against the doorjamb with a smirk pulling at her lips. I notice she's changed into pajamas—loose-fitting shorts and a button-up short-sleeved shirt—and I wonder if I reach my hand up her shorts, I'd be met with her bare pussy.

"Hi, yourself."

She makes her way through my office slowly. "Isla and SJ and their friends are pretty settled. Isla and Sabrina are watching Aladdin and SJ and his friends are playing video games," she tells me as she makes her way to my desk. "I wasn't sure if there was anything else you needed before I went to my room for the night?" Her voice is soft and light but I can see the look in her eyes that tells me she'd meant for the innuendo to come out loud and clear.

"Shut the door," I tell her and she peeks over her shoulder for a second before turning back to me and shaking her head.

"What if someone comes looking for one of us? It may be kind of hard to explain to SJ why we're in here with the door closed. Isla may not think it's odd, if she even knocks."

Fuck. "I need to touch you, Elianna."

"I think I need that too." She practically purrs and it makes my dick hard.

I'm out of my chair, moving toward her until I'm standing in front of her. "I need more than last night." I move so I'm pressed against her and I lower my head to drag my nose along her neck. "I need you to grind your pussy against my dick again." I bite down on her neck gently and she lets out a gasp as I drag my teeth down the slope to her shoulder. "Without clothes this time."

"It's still too early," she whispers even as she tilts her head back. "You should have seen the bag of candy SJ and his friends have already gone through; they're going to be up late."

"They won't need either of us," I tell her before I move my mouth to hover over hers. Her eyes which were closed flutter open revealing those bright brown eyes that I easily get lost in. "But I fucking need you." I look toward my open door, briefly wondering if I could just take her against the wall with my door wide open. I ghost my lips across hers and she lets out a sigh.

"Rowan," she whispers and then I feel her hands under my shirt and dragging up my torso. I pull her harder against me and snake my hand down her back to her ass and grip it hard as I slant my mouth over hers. It takes no time for her mouth to part and I slide my tongue between her lips to find hers, relishing in the taste of her for the first time since last night.

Fuck, she tastes better than I remembered.

Her hands snake around my neck, pulling me harder against her and I can sense her hips moving, searching for friction. A groan rumbles in my chest thinking about the wetness forming between her legs. Keeping my lips on hers, I lift her into my arms, walk her to my desk, and set her on top of it before I sit at my chair in front of her. I prop her feet on my thighs and slowly raise my eyes to hers, taking a moment to catalog the goosebumps on her bare legs, her arms, and her nipples pebbling underneath her cotton sleep shirt.

Her eyes are hooded when I meet her gaze and I hear her take a sharp breath when I rest my hands on her knees and part her legs slowly. "Are you wearing anything underneath these flimsy little shorts?" I ask as I tug on the hem.

She shakes her head and I glide my tongue along my bottom lip lasciviously at the thought that there's only one piece of fabric between me and her pussy. *More specifically my mouth and her pussy.*

"Show me."

Her hands move to rest on top of mine which are still sitting on her knees and she drags her fingertips over my knuckles. "Show you? You mean…my…"

"Your pussy." I nod before dropping my eyes to the apex of her thighs. "Yes. Show me your pussy, sunshine."

She gives me a shy smile, like every other time I've called her that. "I'm still waiting to see your dick, you know."

Remembering her request from last night, I slide my chair back just a little and lean back so her feet are still resting on my thighs but so I have enough space to pull myself out of my sweatpants. I pull myself out and I'm pleased at the sexy gasp that leaves her lips when she sees my dick. "Is this what you want to see?" I ask as I stroke myself from root to tip. I'm already leaking from the head but I hold my hand over my mouth and spit into it, my eyes not leaving hers before continuing to stroke my cock.

"Oh my God," she whispers, her eyes dilating and I watch as she struggles to swallow before she leans back slightly. Her hand leaves mine and though I sense a hint of nerves, her fingers find the hem of her shorts. She moves the fabric covering her to the side revealing her bare cunt to my hungry eyes. Her lips are already coated in arousal making her glisten and the sight causes all the fucking air to leave my lungs.

I grip my dick, squeezing it harder with every stroke downward as I begin to move faster. Her eyes are transfixed on my dick and I notice her breathing becoming even more erratic every time my hand reaches the tip. "Is your pussy getting wet and hot watching?"

"Yeah," she whispers and I watch as her teeth press into her bottom lip hard.

"You need to get off, don't you? You want to rub your horny little cunt right now, don't you?" She nods. "Want me to rub it for you?" Her eyes flutter shut and she nods again. "Use your words."

Her eyes snap open. "Yes. Will you please touch me?"

"Always so sweet and polite." I chuckle as I move my other hand off her knee. "You don't have to be like that with me. Not while we're here. You tell me what you want, understand?"

"Okay."

"Spread your legs a little wider," I tell her and she does as best as she can with her shorts still on but it's enough for me to slide my hand through the leg hole. I touch the top of her mound, dragging my thumb down her short landing strip of hair before making it to the top of her slit. "This is so fucking sexy," I tell her as I push inside and immediately rub my thumb over her clit.

"Shit," she whispers and leans back slightly, opening her legs even wider as I continue rubbing her. I slide two of my fingers inside of her while continuing to rub her clit and she whimpers when I curl my fingers upward slightly. My eyes move back and forth between her gorgeous eyes that now look hazy and full of lust and her pussy that is currently wrapped around two of my fingers, and I don't think I've ever seen a sexier image. "Rowan," she moans quietly and my name leaving those full pouty lips while my fingers are deep in her cunt is enough to send a jolt of electricity shooting through me. I want nothing more than to pull her off this desk and sit her directly on my cock but the wide open door behind us stops me.

"God, I want to fuck you so bad," I whisper as I continue fingering her, praying that my tongue will have the same task *soon*. Her pussy is soaking wet and I wouldn't be surprised if she leaked onto my desk. The thought of getting a whiff of her cunt while I'm in here working turns my already hard dick to granite.

"Maybe..." she lets out a sigh. "We could just for a second?"

My dick twitches and I feel the ache forming in my balls brought on by just those few words. I stand without another thought, removing my hand from her so I can wrap it around my dick dragging her wetness all over it. I use my other hand to grab her by the crotch of her shorts and pull her to the edge of the desk and then without another thought or word letting her know what I plan to do I drag my dick through her wet slit once.

The gasp she lets out is *loud*. Louder than either of us have been the entire time we've been in here together. I snap my eyes to hers and she slaps a hand over her mouth, her eyes wide and nervous. She drops her hand from her mouth after a few moments and I lean forward and brush my lips across hers. "That feel good?" I ask as I swipe my cock through her folds again, slower this time, dragging the tip of my dick up and down her slit as I edge us both. This time I rub the tip against her clit and she squeezes her eyes shut and digs her teeth into her bottom lip.

"Yes," she says before she looks down at where we're connected. "I need more," she begs and I notice she moves closer to me, pushing my cock further past the entrance.

"Fuck." I groan as her gorgeous cunt strangles the tip. "Just for a second."

"Yes. Yes. *Yes*," she says, nodding vigorously, still staring at where I'm two inches deep into her pussy.

"Look at me," I tell her and her eyes float up to meet mine, hooded and sexy as she blinks at me. I slowly push inside of her and she gasps as if the wind has been knocked out of her.

I pull her chest against mine and her nails dig hard into my back. The feeling shoots through my body allowing me to feel the pierce in my dick. *Fuuuuuck.*

"You, okay? Jesus Christ, you're tight."

"I told you," she whimpers as she presses her face hard into my neck. "It's…been…a…while." She pants between words. I stay still, trying to let her adjust to my size, and drop my hand between us, dragging my fingers over her clit to try and relax her. "I've never been this full," she murmurs as she drags her lips along my shoulder.

Fuck. And I'm not even fully inside of her.

I pull her away from my shoulder to look at her, my dick still buried in her cunt with my fingers still lazily rubbing her clit. I watch as relaxation and pleasure take over and I smile as lust fills those big brown eyes.

"You are so beautiful," I tell her.

"You make me feel so beautiful. No one's ever looked at me the way you do."

Her words hit me harder than I anticipated and coupled with me almost being fully seated inside of her and our eyes locked, I feel something change in an instant. Knowing that now is not the time to unpack that, I press my lips to hers and push myself all the way inside, our pelvises pressed together and though we said just for a second, I can't stop myself from sliding out and pushing back in again *and again*.

"Oh my God, Rowan. Don't stop." She moans into my neck, having adjusted to my size and now I want nothing more than to make her come all over my dick. My sweatpants have fully fallen to my ankles and her legs are now wrapped around my bare ass, her heels pressing into it to meet my thrusts while remaining mostly quiet.

"No way am I stopping," I whisper because her tight cunt is wrapped around me so fucking tight, it would take divine intervention to get me to pull out of her right now.

Enter divine intervention.

The sound of the basement door opens and I hear three sets of feet running through my kitchen.

We break apart instantly. My cock is shiny and slick and very angry at me for pulling out of the silkiest and tightest cunt it's ever been inside of. Elianna pulls her shorts back over her pussy and hops off my desk. Her eyes are wide and I can sense the nerves flowing off of her. I move toward her, putting my finger over her lips gently.

Relax, I mouth at her because I know they'll be retreating downstairs just as quickly as they came up.

I hear my son and his friends whispering and shuffling around the kitchen, opening the refrigerator, and the rustling of multiple bags of chips before I hear them running back downstairs and the basement door closing.

"We shouldn't have done that," she says softly and I tilt my head to the side.

"We shouldn't have?" A smirk pulls at my lips and she glares at me.

"You know what I mean. What if..."

"It's okay. Nothing happened," I tell her, not wanting her to obsess over a scenario that has SJ catching us for being reckless.

"I should go to my room."

"Can I come?" I pull her into my arms and slide my hands through her hair tugging gently before pressing my lips to hers. My dick is still hard as stone and the sexy sigh she lets out as she rubs her warm body against me, is making sure it stays that way.

She's about to respond when divine intervention occurs yet *again*.

"Daaaddy!!" I hear screamed from upstairs. "Margot's TV isn't working!!"

"Why are they still up?" I sigh. "Christ, I should have taken River up on his offer," I mumble. "Coming, Isla!" I yell out the door before I turn to look at Elianna who's staring at me curiously.

"And what exactly did River offer?" She narrows her eyes like she knows already.

"To take SJ and Isla to give us some privacy," I tell her as I move toward the door.

"You told River…about last night?"

"Only because the jealousy was written all over my face the second that guy approached you at the game. River can read me like a book and he put it together."

She crosses her arms over her shirt and bites her bottom lip as she tries to hide the smile on her lips. "You were jealous?"

"I spent most of the last week thinking about you and most of last night with you sitting on my dick or with my hand wrapped around it while I pictured you. Yeah, Elianna, I was fucking jealous," I tell her, and I don't wait for her response before I'm out of my office.

I'm somehow suckered into making Isla and Sabrina some popcorn, so it's another ten minutes after troubleshooting Margot's television and bringing them their snack with the order that they need to go to bed *soon* before I'm in front of Elianna's door. I knock softly once, hoping she's not asleep when she opens it with a shy smile on her face. She keeps the door mostly closed while she stands in the doorway blocking the entrance.

My hand reaches up, unbuttoning the top button of her shirt, dying for a glimpse of those perky tits I've never seen but haven't stopped picturing since the second I laid eyes on her. "You going to let me in?"

Her eyes peer down the hall before looking back up at me. "Can you be quiet?"

"Can you?" I ask her. "I recall you being a little…sensitive." I lean down so I'm eye level with her chest and drag my tongue between the valley of her breasts. I hear a quiet gasp leave her lips and then her hands are at the back of my neck guiding my mouth to hers. She pulls me into her room, closing the door behind me, and it only takes us a few steps for us to be on her bed, me on top of her and her legs wrapped around me, our lips still attached. Her fingers run through my hair, and I feel the gentle sensation of her nails on my scalp spurring me on, making me kiss her harder. The room is quiet, save for our heavy breathing and the sounds of our bodies grinding against each other. I'm really fucking glad I replaced the bed in here before she moved in because it barely makes any noise.

"Rowan," she breathes out quietly. "Please *please*, fuck me."

My dick throbs at her begging; hard and leaking and dying to be inside her like she wants. "I need to do something first," I tell her as my hands find the front of her shirt, unbuttoning the second and third buttons. My face is tucked into her neck, breathing in her spicy scent and I drag my teeth along the skin desperate to mark her there.

"What's…that?" she says, her voice breathy and full of need.

She has a small lamp on her nightstand sheathing the room in a soft glow, but bright enough for me to see everything I need to see when I pull back to look down at her. "Taste you."

CHAPTER FIFTEEN

Elianna

I SWALLOW NERVOUSLY, BEFORE MEETING HIS GAZE. My breasts aren't exposed yet, but I feel his hands dancing just beneath them, like he's waiting for me to respond to what he said. I bite my bottom lip trying to temper the frenzy of nerves coursing through me. A combination of excitement, lust, and worry flows through me, and I think he feels the last of those emotions because he pulls back slightly and moves his hands away from my breasts.

"What is it, gorgeous?"

My eyebrows pinch and a fourth emotion—embarrassment—flares up that I have to tell him.

Maybe I don't need to?

Well, you have to say something now.

"I haven't..." My voice wavers and I clear my throat, trying to remove the nerves from it. "No one has ever done *that*, so I'm just a little nervous."

He stares at me for a moment before he rubs a hand over his mouth. "We need to have a talk about the men you've been dealing with because…*excuse me?*" He's pulled back so he's seated on his heels as he looks me over. "First things first, is it because you don't want anyone to?"

"No." I shake my head. "It's not that…it's just…no one has ever wanted to, I guess."

"Fucking idiots," he grumbles. "Okay, follow-up question. Elianna, have you ever had an orgasm?"

"Yes," I respond quickly. "Of course."

"Not one you gave yourself."

My cheeks heat at having to admit this. "Well…no." I watch as he closes his eyes slowly and lets out what sounds a bit like a groan. "It's fine!"

He snorts and gives me a look like he's ready to scold me for saying that. "It's absolutely *not* fine, but we will dig into why you think it is after you come all over my tongue." The shock from his words quickly turns to lust as tingles immediately flutter through my pussy. My eyes trace his mouth thinking about those soft lips pressed against the space between my legs. His hands find my shorts and his eyes look at me for reassurance that I'm okay with him taking them off. I nod once. He slides them off and tosses them behind him before he swallows hard. "I can't believe a man was lucky enough to touch you and wasn't begging you to let him do this." He looks up at me before undoing the last button of my sleep shirt and letting it fall open.

I'm now completely exposed in front of him and with the look he's giving me, I don't feel nervous or self-conscious because he's staring at me like I'm the most beautiful thing he's ever seen in his life. "You're so perfect. I knew your tits would be as pretty as the rest of you." He leans down and brushes his lips against mine once. "Since it's your first time, I won't make you sit on my face, yet," he whispers against my lips. "But make no mistake, having your wet cunt ride my tongue is next."

A gush of air leaves my lungs and I feel every hair on my body stand on end because no one has ever talked to me like this before. So nasty and dirty and *hot*.

Thoughts of how I taste briefly enter my mind before I feel something pressed right against me and when I look down, I see his nose pressing against my sex and then I hear a deep inhale. "You smell so fucking good." He opens me up, exposing every inch of me to him and then I feel his finger rubbing over my clit again. "I am going to enjoy every fucking second of making you come. Fucking honored that I get to be the first man to do it." And then with his eyes still on me, he lowers his mouth and takes one slow lick through my slit.

Holy shit! Pleasure clouds my vision and I struggle to keep my eyes open as a tremor moves through me. "Oh fuck!" I moan while still keeping my voice barely above a whisper. My eyes slam shut as fireworks shoot through my body and I fall to my back as my arms give out in response to the pleasure.

"Stay with me, sunshine," he groans with his face buried between my legs. "Keep those eyes on me. I want to watch you come while I'm tasting it." I lift my head and try to open my eyes but the way his tongue keeps flicking my clit makes it fucking impossible. He chuckles and the feeling vibrates through me. "Okay, we'll work on it," he says before he slows down his efforts. He takes long, slow licks against me from the bottom of my pussy all the way to the top of my mound, leaving no inch of me untouched.

Fingers find my stomach and begin to slide upwards and then his warm hands palm my breasts and something glides across both nipples. "Oh God, Rowan. It—it's too much…" I stammer, trying my best to keep my voice as quiet as possible but I slowly feel everything logical leaving my brain. One of my hands drops to his head, and I pull some strands gently while raising my hips harder against his mouth.

"That's right, baby. Show me where it feels good."

"Everywhere," I whisper. "Nothing has ever felt…this amazing."

That familiar feeling begins to build in my toes when I feel two fingers slide inside of me all while his tongue continues to lap at my clit and every time he glides over it, it throbs with pleasure. I'm already nearing the edge when he touches something inside of me and I have to slam a hand over my mouth to stop myself from crying out.

"Oh, fuck fuck fuck. Oh God, I'm going to come."

"Good girl. Give me what I fucking want, Elianna." He grunts and the use of my full name pushes me even closer to the edge.

I am going to come for the first time against this man's mouth… who happens to be my very gorgeous boss who is almost twenty years older than me.

I moan at the thought, feeling so turned on I can barely think, and I have no idea how loud I am over the pleasure currently shooting up my spine and burrowing into my brain as he continues to lick my aching cunt. "Right there. Oh my God, Rowan. Yesss, I'm coming. Fuck." I moan. One of my hands finds my nipple while the other tangles in his hair as I roll my hips against his mouth and fingers so fucking desperate to come, the idea of sitting on his face comes to mind and I suddenly want nothing more than to do that.

"Want…" I breathe out as my orgasm washes over me. "Oh God, I want to ride your face," I tell him and the sound that comes out of him in response is so fucking sexy. I feel my orgasm subsiding but my body feels like it's floating and I am so content, I could cry. "Wow," I whisper. My clit is still throbbing like it has a heartbeat of its own and a shudder moves through me when I feel a light kiss on it.

He finally pulls away, his lips and chin shiny and coated with a layer of me. His eyes are hungry as he slides his tongue through my slit again and then drags it up my body to each of my nipples, leaving them wet and tingling from the cool air of the room. He doesn't say anything else and I assume he's waiting for me to respond but my brain is still slightly out of sorts.

"Holy shit," I whisper, still trying to slow my breathing. "I didn't know it could feel like that."

"I think I just figured out what I like to do to relax," he says referring to the conversation we had when I first started working here. "Pretty sure I'm already addicted to the taste of your cunt." He holds my gaze while he runs a digit through my folds and proceeds to lick me off of his fingers. "So, are you ready to sit on my face?" He moves to lie on the bed and I realize I'm probably being a little selfish.

"No...I think I was just caught up in the high of everything." I bite my bottom lip. "Can I... take care of that?" I nod toward his dick which is very hard and pointed at me.

"You can after I make you come again."

Realizing he's still clothed while I'm completely naked, I cross my hands over my naked chest. "Take your clothes off first." He gets off the bed and does as I ask, slowly pulling his shirt over his head, followed by his briefs and sweatpants leaving him completely nude and gorgeous, and I realize it's the first time I've not only seen his bare torso but his entire body. My eyes go from his muscular legs to his chest with the amount of chest hair that I find so hot, to his toned arms to his dick before moving to his handsome face that has a smile on his lips.

"You done?" he asks as he rejoins me on the bed and lies on his back, bringing me with him to straddle his face. I can see the smile in his eyes as he holds me over his mouth but I squirm out of his hold before his tongue can rub against me.

"I want to face the other way..." I tell him. "So, I can play with you too."

I'm still hovering over him, straddling his neck. He kisses my inner thigh and gives me a smile. "Baby, you don't have to do that."

I frown, confused at why he thinks I wouldn't. "Oh... *oh*," I say recalling his question earlier. "Do *you* not like it?"

His eyes widen. "Yes, I do. And the thought of your sweet mouth wrapped around it..." He trails off and clears his throat. "I just know a lot of this is new to you and I don't want to introduce you to too much all at once."

Ohhh.

I shoot him a wicked smirk and then I move so that my face is hovering just above his. "I've done it before." I drag my tongue lightly across his bottom lip before pulling back.

His gaze darkens as he sits up slightly. "You have?"

I nod. "Yes. More than once." I'll admit I may have added that last part because the look in his eye that I'm pretty sure is fueled by jealousy is kind of hot.

"And he didn't eat your pussy?" he asks in shock.

"We've covered that already."

"Elianna," he says like he's warning me.

"Mr. Kincaid," I sass.

A sinful look flashes across his face before it fades into a sweet smile. He rubs my cheek and drags his thumb over my bottom lip. "I hate that no one has taken care of you." Those words sound very similar to something he's said before and I don't know if there is a double meaning to his words but I try not to focus on it.

I look away from his gaze and move myself down his body. "Can I suck your dick now?"

"Yeah," he says between ragged breaths. "Come sit your pussy on my face."

Heat flashes through me. Despite knowing what that mouth can do, I don't think I'll ever get used to the things that come out of it.

I spin around to straddle him and I instantly wrap a hand around his dick as a groan leaves his lips. "Oh *fuck*," he says and a surge of pride moves through me that just my hand causes this reaction. I lower my mouth and drag my tongue over the tip of his dick collecting the pre-cum that's leaking from the head.

"Shit, you're killing me, baby," he whispers and then he drags the tip of his tongue along my sex. I clench, my body tightening at the thought of what's to come. I wasn't lying when I said nothing felt like that. I have what I think to be a pretty decent vibrator that is solely meant for suction and it didn't even come close to how his lips felt wrapped around my clit.

I drag my tongue up his shaft, wondering how I'm going to fit his entire dick in my mouth when three beeps followed by the sound of the alarm indicating someone is coming in the house ring through the air.

Rowan's tongue which had been deep inside my pussy, immediately freezes and I feel the cool air hit my sex as I assume he pulls back.

"Tell me, I'm hearing things."

Next is the sound of more beeps, indicating someone is deactivating the alarm and immediately I scramble off of him to get off the bed. I pull on my shorts and my sleep shirt in seconds.

"What the fuck? Is that Margot?" Rowan whispers as he pulls on his sweatpants and t-shirt. "What time is it?" I spy my phone on the nightstand and grab it noting the time of just after one-thirty and show it to him. He growls in response. "She knows better than to be driving this late at night by herself."

He listens by the door waiting to see if she goes upstairs, knowing that he can't just walk out of my room at this hour when we both hear the sounds of her making her way toward my door.

My eyes widen and he shakes his head. *It's okay*, he mouths and we hear her shuffling outside before a light tapping on his office door.

"Dad, are you in there?" she says softly and I bite my lip nervously before I hear her retreating down the hall.

"She probably thinks I'm sleeping. It's fine," he whispers before he runs a hand through his hair. "But I should go. I need to figure out what she's doing here and if she's okay. I swear she better not have been drinking."

I had an inkling she may be experimenting with alcohol but

I'm not totally sure. I sincerely hope if she has been tonight, she wouldn't have driven her car home.

"I can't tell where in the house she is," he whispers and reaches into his pocket. "Fuck, and I don't have my phone. I left it in my office." He swallows and I can sense the nerves flowing off of him. "What if she called me to come get her and I didn't?" His voice is laced with worry and I look down at my phone.

"Then she would have called me, I would think?" I show him my phone which shows nothing but a few Instagram likes, an email, and a *Monopoly Go!* notification from the ongoing game I've had with my sisters for years.

"I'm sorry," he says.

"Don't be." I nod at him. "Maybe just wash your face before you go see her?" I add weakly.

"Right." He murmurs but I still see the anxiety all over him. "I just panic about her driving."

"I know." I reach for his hand and give it a squeeze. "She's okay. She's here and she's safe, that's all that matters."

He nods before he turns my doorknob and slowly peaks his head out of the door. I look after him, breathing a sigh of relief when I don't see anyone in the direct line of sight in the hallway. He turns back once to look at me and gives me a nod before he moves down the hall slowly and quietly. A few seconds later, I hear the gentle click of his bedroom door.

CHAPTER SIXTEEN

Rowan

I WASH MY FACE AND BRUSH MY TEETH QUICKLY, AFTER checking my phone where I see a message from Margot telling me she was coming home early and that she was fine *but that is absolutely not fine*. I'm up the stairs moving toward Margot's room, surprised to find the door open, and only then do I remember that Isla and Sabrina were in her room. Margot doesn't usually mind when Isla sleeps in there when she is gone, so I doubt she's mad but I also don't know what kind of mood Margot is in right now. When I move inside, I see Isla and Sabrina with sleepy eyes collecting their blankets and stuffed animals and moving off of Margot's bed.

"Hi, Daddy." Isla yawns as she sleepily pads by me with Sabrina in tow.

"Hi, Princess." I smile at her. "You need help?"

She shakes her head and I watch as they move to Isla's room down the hall.

Margot is in her ensuite bathroom so I walk through her room and knock on her door. "Margot, honey. Are you okay?"

I hear a tiny yelp and then Margot opens the door, her eyes wide and unblinking. "Yeah, Dad, I'm fine."

"Then, *what* may I ask, are you doing here at almost two in the morning when you were supposed to be staying at your friend's house?" I cross my arms over my chest, my previous worry slowly morphing into anger at the thought of her driving this late at night by herself. "You know I don't like that. Your curfew is midnight, it does not matter whose house you are staying at that night."

"I know," she says, her eyes welling up with tears. "I just wanted to come home."

"Why?"

"Mel and I got in a fight and…I just wanted to go."

"She's your best friend and you have gotten into arguments before and did not need to come home. Try again."

"Dad? Can you not? I got home safe…"

"Not the point. Mel lives a good fifteen minutes from here." I take a step closer to her and lower myself to look her in the eye. "Are you under the influence of anything?" I ask her, knowing that alcohol has the power to exacerbate even the silliest argument between friends. She shakes her head slowly and I narrow my eyes at her. "Breathe."

Her eyebrows pinch together angrily. "What? You don't believe me? Since when do I lie?"

"Oh, so you don't drink when you're at your friend's house?"

She tilts her head to the side. "Are you asking?" The sass is evident in her voice and I am not in the mood for it.

"Margot Juliette," I warn her.

"Oh my God." Her tone is full of exasperation as she moves away from me and starts moving her pillows around on her bed and throwing a few of her decorative ones on the couch in the corner of her room. "Yes, I've tried alcohol at friends' houses and parties, but I didn't tonight. I wouldn't have driven if I had."

I'm inclined to believe her but I'm still not buying everything she's trying to sell. "I don't care if you and Mel got into an argument. You cannot be out driving around at this hour, especially without talking to me. You know better."

"I texted you."

"I didn't respond. That doesn't count and you know it doesn't." I point at her. I tried my best not to be unreasonable about her driving, but given what happened to their mother I am never more anxious than when she is behind the wheel. So naturally, I am worked up about her doing anything this late at night without talking to me first.

"Okay…I figured you were just caught up working. You're a light sleeper and I know you sleep with your phone on loud, so I assumed even if you were asleep, my message would have woken you up, but then I went to your office when I got here and you weren't there."

"Yeah, I…I was asleep," I tell her. "You should have called." *Not that I would have heard that either*, I think, annoyed with myself for not having my phone close by. "Or called Elianna," I add after.

"Sorry." She shrugs, and call it a father's intuition, but I feel like there's a lot more to this story than she's letting on.

"Can you and Mel work it out?" I ask her and she shrugs again. I raise an eyebrow at her because she knows that's not going to fly.

"Probably." She climbs onto her bed and lays down before turning on Netflix. "Can we finish this tomorrow? I'm so tired."

"Fine." I turn toward the door. "You know you can talk to me if something is bothering you, right?" I tell her and she nods without looking at me.

"Sure, Dad," she says. "Close my door, please."

I shut the door behind me, confused by Margot's behavior, when I come face to face with SJ. "And now why are *you* up?!" I look at him and he rolls his eyes.

He snorts and takes a sip from the can of Coke in his hands. I wonder how many of those he and his friends have had tonight. "Is she okay? I missed her text to turn off the alarm so it wouldn't sound and we had our headsets on so I didn't even hear her come in." He looks behind me at the closed door. "Why is she home?"

"I don't know. She said she got in a fight with Mel but I feel like there's more to it."

"Sounds like bull."

"SJ." I glower at him as we move down the stairs and I remove the can from his hand. "No more caffeine. How many of these have you had anyway?"

He looks up in the air. "This is like my second."

"*Like* your second?"

"Or third?"

"SJ, knock it off," I snap at him.

"Fiiiine," he says as he makes his way back to the basement door.

"Off the game before three a.m."

He turns around and his eyes widen in shock. "What?! But we are in the middle of a tournament!"

"I don't care. Finish it in the morning. You're ten years old!"

"We're up against people on the West Coast! We can't forfeit!" he retorts and I imagine he's probably cursing Margot and himself for being nosy at the moment because I may not have realized they were still up otherwise.

Especially if I was still face-up in Elianna's pussy.

"Three a.m., Sawyer. Don't make me turn off the WiFi."

He grumbles before he's through the door closing it behind him and I hear him running down the stairs.

Back in my room, my nerves are still running through me when my mind drifts back to the woman down the hall. I wonder if she's asleep by now and I'm grateful to see a text from her when I pick up my phone.

> **Elianna Riley (Nanny):** Is everything okay? What happened?

I press the call button and hold my phone to my ear. She picks up immediately.

"Hey," she says, completely alert and I'm glad I didn't wake her up. "Is she okay?"

"She's fine. Said she and Mel got into a fight, but...she seems off."

"I see. Did she tell you what the fight was about?"

"No, she wouldn't tell me." I let out a sigh. "Maybe you could try tomorrow?"

"Of course. I'll talk to her."

I think Margot still has a bit of her guard up when it comes to Elianna, but I do think she may open up to her if she wants to talk. Especially if it's something she doesn't feel comfortable talking to me about.

Neither of us says anything for a moment while I drop to my bed and fall to my back. "I was so relaxed earlier," I chuckle.

"I'm sorry you didn't...you know...come." She giggles nervously and just that one word falling from her lips has my dick twitching in my pants.

"Trust me, tonight was still the most relaxed I've been in...a long time."

"How long?" she asks, and I realize she isn't aware of how long it's been for me.

"A little over a year," I tell her. "Before Bianca died."

"Oh," she says sadly.

"I've just been busy and...tired," I tell her.

"I get that," she whispers. "Maybe I can...still help?"

"We will find a time to resume what we started; don't you worry."

"Well, I meant...now?"

"I don't think I should come back tonight," I tell her, even though my entire body is not at all in agreement with that.

"I don't either but...there are other ways I could help..." She trails off and a smile finds my face thinking about having phone sex with her when she seems to struggle even saying the word *pussy*.

"What did you have in mind?"

The sound of my FaceTime ringer comes through the phone and the thought of getting to see her naked has me answering it immediately.

"Hi," she whispers with a sexy smile on her face. It's obvious she has turned on another light, illuminating the room a little more and allowing me to see everything from the stomach up. Her lips are glossy like she's put something on them and she's pulled her hair up into a loose ponytail. Her dusty rose nipples appear to be hard and I wish I was wrapping my lips around them. "Take off your pants."

I turn on my dimmest lights and prop my phone up on my nightstand before reaching for my AirPods. I put one in so I can hear if someone is outside my door but so I can also hear Elianna's voice clearly. I do as she says and position myself so she can see me as well. "Can you see?"

She nods. "But this is about you." She smiles. "As long as you can see me."

My hand immediately finds my dick and I begin to stroke it slowly. "I can't see your pussy," I whisper and she giggles before she moves back slightly and I realize she must have her phone on a tripod or something. "Spread them," I tell her and she nods slowly before spreading her legs obscenely giving me the perfect view of her pussy. Memories of my fingers, tongue, and cock buried inside of it come flooding back to me and I already feel like I could come. Two fingers find her mouth and I watch in shock and fascination as she drags them along her tongue and slides them down her body between her legs.

"Holy fuck."

"I really...liked that earlier," she tells me. "I love the way your fingers feel inside of me...your tongue..." She lets out a shaky breath. "*There.*"

"Your pussy." I grunt as I begin to jack myself faster. "Say it," I grit out, wanting to see and hear that word fall from those shiny lips.

"My pussy," she says and I groan in response. It must spur her on because she begins rubbing her clit faster. "I want more." Her voice is breathy and full of sex and I wonder if she's nearing her climax.

"Fuck, so do I, baby."

"I want to suck you until you come down my throat."

"Shit."

"You're big...but I want to try to suck all of you." She clears her throat. "Get all of your dick in my mouth," she whispers, probably assuming I want to hear her say that specific word too.

"Jesus. You're going to make me come, Elianna."

"Good," she purrs. "Pretend you're inside of me." She gets on her knees and moves closer to the camera so the focal point is her cunt. "I'm riding you right now. And"—she gasps—"you're in so deep, Rowan. Fuck me." She moans and my teeth bury into my bottom lip as I watch her spread her sex open revealing her wet, ripe clit.

My eyes flit away from the camera to my bedroom door, wondering if maybe I could make it to her room without making a noise. "Ellie, fuck me, baby. Right there."

She gasps in response and moves so her face is back in the camera. "Is that...oh God...the first time you've called me Ellie?"

"Maybe out loud," I tell her as I fuck my fist faster.

She sits back down and spreads her legs again, giving me the perfect view of all of her. "I love it," she says as she rubs herself harder. "Say it when you come."

"Fuck yes," I tell her. "Can I come in your pussy?"

She nods. "*Please.*" Her voice is pleading and desperate as she chases her orgasm which I think is nearing.

"Are you close, baby? Rub that sweet little clit harder for me. God, it looks so wet and perfect. If I were in there, I'd lick you fucking dry." I pull at my dick in a bit of frustration, wishing I could still taste her on my tongue.

"Right there…Rowan…can I…"

"Can you what? Tell me, sunshine. The answer is yes whatever it is."

"Can I…come all over your dick now?" she asks and the breathiness in her voice sends me over the edge as ropes of cum shoot out of my dick and onto my stomach.

"Fuck fuck fuck, yes come for me, Ellie." I groan out through my climax and I hear her moaning in my ear a beat behind mine.

"Oh yes, *there,*" she says and I watch as her tits shake with the force of her orgasm. Her head is thrown back and she has one hand behind her to hold her upright as she thrusts her hips against her hand. I'm certain I've never seen a sight more sinfully gorgeous.

She rides out the rest of her climax before she slowly lifts her head to look at me with a mischievous twinkle in her eye before she drags her eyes down my torso. She runs her tongue along her bottom lip and I let out a grunt in response. "Do not fucking tempt me. It's taking everything in me not to rip both of our doors off their hinges to get to you right now."

Her hand that was just between her legs moves up her body and slides between her lips and I watch in fascination as she sucks herself off of her fingers. My dick jerks at the idea of following suit.

"I should go to bed."

I nod, wishing like hell she meant *my* bed. "Right, same."

"I'll talk to you in the morning."

"Can't wait." I smile and she returns it before blowing me a kiss and ending the call.

I don't know how much longer I'm awake, staring at the ceiling thinking about Ellie and also what River said. Is this just sex? Does she want more? And if she does, how would the kids take it? The idea that my relationship with Elianna, *whatever kind that may be*, is getting more complicated by the moment is the last thing that crosses my mind before I fall asleep.

CHAPTER SEVENTEEN

Elianna

I'M UP EARLIER THAN USUAL BECAUSE I SPENT THE REST OF the night tossing and turning thinking about the line I crossed with Rowan last night.

The hundreds of lines we crossed.

Memories of me sitting on his face and him fucking me on his desk played through my mind on a consistent loop for another hour before I finally fell asleep. Now, I'm awake and horny despite the two delicious orgasms I had last night. I take a shower, doing my best to avoid giving too much attention between my legs so that the lingering tingly feeling will subside, but it's no use. Every move I make, I feel Rowan and where he'd been. I ignore the pesky voice inside my head telling me things are going to get messy really fucking soon if we continue down this road.

Rowan is not only charming and gorgeous and pretty much

walking sex, but I'm really into him, and he seems obsessed with putting his mouth between my legs.

Things are already really messy.

I make my way out of my bedroom at a quarter to eight and sit at the kitchen table with my laptop to get some homework done. I'm not sure how late everyone was up, so I'm not anticipating anyone up this early which is why I'm shocked to see Margot walking through the kitchen only twenty minutes later.

"Hi." I smile at her. "You're up early."

"Yeah…I…didn't sleep well."

"I imagine. I…heard you come in last night," I tell her, having decided I wouldn't pretend I didn't know she came home in the middle of the night.

"Sorry, if I woke you up."

"You could have called me, you know. I would have come to get you…" My brows pinch in both question and worry. "If you didn't want to call your dad?"

"It was fine," she says as she grabs some orange juice from the refrigerator.

"Do you want to talk about it?"

"Are you going to tell my dad?" she asks.

"Is it illegal?"

She snorts as she pours herself a glass of juice. "No."

"Then we can keep it between us."

She moves through the kitchen and sits down. "I saw some weird stories on Instagram…with Gabe."

Ahhh. Okay. I hadn't anticipated him being a part of this with him supposedly out of town, but this makes sense.

"What did you see?"

"He plays for a travel soccer team, not for our school. And I guess the team went to some party. I follow most of the guys and in the background of one of the stories…some girl was in Gabe's lap and it looked like they were kissing."

"Looked like it? Or they were?"

She pulls out her phone and slides it across the table. "I took a screenshot, what do you think?"

I look at the photo, and while it isn't totally clear, it certainly looks suspect. She's definitely in his lap and the way she's turned it could be that they're just talking, but with the amount of beer cans on the table in the forefront of the picture, I'm going to assume they aren't exactly sober.

"Have you talked to him?"

"Of course. I called him and flew off the handle!" She lets her head drop to the table. "He claims they weren't kissing and he made her get up as soon as she sat down and the story just happened to catch it. Of course, now it's gone."

"What do you think about that?"

"Sounds a little too coincidental." This thought makes me breathe easier. I know Margot is a smart girl but even the smartest girls get the wool pulled over their eyes.

"Okay, so how does your argument with Mel fit into that?"

Her head perks up from the table and narrows her eyes at me curiously *or maybe suspiciously*. "How did you know about that?"

Dammit. I should not have said that. "Oh, I talked to your dad last night. I wanted to know if you were okay."

"Oh." She shakes her head. "Right, of course." She gives me a guilty look. "I made that up because I didn't want to tell him about Gabe. I don't know what I'm going to do yet. I mean he says it was nothing, but I don't want Dad to hate him if I'm not going to break up with him."

"Does it feel like nothing?"

Her lip trembles slightly and she wipes a finger under her eyes. "I don't like that she was in his lap."

"Of course. I wouldn't either."

"Can you just tell me what you think?" she asks. "I don't... have anyone else that I can talk to about this." I hear the sentiment loud and clear that once upon a time she would have gone to her mother.

"You've been with Gabe for a year, right?"

"A little over, yeah. We were friends for a year before that though. I just didn't realize he liked me the entire time. And then… when everything happened he was just…so great to me. He barely left my side when she died, and I guess I just…liked that he took my mind off of it? And now I do love him."

"Can I ask you a personal question?"

She puts her head in her hands before peeking at me through her fingers. "Can it not be about sex?"

"Sorry, but I need all the facts before I can give you my opinion." I close my laptop.

"We haven't had sex," she tells me. "We've come close…a few times."

"I see. What's stopped you?"

"My dad called once. His mom came home…and…one time it just didn't feel right."

"Do you think it's your subconscious telling you he's not the right person to give your virginity to? You know you only lose it once." I clear my throat. "And as someone who didn't have a pleasant first experience, unfortunately, that memory of your first time sticks with you forever."

A sad look crosses her face and she lowers her eyes to the glass in front of her. "That sounds like something my mom would say." I watch as she slowly blinks tears from her eyes.

"I'm not going to tell you what to do and it's easy to pass judgment and give advice on relationships that your heart and emotions aren't invested in. What I will say, however, is if something doesn't feel right, it usually isn't. I don't know what the situation was, but maybe the question you should ask is why that girl felt so comfortable to hop in his lap even if it was just for a second. Did she know he had a girlfriend? Had he been flirting with her? Unfortunately, in this situation, you can only go by what he tells you, so it's going to be up to you if you believe what he's saying and if you trust him. Has anything like this happened before?"

"No…" she says with a hint of hesitation and I can't tell if she's telling me the truth or if the hesitation implies, *not that I know of.*

"Margot, you are a catch. You are smart and kind and one of the most considerate people I've ever met, let alone for someone sixteen. You are beautiful and popular and charming and I bet guys are waiting in line for Gabe to mess up. Don't take any nonsense from anyone."

A smile pulls at her lips and she nods just as the sound of a door opening breaks through our conversation. Margot's eyes widen and she shakes her head at me just before Rowan walks into the room. I try not to focus too much on how gorgeous he looks even at eight-thirty in the morning. "Good morning, ladies," he says looking back and forth between us.

"Hi, Dad." Margot gets up, shooting me one last glance. "Thanks, Ellie," she says, and then she's gone without another word.

Rowan looks at me and then points behind him where I can hear Margot walking back upstairs. *Did you talk to her?* he mouths and I nod.

"For now, you're on a need-to-know basis." I stand up and make my way to where he's standing.

"Elianna." He glowers. "Last night was not acceptable."

"And she knows that."

He puts a hand over his eyes before dragging it through his hair. "My daughters are going to be the death of me." He lets his hand drop and his soft eyes find mine. "She's okay?"

"She's okay. Just a rough night."

"Fine," he murmurs before his eyes slide over me slowly. He takes a look behind him before grabbing me by the hand and tugging me closer to him. "How'd you sleep?"

"Okay, you?"

"A little restless thinking about you down the hall when I wanted you in bed with me but I survived." He sighs. "I don't know when we'll have another night alone. Might be harder when Margot is home."

"I know," I whisper. He reaches up to gently stroke my face and I can't help but lean into his touch. My eyes flutter shut and I feel the gentle brush of his lips across mine and then my cheek leaving dozens of sparks in its wake. "Rowan," I whisper.

"Sunshine." His nose rubs against mine and then down my neck when he grabs me by the waistband of my drawstring pants and tugs me even closer to him. His hand reaches inside both my pants and my underwear and drags a finger through my slit. "I thought about this all fucking night. Your wet cunt dripping all over me," he murmurs low in my ear and then I feel his palm rubbing against my clit while two fingers push through my opening.

"Rowan…" I press my face into his chest to muffle the sounds.

"You're so wet and I've barely touched you. I fucking love that."

I grip his forearms in an attempt to steady myself while pleasure sizzles beneath my skin. "Oh fuck," I whisper as I feel myself nearing the edge already.

"You're not so innocent, are you, baby? Letting me finger you in the middle of the kitchen." He grunts. "I need you to fucking come though. I need something to hold me over until I can get my mouth back down there." He replaces his palm with his thumb and applies more pressure, rubbing me in circles and I find myself sinking my teeth into his chest. "Oh fuck." His mouth is right at my ear and he bites down on my lobe in response. "Knowing that I'm the only man that's ever licked your hot little cunt has made me fucking feral, Ellie."

His dirty words send me over the edge and I slap a hand over my mouth to make sure no noises escape me, but even in the high of my very delicious orgasm, the sound of a door opening somewhere in the house breaks through the haze. I'm disoriented while I come down from my climax, but I feel his hand leave me and then he's no longer standing in front of me. My eyes flutter open, just as Isla and Sabrina come through the kitchen still in their matching pajamas.

"Hi, Ellie. Hi, Daddy!" Isla climbs up on one of the bar stools and Sabrina follows suit. "Ellie, are you okay?" My eyes snap to hers and I nod enthusiastically while trying to calm my still-racing heart.

"Yes. Sorry. Breakfast?!" I resist the urge to glare at Rowan who is chuckling to himself while he washes his hands. He gives me a subtle wink when I meet his gaze and the space between my legs that is still sensitive from his assault pulses with need.

The next morning, it's almost eight-fifteen, and while Sawyer is downstairs devouring the pancakes I made, I'm surprised Isla hasn't come down yet. I don't usually need to move her along; she knows when she hears Sawyer heading downstairs that she needs to as well but sometimes she's still picking out her outfit and needs some help. I jog up the stairs and into Isla's room to see her sitting on the edge of her bed, still in her pajama top with a pair of cobalt blue leggings like she'd gotten tired halfway through getting dressed.

"Isla? Come on. I made pancakes." She looks up at me and I see the exhaustion all over her face. "Oh, honey, are you not feeling well?"

She shakes her head and I watch as tears well up in her eyes. "But today is Art Day. I can't miss it."

I kneel in front of her and put my hand on her forehead and then on her cheek; she definitely has a fever. "Oh Isla, you are burning up. You cannot go to school."

"But..."

"I know..." I rub her back gently knowing how much she was looking forward to Art Day. "But we can have an Art Day here when you're feeling better."

"It's not the same."

"I know." I touch her face and gently help her pull her leggings off. "But we can invite your friends from school."

"Like...a party?" she asks, but the usual excitement in her eyes isn't there.

"Yes." I nod, hoping that will cheer her up some. Remembering that both Rowan and Margot are gone, I realize Isla will have to go with me to take Sawyer to school.

Rowan left before I was even awake this morning. He'd sent me a text calling me beautiful, that he couldn't wait to see me later, to have a good day, and to let him know if we needed anything. "Honey, are you hungry?"

She shakes her head and rubs her eyes and I can see her fading fast. "Okay, we have to take Sawyer to school." I grab a fresh pair of sweatpants for her and pull them up her legs. We're going out in colder temperatures, so I swap her pajama shirt for a t-shirt and hoodie that I pull over her head.

"Are you going to be sick?" I ask, wondering if I should just let Sawyer stay home from school to avoid taking Isla out.

"No."

"You sure? It's okay if you are."

"I'm okay." She gets off the bed but looks like she's about to pass out. I pick her up and she rests her head on my shoulder instantly. I rub soft circles on her back as I make my way down the stairs to see Sawyer playing on one of his portable video games.

"You know you can't be on that before school."

He puts it down and gives me a guilty look. "Sorry!" He frowns immediately when he sees Isla in my arms. "What's wrong with Isla?"

"She's sick, so she's not going to school today, but we're going to take you to school."

"Oh, we can call Uncle River. Whenever one of us is sick, he usually comes to take the other one of us to school or I can text Margot."

"Margot is in class!"

"So? I'll text Uncle River first." Sawyer snorts as he types away on his phone. "This way you don't have to take Isla out." He comes closer to me and reaches up to rub Isla's back. "Isles, you, okay?" She nods slowly, not lifting her head from my shoulder and I notice her thumb has found her mouth which I've never seen her do before. "Can you just write me a note since I'm going to be late?" He picks up his phone. "Hey, Uncle Riv." *Damn, that was quick. Isn't he a teacher? Maybe he doesn't have a class right now.* He leans over the counter. "Mmmhmm, okay hold on." He hands me the phone.

"Hi. I was going to take her with me, but Sawyer said maybe you could come? It's totally fine if—"

His voice—which I realize for the first time sounds so similar to Rowan's but doesn't have the same effect on me at all—comes through the phone. "No sweat. I have a free period now so I can be there in ten. Is she okay?"

"She has a fever, but she'll be okay."

"Did you call Rowan?"

"Not yet."

Realizing I'm not going to take Isla out, I walk with her to the couch in the living room and lay her down on it, pulling her sweatshirt over her head so she doesn't overheat.

"Let me talk to her real quick."

I hand Isla the phone and she blinks up at me with sleepy eyes. "Is it Daddy?"

"No honey, it's your uncle." She nods and takes the phone from me. I walk back into the other room, grab a pad of paper from one of the drawers in the kitchen, and write Sawyer a note for his tardiness. "Is there anything specific I should know about her being sick?"

"She gets really clingy."

"That's normal." I nod, knowing that most children that age are that way.

"She'll want our mom," he says sadly. "Or dad…" He sighs. "Maybe I should stay home. She really likes you and all but… you're not either one of those people."

While those words are true, they hit me harder than I

anticipated, and I try to tell myself that I'm not hurt by them. "I get that," I whisper.

"Ellie!" I hear her voice from the other room and unlike the loud exuberant voice I'm used to, she sounds soft and weak. Sawyer follows me into the living room and Isla holds Sawyer's phone out for one of us to take.

"Isla, you want me to stay home with you?" he asks her and it warms my heart that he's so protective of her. I was the same way when either of my sisters were sick and something tells me if Margot was aware of what was going on, she'd be the same way.

She blinks at us curiously. "Ellie, will you be here?"

I nod as I sit at the end of the couch and rub her leg gently. "Of course. I'm not going anywhere."

"I'll be okay then." She reaches for the blanket that is draped over the back of the couch.

"You sure?" he asks and she nods but not before she moves across the couch and rests her head in my lap.

Twenty minutes later, Sawyer is gone, I've given her some Tylenol, and she's lying on the couch moments from sleep when I decide it's time to call Rowan. I'm not sure if he's talked to River or Sawyer at this point, but he hasn't called me, so I assume he hasn't.

"Hey," he says and I can't stop the flutter in my chest at just that simple word.

"Hi."

"How are you, gorgeous? Everything okay?" I can hear the smile in his voice and I love that I'm the one that put it there.

"Well...yes. It's fine. I have everything under control, but... Isla is sick."

"What's wrong?" he asks and I hear the sound of a door closing.

"She has a fever. It's that time of year that some type of bug goes around but she's going to be fine. I gave her some Tylenol and some Pedialyte and she's resting on the couch as we speak." She'd moved back to the other side of the couch when she got hot, and now she's half asleep under a cool sheet.

"Where's Sawyer?"

"Your brother came to get him. They just left."

"Shit, I'm sorry. I don't think I ever went over this contingency plan."

"It's okay. Sawyer knew what to do. And I've been alone with kids where one kid is sick and the other isn't enough times to have my own plan. I usually just pack the sick kid up with me and take them if the other has somewhere to go. It's not ideal but there isn't always another alternative."

"Is she awake?"

"Barely. She did ask for you earlier when your brother called."

"Can I talk to her?"

I look toward Isla who seems to be a little more awake probably because I've been talking. I get off the couch to kneel in front of her. "Hey there!" She gives me a sleepy smile and a tiny wave. "Your dad is on the phone."

I put the phone to her ear and she takes it. "Hi, Daddy. Mmmhmm. Mmmhmm. Yeah." I chuckle to myself because these are the fewest words I've ever heard her speak. "No, I'm okay. Love you too." She hands the phone back to me.

"I'm surprised she didn't ask me to come home," he tells me, and I remember what Sawyer said earlier. I'm happy that I can serve as a substitute. "She can be a little clingy when she's sick."

"I am a nanny, you know. I am familiar." I giggle.

"Right. Of course. Well, you'll call me if you need anything?"

"Yes, but we're okay. Please try not to worry."

"I've never known her to get sick and not need me or…her mom." He pauses before clearing his throat. "Thank you. She must feel safe with you."

"Well…good. That means I'm doing my job." I smile and I'm glad he's not here to see how forced my smile is because I don't think this feels like a job anymore.

Isla managed to drift off to sleep for most of the afternoon which gave me a chance to make a pot of my grandma's chicken soup, grateful that I'd already had the oversight to take some chicken out of the freezer last night. She hasn't eaten anything more than a few bites of toast and I'm hoping that she'll be a little hungrier when she wakes up.

I'm sitting on the couch with her, reading on my phone when she stirs next to me and I hear a little whine leave her. I get up and kneel in front of her again and notice she's starting to sweat. I hope that means her fever is breaking. A murmur leaves her lips and my heart breaks when I realize what she's saying.

"Mommy..." she whines and I wish there was a way for me to take this particular pain away. I rub her cheek gently and her eyes flutter open, blinking them several times like she's trying to focus.

"Hey, sleepyhead. Are you feeling any better?"

"Ellie..." She gives me a sad smile. "Kinda."

"I made some soup." I push her hair gently from her face. "Do you think you can have a couple bites of that when it's ready?"

"Chicken noodle?"

"Of course!"

She looks toward the kitchen and sniffs, probably sensing the smell of it in the air. "You made it?"

I nod. "My grandma's recipe."

"Okay."

"And then after, maybe a bath? It will help if you're hot."

"Okay," she repeats.

"You're being so brave!" I tell her. "No tears or anything. I should have known you were a big girl."

She giggles before a tiny cough leaves her followed by a pitiful little groan. I grab the glass of water from the coffee table and hold the straw to her lips. "Thanks, Ellie." I get up to go check on the soup when I hear her voice again. "You won't leave, right?"

"Of course not. I told you I was staying."

"No, I mean ever. You won't ever leave?"

My heart squeezes in my chest. I've had this conversation with every single child I've ever nannied for. It's a tough one to have, but I always find it better to prepare them that one day I will leave. I go over the spiel in my head that I've given several times but the words get caught in my throat and very different ones come out.

"I'll be here for as long as you need me."

A few hours later, Sawyer comes walking through the door with River right behind him and immediately they go to the kitchen.

"This soup smells so good. Is it just for Isla?" River calls out, and Isla, who seems to have a little more energy than she did this morning, giggles. She'd managed a few bites of soup but most of it was still sitting on the coffee table with her crackers and juice.

River and SJ walk into the living room each holding bowls and Isla sits up and frowns. "Don't eat all my soup!"

"I can make more," I tell her.

"Yeah, make more. Row is going to love this." River nods before he walks through the living room and sits on the couch on the other side of her. "What's going on, Isles? Are you ditching school already?" he asks.

"I'm siiiick," she whines.

"A likely story," he jokes, and she scowls at him.

"You look better," Sawyer says as he sits between me and her before taking a bite of the soup. He immediately looks at me. "Seriously? What can't you make?"

"I take that to mean you like it."

"So good," he says between bites. "I think we need this in the house all the time."

"You don't think you'll get tired of it?" I raise an eyebrow at him and he shakes his head.

"No way," he says before he gets off the couch and presses a kiss to Isla's cheek. I slap a hand over my forehead. "Okay, sir, she's sick. Would you like to be next?" I call after him. "You're taking some Tylenol!"

"Whatever I gotta do to keep this in the house." He points at the bowl before he disappears.

"Everything was okay though?" River asks, and I nod. "Seems you have everything under control here. Never thought I'd see the day when this house wasn't in a state of constant chaos." He looks down at Isla who's back to staring at the television now that another episode of *Bluey* is on. "I'm really glad they have you." He stands up, and like Sawyer, presses a kiss to her cheek. "And I am very much looking forward to holding this over my brother's head forever. I mean I knew you'd be perfect," he says with a knowing grin and I remember that River is aware of mine and Rowan's recent change in our...relationship.

"Are you leaving?" Isla asks and River nods.

"I am. I have practice, but you call me later if you want me to swing by after?"

She nods. "Okay."

"Love you, munchkin." He looks at me. "Catch you later, Ellie."

CHAPTER EIGHTEEN

Rowan

I MANAGE TO LEAVE WORK AT A DECENT HOUR SO I CAN BE home before Isla goes to sleep, but when I walk through the back door, SJ is at the kitchen table doing his homework and Isla is nowhere in sight. "Where's your sister?"

"Which one?" he asks, not looking up from his paper.

I glance at him, annoyed. "Isla. Last I checked, Margot isn't home yet."

"She's upstairs with Ellie." He looks up at me. "You have to try the soup she made for her by the way. Dad, we can't let Ellie go *ever*."

Wasn't planning on it.

"Noted. School was okay today?"

"Fine." He shrugs. "Had my meeting with the shrink. When can I stop doing that anyway?"

"I'm guessing when your behaviors improve," I tell him as I slide my jacket off and hang it on the back of one of the chairs.

"They have!"

I fold my arms over my chest. "Don't you have detention this week?"

He drops his forehead and taps it against the table in three consecutive taps. "This is the worst."

"I'm sorry, bud. I did my part and stopped you from getting expelled." I ruffle his sandy brown hair before I make my way upstairs. When I get to Isla's room, she's lying in her bed with Ellie sitting next to her reading a story. For the first time, I really see Ellie as not just the nanny but someone my kids are falling in love with by the day.

Ellie must sense my movement because her eyes dart to mine and she gives me a soft smile.

"Daddy!" Isla's eyes light up and while her voice isn't as enthusiastic as it usually is, I know she's still excited to see me. She sits up and raises her arms toward me as I make my way to the other side of her bed and pull her into my arms. She climbs into my lap and tucks her head right under my chin while I squeeze her tight.

"How you feeling, Princess?"

"Mmm, I still don't feel good."

"You don't have a fever though, so that's good," Ellie says as she presses the back of her hand to Isla's forehead followed by her cheek.

"Do you think she needs to stay home tomorrow?" I ask her and she gives me a look that tells me she's not sure.

"It may not hurt? Especially if she's still not feeling great? I planned to just see how she felt in the morning."

"Okay. I was thinking I would work from home tomorrow…" I stroke Isla's hair and press a kiss to the top of her head. "Whether she's home or not," I continue and watch as Ellie's pupils dilate before she licks her bottom lip. I take it she understands what we'll be doing if we have the house to ourselves.

A smirk finds my face but it falls instantly when I hear Isla's voice. "Daddy, we aren't finished. Shhhh."

"Oh, I'm sorry." I try to move to let them get back to their story but Isla just squeezes me tighter making me believe she wants me to stay.

I can't help but watch Ellie while she reads, and although I know it's her job, there's something about watching her with my sick daughter that does something to me. We're nearing the end of the story, with Isla teetering on the edge of sleep when Margot walks in the room, and when I look up, she's staring at us confused like she's not sure what she's seeing.

"I heard Isla wasn't feeling well. Is she okay?"

"She had a fever but she's much better now," Ellie tells her and Margot's lips form a straight line as her eyes dart back and forth between me and Ellie.

"Dad, you're home early. When's the last time you beat me home?" she jokes but I can hear the underlying snark in her voice.

"Well, it's nothing new. Who else has been here when one of you guys has been sick?" I ask her.

She adjusts her backpack that's hanging off one shoulder. "Right," she says in a way that makes me think she doesn't agree with what I said but doesn't want to get into it. "Feel better, Isla."

"Night, Margot," Isla says softly as her eyelids begin to droop.

I'm still in my office at almost two in the morning, as I still have a mountain of work to do after leaving work early, when I see a soft light streaming from under the crack of Ellie's door. I wonder if she's awake or if she fell asleep with her light on. I don't want to wake her but we haven't had a moment alone in two days and I'm desperate for one. I walk quietly across the hall, knowing that while unlikely, Margot could still be awake.

I tap gently on her door and I hear movement on the other side. *Thank God.*

When she opens the door, she has a shy smile on her face. "Yes?"

"I haven't touched you in two days. I can't go another second," I growl as I push her back into her room and close the door behind me. I waste no time pressing my lips to hers and sending her pajama pants and underwear down her legs before yanking her top off over her head leaving her completely naked.

"Now?" she gasps.

"Fucking *now*," I tell her as I pull her to the carpeted floor and press my lips to her pussy hungrily. After a second, I pull back and give her a salacious look. "I was planning to spit on your pretty pussy to get you ready but you are already very wet, Elianna." I run a finger down her slit. "By any chance were you playing with yourself in here?"

She props herself up on her elbows and blows a hair out of her face. "Maybe."

"Fuck." I drag my tongue through her slit. "Were you thinking about me?"

"Maybe," she repeats.

I suction my lips around her clit and pull gently causing her breathing to change. "Maybe, huh?" I pull back and blow on her and a shiver wracks her gorgeous body.

"Rowan, I'm already so wet and we don't have time for teasing. Please just fuck me," she begs.

I push my sweatpants and briefs down, freeing my dick, while also hating the fact that I'm not making her come on my tongue first. I don't waste a second before driving my dick inside of her and she must not have been expecting it or she forgot how I felt from the one time we've done this because she lets out a yelp in surprise. I press my hand over her mouth and lean down to whisper in her ear. "Are you going to be a good girl and stay quiet or do I need to keep my hand over your mouth?"

She raises an eyebrow before reaching up to put a hand over mine, telling me she wants it there. I thrust slowly trying not to make any noise at all when I notice her discarded underwear next to us. Using my other hand, I grab them and slide them into her hand and she looks at me curiously, not understanding what I want.

I lean down and whisper low in her ear, "Give them to me. I'll taste your cunt however I can get it."

Her eyes are wide when I pull back, but they flutter shut momentarily after I push inside the deepest I've gone tonight. She reaches up, pushing her panties into my mouth and holding her palm over my mouth to keep them there. I begin moving faster, my orgasm building from her wet underwear in my mouth and the mere fact that I am fucking her on the floor of her bedroom at two in the morning because I couldn't wait another day without being inside of her.

I put a hand down by her head, to rest most of my weight on that, as I begin fucking her harder and I can feel her moan behind my hand. She tightens her hand over my mouth and I feel her clenching around me. I nod at her, doing my best to coax the orgasm out of her without words. Her other hand reaches up and grabs the back of my head, stroking it gently before her eyes slam shut and she clamps down hard on me.

Fuck yes, give it to me.

Her eyes are closed as she thrusts upwards to meet me, sucking my dick deeper inside her slick pussy with every stroke. Pleasure shoots through my veins and I feel myself nearing the edge…and in that final second, it hits me that we haven't talked about whether she's on birth control and I only have a moment to make a decision. I pull out of her at the *very* last second, removing my hand from her mouth to grab my dick and shoot it all over her stomach and luscious tits.

She gasps, her eyes wide while she pulls her hand away from my mouth and the silky fabric as well. We are both trying to slow our breathing but I manage to stutter out, "Baby, I'm so sorry…didn't know if you were on anything, and…"

"That was so hot," she whispers. "I…I've never come that hard." I resist the urge to preen at that because I fucking love that I'm responsible for so many of her firsts. She looks down at her body that's covered in my orgasm. "I'm on birth control…" she tells me. "Helps with my cramps." She drags two fingers through the mess I made on her and I watch in fascination as she drags those fingers through her pussy, rubbing my cum on her clit.

"Oh, *fuck.*"

She leans up, pushing me onto my back, and straddles me. I'm still wearing a shirt so she leans down and does a halfway job of cleaning herself up using the bottom of my t-shirt. "Can you get hard again?" she asks me.

"With some help, yeah." I smirk at her and she gets off of me to kneel between my legs.

She wastes no time dragging her tongue up my softened shaft and I can already feel it perking up at the feel of her warm mouth. She swirls her tongue around the tip, her eyes trained on mine as she hollows out her cheeks and sucks me harder. "Fuuuuuck." The word comes out with a gust of air because this is undoubtedly the best head I've ever gotten. She laps at the head as soon as pre-cum forms and lets out a quiet moan like it's the best thing she's ever tasted. She pushes herself slowly down my entire length until her lips hit my pubic bone and when she gets there she swallows, sucking me as far back as possible and I swear I lose my fucking mind.

"Ellie…baby…wait…pull back…fuck…gonna come," I sputter as I pull on her hair gently, trying to get her off my dick but she shakes her head, sucking me harder. "You want it in your mouth?" I close my eyes as the feeling is already pulling me under. "Not your pussy?"

"Next time," I vaguely hear her whisper, but my climax is

thundering through me. My hand tangles in her hair and I'm vaguely aware that I'm holding her head down after I thrusted upward as ropes of cum shoot out of my dick into the hottest mouth it's ever been inside.

Fuck. Fuck. Fuck. I let go of her hair and rub her cheek gently, praying I didn't hurt her. "Shit." My eyes fly open and I look down to see her grinning at me, her brown eyes glazed and gorgeous. "Was that okay?"

"I loved that. Are you kidding? It was so hot…it was like you were using me to get off."

I narrow my eyes in shock because how is this the same woman that told me last week, she'd never dry-humped anyone or had her pussy licked. "You've come a long way in a week, sunshine."

"I never said I didn't like sex. I very much enjoy having an orgasm." She smirks as she leans down and rests her body on top of mine. "I just hadn't found the right man to do it with."

The fact that she finds me right for her in any sense makes me want to beat my chest with pride despite how complicated our situation is.

I reach up and move some hair from her face. "Wednesday," I blurt out.

"Wednesday?" she questions, clearly confused by the lack of context.

"I'll say I'm working late." I rub my thumb over her bottom lip. "I know it's the day you have to go to campus. Have dinner with me after you leave. River can come hang out with the kids after his practice. I need more uninterrupted time alone with you. Time where we can talk louder than this," I tell her.

"Okay…" She nods and I'm happy that it didn't take much convincing. "As long as Isla is feeling one hundred percent better," she tells me and I'm pretty sure at that moment, I fall in love with my nanny.

I wake up the next morning feeling lighter than I've felt in months. *I guess that happens after having two back to back intense orgasms with someone after a year hiatus.*

But the larger part of me knows it's because I felt something shift last night. I turn on my side, blindly reaching for my phone and I'm surprised to see what time it is. It's nearing almost nine and I can't remember the last time I slept this late on a weekday. I had already let my office know I'd be working from home today, so no one is looking for me past the standard morning emails. I hear shuffling coming from the kitchen followed by two voices and I realize Isla must have stayed home again.

I quickly brush my teeth and use the bathroom before I make my way out to see Isla sitting at the table eating pancakes. She's wearing her favorite yellow sunglasses and watching something on her iPad which is something I don't usually allow at breakfast, but when I see Ellie pouring more batter into the pan, I assume she allowed this.

"You don't look very sick," I tell Isla, tilting my head to the side before looking at Ellie.

"It's just a precaution!" Ellie says. "She was still coughing a little this morning and I just wanted to be safe."

"Sunglasses at the table, miss." I give Isla a look because she knows better and she pulls them off her face with an innocent smile.

"Hi, Daddy!"

I sit down next to her and put my hand over her forehead and on her cheek. "How are you feeling, honey?"

"Okay," she says before taking a bite of her pancakes, still completely engrossed in what she's watching on her iPad.

"Did you take her with you to take SJ to school?" I ask Ellie and she gives me a dry look.

"I would have woken you if I was leaving her here, but since she's feeling better, I wanted to give her a little fresh air. We even went on a short walk, right?" She looks at her and Isla nods.

"I'm glad you're feeling better, munchkin." I press a kiss to her head before moving across the kitchen toward Ellie.

"Pancakes?" She points at them. "I thought you might be hungry," she says softly with a tiny lift of her eyebrow and I can't stop the smile from pulling at my lips.

For you, I mouth at her before I make an obvious show of trailing my eyes down her body. "When she takes a nap," I whisper so Isla doesn't hear me as I make my way around the island. When I walk by her, I slide my hand across her ass, gripping it before landing a light smack on it and she giggles.

It's almost one in the afternoon when Ellie appears in my doorway. "Hey," she says and just that one word makes my dick hard. "Isla's asleep," she tells me with a sexy gleam in her eye. "I was going to take a shower." She bites down on her bottom lip. "Want to join me?"

CHAPTER NINETEEN

Elianna

IT TAKES US ABOUT THIRTY SECONDS TO END UP IN ROWAN'S bathroom which may be the most gorgeous I've ever been in. I expected us to use my bathroom but Rowan lifted me into his arms before I could take even a step into my bedroom and carried me down the hall to his room while his lips devoured mine.

"I've never been in your bathroom…or your room," I say as he helps lift my shirt off over my head, his lips dropping to my neck and trailing kisses down my shoulder.

"Don't remind me." He cups my face and presses his lips to mine, pulling my bottom lip gently with his teeth. "You are not leaving this room without letting me fuck you in my bed."

I nod excitedly. Last night unlocked something inside of me. Maybe because I was already so worked up—because as he'd guessed, *I had been touching myself earlier that night*—but I feel like my pussy is still throbbing from where he'd been. I want him again. *And again.*

He turns on the water in the massive shower but I can't stop my eyes from staring at the marble sunken tub on the other side of the bathroom.

"You want to take a bath instead?" he asks while kneeling behind me to slide my leggings down my legs before he drags his lips over my ass cheeks, nibbling gently.

"No, but maybe next time if there's an opportunity?"

"Next time we're completely alone," he says as he pulls off his shirt, and it will never get old seeing this man's naked chest. When he slides his sweatpants down his legs revealing his bare cock, I let out a choked breath.

I slide my underwear down my legs and make my way into his shower which is large enough for a group of people. There's a rain shower feature in the center as well as different retractable shower heads shooting water from the sides. "This shower is…so nice."

"You're my first guest in here," he tells me and I gape at him because while I know he said it had been a year, I know he's lived here since his divorce.

"Am I?"

"Why do you sound so shocked? Do you think I'm a manwhore, Miss Riley?" he jokes.

"No! I just…you're…I know you've lived here since your divorce and I just assumed…"

"I rarely brought women into my house. It just felt too personal with all of the kids' stuff here and I was never super serious about any of the women I dated in the three years since my divorce."

"Oh." I don't have anything else to say, because what could I? It's like he's telling me I'm the last woman he's been this intimate with since the woman he was married to. "So, this is a pretty big deal for you?"

"It is. But it doesn't need to be for you..." he says. "Please don't panic on me. I know I'm older and maybe you don't want more..."

I press a finger to his mouth, silencing him. "You do remember I hadn't had sex since...more than likely before your youngest was conceived?" I stand up on my tiptoes and wrap my arms around his neck to bring his lips to mine. "This is a pretty big deal for me too." His lips crush against mine, pushing me against the wall, and I whimper when I feel the cool marble against my back. His lips leave mine and he trails kisses down my neck. He lifts me into his arms and my legs immediately wrap around him. When his lips find one of my breasts, he pulls my nipple between his lips and rolls his tongue around it.

"Rowan," I say through a shaky breath when I feel his teeth graze against the nub and bite down.

"Oh, fuck me, sunshine. I love your pretty tits," he says before switching to the other to pay it the same attention. "I haven't had nearly enough time with them." He flicks my nipple with the tip of his tongue before dragging his lips back up to my mouth. My pussy is resting right against his torso and I grind myself against it, trying to stimulate my clit and he groans in my mouth. "You drive me crazy; you know that?" I whimper when his fingers find my sex and glide through my folds. "You did know that, didn't you? You know that when you walk into a room, I can barely take my eyes off of you. You've been here for a month and you've got me struggling to even focus at work because I'm thinking about you and this and the fact that you walked into my life so effortlessly and somehow both fixed everything and turned it completely upside down."

"Oh my God." I moan, both at his words and from the feeling between my legs as he continues to stroke me. He sets me on my feet and pulls his fingers from me, immediately sliding them into his mouth. I don't even have to question what he's about to do because he's on his knees with my leg over his shoulder, instantly attaching his mouth to my pussy.

I press a hand over my mouth, still not wanting to be too loud even though the sounds of the shower should drown out any noise we make. I run my other hand through his hair, pushing it back off his forehead, and stare down at this man I'm developing stronger feelings for by the day. "This…" I moan. "This is what I was thinking about last night while I got myself off." His eyes meet mine and I can see the smile in them as he worships my pussy with his mouth. He pushes against me harder, sliding his tongue as far inside as possible like he's trying to touch every inch of me he can. "Oh fuck, I'm going to come." I sigh and those words must spur him on because he moves back to my clit with faster and more uncontrolled strokes.

"Fuck yes, you are. Give me what I want and come all over my tongue and then you're going to come all over my dick again."

Memories of fucking him on my bedroom floor after shoving my wet underwear through his lips come back and my climax hits me hard and slow, starting at my toes and moving through the rest of me. "Oh my Goddd." I groan as I drag my nails against his scalp. "Yes yes yes. Fuck yes." I grind myself against his mouth through the rest of my orgasm, trying to wring out every ounce of pleasure. I let go of his hair just as he places a final kiss on me and stands up.

"Let's finish up in here. I need to fuck you in my bed."

We finish showering, which I'm surprised didn't end in round two with the way Rowan used his hands to rub the soap into my skin everywhere. My breasts, my cunt, he'd even slid his hand between my ass cheeks to circle the hole back there and when I shuddered in both lust and nerves, a grin found his face that had such promise.

We're on his bed now, and his firm hands are rubbing lotion into my skin that I made him retrieve from my bedroom. Thankfully, he had decent body wash that wasn't a three-in-one, nor was it something so overly manly that it would have been obvious I'd used his, but I needed my specific lotion. I had been applying it myself before he grabbed it from me for being 'a tease' so he could do it himself.

He glides his hand up my leg, smoothing the cream into my skin. "You always smell so good," he says pressing his nose against my ankle before placing a kiss there. The bottle of lotion hits the ground with a quiet thud as he climbs up the bed and rests on top of me.

"Can I be on top?"

"Whatever you want, sunshine." He presses a kiss to my lips and lies in the center of his massive bed stroking his cock slowly. He's been hard since we got in the shower and it hasn't lessened at all so I know he's ready for me. I replace his hand with mine as I straddle his waist and hover above him. I drag him through my slit once and he takes a deep breath in through his nose and out through his mouth. "Don't tease me, baby. Let me in that wet cunt."

I push down on him and I feel like the wind is momentarily knocked out of me because this position somehow feels deeper than last night. I don't move right away to give myself a chance to adjust to how full I am.

"You alright?" He grabs my hands, yanking me forward and I fall to his chest but keep him snug inside of me. He cups my cheek before giving me a light kiss on my lips. "Does it hurt?"

"No...just...I need a second. I've never done it in this position...but I'm good."

"Take your time," he says against my mouth and I fucking melt.

I sit back up, placing my hands on his chest for leverage as I slowly move up and down on him. Every time I take him all the way in, I grind my clit against the base of his cock and a spark shoots through me.

"That feels good, doesn't it?" he says as his hands find my hips and he pulls me down harder with every thrust. He's not controlling the pace, but the pressure, allowing for even more friction between us.

"Yes yes yes." I toss my head back and pull my hair from the bun I'd had it in and my curls fall around me.

"God, you're fucking sexy, baby." He glides his palm up my torso dragging his thumb over one of my nipples. "I can't believe you're mine."

Hearing those possessive words fall from his lips spur me on faster and I move up and down quicker as I feel the beginning of my climax brewing. "Does this work both ways?" I ask him.

"Fuck yes." He groans. "I'm yours, sunshine. Think I have been since the first time you walked through my front door."

"Rowan!" I cry out. I actually feel the tears forming in my eyes as my orgasm approaches and also at his words. "I'm close."

"Me too. Take me with you, Elianna."

Our movements are fast and erratic as we both chase our releases and my orgasm comes a beat later, like that command in his voice had the power to force it out of me. I wonder if I could come from the sound of his voice alone.

"Fuuuuuck," he groans and I feel the delicious sensation of his dick pulsing inside of me.

"I love feeling you come," I tell him.

I look down at where we're connected and I stare in amazement while I lazily ride him through the aftershocks of our orgasms, watching as his cock disappears inside of me with every stroke.

"So, fucking perfect," he murmurs and when I look up, he's staring at the same thing I was. His eyes find mine, slowly tracing my face and then he reaches up to drag his knuckles down my cheek and the movement is so sweet I want to cry. *Who knew I'd end up being so emotional after sex?* "Hi, sunshine."

The next day is Wednesday and Margot is used to coming home right after cheer practice so I can leave for my weekly meeting with my advisor, but because I'm meeting Rowan for dinner afterward, I've dressed up a little more than usual.

"Someone has a hot date?" Margot calls from the living room where she's got her laptop perched on her lap.

"No…a few of us are just getting dinner after."

"Well, you look really nice for someone just going out with school *friends*," she emphasizes as she looks me over. Maybe I have gone a little overboard, but this is our first official date and I saw the way he responded to what I was wearing when I went out last weekend. I'm wearing a short but tight, long-sleeved, open-back dress. *I had the foresight to put on my coat in my room so Margot isn't aware that my dress is backless. Hopefully, it doesn't look quite so sexy.* I'm currently wearing knee-high boots, but I plan to change into black pumps once my meeting is over. I usually wear my curls naturally, but tonight I straightened them and added curls from my wand giving it a glossy blowout look.

"I'll take that as a compliment?"

She shrugs with a smile and I feel like things have been off with Margot lately. I wonder what's bothering her. "How are things with Gabe?" I ask her and she scrunches her nose.

"Fine." She looks toward the television, I think as a way to end the conversation.

"Are you still together?"

"Yeah. Homecoming is in two weeks. I wasn't dumping him before that."

"But…you want to?"

"I don't know. He says that whole thing with the other girl was just a misunderstanding," she says glumly and I wonder if she doesn't really believe that.

"I told you he was a loser," SJ interrupts as he walks into the room eating an apple obnoxiously before jumping on the couch next to Margot and taking the remote from her.

"Hey!" She goes to reach for it but he moves to the end of the couch out of her reach. "This was a private conversation, you jerk."

"Then have it in your room next time! Living room is fair game," he says before changing the channel to ESPN.

"You have an entire television in the basement that is basically just yours. Go away." She puts her laptop on the coffee table and moves closer to him to smack the back of his head before snatching the remote.

"What did he do anyway? I have friends with older brothers, you know," he says before dragging an imaginary line over his throat.

"Nothing. God, you're annoying. And don't tell Dad. He'll just get all up in arms."

"Because he *also* knows your boyfriend is a loser?" SJ says through another bite of his apple.

"Okay enough," I tell them. "Where's Isla?"

"Here I am!" she says coming through the living room with a coloring book and a box of crayons. She drops her things to the ground and lies on her stomach before opening her book.

"Okay, so you know your Uncle will be here at about seven? The food is ready whenever you want to eat it." I'd started chili in the slow cooker earlier this morning much to everyone's excitement as I learned it was one of all of their favorite meals.

"You do this every week, you know. It's not like we were never here alone before you came into the picture," Margot says before turning the television back to what she'd been watching and I can't exactly tell if I detect sass in her voice or not.

"Okay. No one in the house. Don't answer the door," I remind them.

"We know. Enjoy your dinner," Margot says without looking at me.

Isla gets up and comes over to hug me. "Only crayons in here." I point to where she was previously lying. "No markers." I give her a knowing look and she puts a hand over her mouth and giggles.

"Okaaaay!" She nods. "Will you wake me up when you get

home?" This is the first time she's asked me that and I try to ignore the way my heart squeezes in my chest at her request.

"It might be very late."

She shrugs. "That's okay."

"If I don't, I'll see you first thing in the morning."

"Okay." She wraps her arms around my neck and presses a kiss to my cheek. "Bye, Ellie!"

"Bye, munchkin."

A few hours later, I'm pulling up to the Italian restaurant that Rowan picked. It's technically still the city but more on the outskirts; we didn't want to go somewhere too close to home in case someone recognized us. We know there isn't anything necessarily wrong with our new relationship, but we don't want anything to get back to the kids before we talk to them about it, and as we quickly learned from the instance with SJ, it's that parents talk and so do the kids.

I pull up to the valet, per Rowan's...*advisement* because he didn't want me walking around at night by myself after dealing with street parking in the city, and before I can even turn the car off, my door opens. I yelp, having not noticed anyone approaching the vehicle when I see Rowan's breathtaking smile.

"Sorry, baby, I thought you saw me. I didn't mean to scare you." He holds his hand out for me to take.

"Were you outside waiting for me?"

"Of course." He cups my chin and drags his thumb gently over my bottom lip. "Hi, beautiful."

I get out of the car and he pulls me into his arms and presses his lips to mine. He slides his tongue against mine once, touching it lightly and then pulling away before either of us can try to deepen it. "Finally. I've been thinking about kissing you all day." He runs a thumb over his own mouth and it amazes me that even his simplest moves are so fucking sexy. "I love when you wear this color. Is it on me?" he asks and I shake my head.

"No, it's a stain. We'd have to do some heavy kissing for it to transfer to you."

"Damn. I was hoping to have your mark on me." He winks before dragging his fingers through my strands gently. "I love this."

He hands the valet my keys and we make it inside and up a flight of stairs to our table that's nestled in the corner up against a window that gives us a view of the waterfront. He helps me out of my jacket and the sharp intake of air I hear behind me is just the reaction I was going for. He moves to stand in front of me before taking a step back and dragging his eyes slowly up my frame. "You look beautiful." He smiles. "Stunning actually."

"Thank you," I tell him as I take a seat. "You look really nice too." He's wearing an all-black suit and shirt without a tie, and the top two buttons of his shirt are undone. I just want to run my lips over the exposed skin. "Better than nice, actually." I prop my head up on my hand and eye him up and down. This man can wear the hell out of a suit.

He bites his bottom lip and leans back in his chair. "Stop it, or we won't make it out of the restaurant."

After the waiter comes by to bring our water and take our drink order, I broach the subject I've been curious about. "Can I ask you something?"

"Anything," he says before taking a sip of his water.

"Can you tell me what happened?" I wince, nervously. "Why did you get divorced? I'm sorry if that's insensitive."

"It's not. It's natural for you to be curious and I've been waiting for you to ask." He clears his throat. "There really wasn't one specific thing but a lot of things. We just…fell out of love, I guess? We had kids and I started working like crazy and…I definitely didn't prioritize her and our marriage; I'll own that. She stopped wanting to be intimate and then I stopped trying. We started fighting all the time about everything…" he winces, "and then we kind of became complacent?" He looks a little nervous before he continues. "Very much between you and me, we were planning to separate after SJ, but one night, we'd gone to an event for my job, we'd been drinking, and one thing led to another and…then we had Isla. We lasted another two years after she was born and then one day, she told me she was moving out and I…didn't try to stop her."

"Did you ever try counseling?"

"No." He shakes his head. "I didn't want to try and neither did she. I had *and have* so much respect for her as their mother, but we didn't grow together. Not the way a successful marriage should. She wanted more from me and I didn't have more to give. Looking back, I wonder if I should have tried more or if it would have made a difference. If maybe we had just gone too far down separate paths that we couldn't come back together." A look of disappointment crosses his face and I wonder if there's any part of him that would have been willing to try again if she were still alive.

"Do you think you just didn't like being married?"

"No, I loved the companionship and having someone to come home to and raise a family with. Sometimes certain marriages just don't work."

"I see." I nod. "Do you see yourself getting married again?"

"I'm not ruling it out," he says. "I know I'm probably not selling myself on being a great husband…" Someone brings us our drinks, setting his scotch in front of him and my cosmopolitan in front of me before they disappear quickly. "Neither of us were happy."

"I get it." I nod. "Well, that's all I wanted to know." *Hardly. I did have some other questions but I didn't want to ruin our one night of true privacy by talking about things that could wait.*

"Now I have a question." He leans forward, dragging a finger over my knuckles before he brings my hand to his mouth and kisses it gently. "I know there's a pretty big age gap here and I have children and…I guess I just want to know where your head is at about all of this."

"Well, I know you have children," I joke.

"You know what I mean. Do you just want to have fun? That's fine if you do. I just feel like we should talk about this."

I shake my head slowly. "No, I want more than that…with you, if that's something you're interested in."

He gives me a smile that damn near takes my breath away. "I think you know I'm more than interested."

Excitement courses through me at the thought that we are on the same page. "Maybe we just shouldn't tell the kids yet?"

"No…" He shakes his head. "I think we should wait a bit."

"Do you think Margot suspects something?" I fidget nervously with my hands. "It's just a feeling."

I see a hint of worry in his green eyes. "I thought the same, but…Margot is pretty good at not beating around the bush. If anything, she might suspect that I have feelings for you but that nothing has happened."

"We just need to be careful, especially at home."

When we finish the heavy talk, we move on to lighter things and I can honestly say it is the best first date I have ever had.

"So can I see you again?" he asks with a cheeky grin as we walk out of the restaurant hand in hand.

I roll my eyes. "Like another date?"

He nods. "Something like that."

An hour later, we are in an abandoned parking lot twenty minutes from home, kissing in the back of his Mercedes like two teenagers who are sneaking around behind their parents' backs.

"I should get back," I tell him between kisses. I'm in his lap straddling him, grinding against his dick as we kiss and a part of me wants to take him out of his pants so we can go past dry humping. It's nearing eleven-thirty though, and the plan was for me to come in at least twenty minutes before him.

"Okay," he says even as he continues to kiss me.

I cup his stubbled jaw, dragging my fingertips over the skin as our mouths devour each other hungrily.

"Rowan."

"Sunshine," he grumbles against my neck before sinking his teeth into the skin and running his tongue over it.

"It's getting late."

"I know, fuck. Can I come to your room later?" he asks with a hint of desperation in his voice.

"I thought we said we were going to be careful."

"We are. I'll be quiet. We don't have to do anything, I just… like being near you, and I spend so much time away from you. And what's worse is I spend more time around you but not being able to touch you like I want to." He drops his forehead to my shoulder and lets out a breath.

"Okay, but not until we're sure everyone's asleep again."

I'd thought ahead, especially with the lipstick I was wearing, and brought makeup wipes to help fix both the inevitable ring I knew would end up around my mouth and the bright red all over his from all the kissing we'd done tonight. Once we're both cleaned up and my lipstick is reapplied, I'm on my way back to the house.

When I walk through the front door, I see River and Margot on the couch watching a slasher movie. Well, River is watching and Margot seems to be peeking through her fingers and half-opened eyes. She yelps when I walk in and lets out a sigh when she sees it's just me.

"This seems like a good idea to watch right before bed?" I ask, glaring at River for subjecting her to something that is clearly scaring her.

"It was her idea!" River says with a chuckle.

Margot pauses the movie and looks at me. "How was…your dinner?" She blinks at me.

"Great," I tell her.

"Well, Row isn't home yet," River says as a part of our cover, "but now that you're here, I am going to head out."

"Thanks so much for staying so late," I tell him and I hope he can read between the lines. *Thanks for helping us tonight.*

"We would have been fine for the record. It's not even midnight," Margot adds as she pulls out her phone.

"So, I can't come hang out with my favorite nieces and nephew?" River shoots her an incredulous look as he slides on his leather jacket.

"We're your only nieces and nephew," she replies dryly.

"Which is why you're my favorites!" He leans down and presses a kiss to her forehead. "Turn off the movie and go to bed," he tells her.

I follow him out the front door, closing the door behind me. "Everything went okay?"

"Oh yeah, all good," he tells me with a smile. "Where's Rowan?"

"Around the corner."

He chuckles. "Man, he's really crazy about you. He hasn't been like this in…years."

"Like what?"

He hesitates for a bit and scratches the back of his neck. "Light, I guess you could say? He's been so tense and stressed the last few years. Like he didn't have time to take a breath, or like he didn't even know how to breathe for that matter. The kids are his main source of happiness but I'm his brother and I've known something was missing for him for a while. Remember I told you he was drowning?" He nudges my shoulder. "It's like you threw him a life raft in more ways than one."

"Wow." I already had a feeling about some of this, but it's different hearing it from the person closest to him.

"Oh, and Isla?" He nods at the house. "She's crazy about you too." He pauses before starting to walk backward toward his car. "Really glad we bullied you that day at the grocery store," he says with a final wave before he jogs down the steps.

When I'm back inside, Margot is still sitting on the couch. "You're not going to bed?"

"In a minute. I just wanted to talk to you."

"Of course, what's up?" I ask and her chestnut eyes immediately begin to water. "Margot, what's wrong?" I sit next to her on the couch and pull her hand into mine but she immediately scrunches her nose and pulls her hand back. "Isla was really upset that neither you or my dad were here to tuck her in tonight."

My eyes dart to the stairs thinking about the tiny person upstairs that I knew I already loved while figuring out my feelings for her father. "I thought she'd be okay for one night."

"Me too and maybe it was just a one-off, but…Isla is already really attached to you and I just hope you're not planning to hurt my little sister."

"Margot, you don't have to worry about that. I would never."

"Even if you left or something happened that made you want to leave…" She trails off. "She's only six and she's lost so much. Please don't be another thing she has to get over losing," she says before she gets up and makes her way upstairs without another word.

CHAPTER TWENTY

River mentioned that Margot is probably still awake so as soon as I get home, I go upstairs to say goodnight. When I get to her room, I'm surprised her door is wide open.

"Knock, knock," I call from the threshold.

Margot is lying on her bed scrolling through Netflix. "Hey, Dad," she says without looking my way in a tone that makes her sound almost bored. I close the door behind me and fold my arms over my chest.

"Alright, you want to tell me what's been going on with you lately?"

"Nothing." She shrugs and I move to stand in front of her television. It's mounted on the wall behind where I'm standing, but I know I'm still blocking most of her view.

"Margot." My tone is even yet stern because while I am not mad at her, I am not loving her attitude.

"Well, since I told Ellie and Uncle River will probably tell you, Isla had a tiny meltdown when it was time for bed because neither you nor Ellie were here to tuck her in. She calmed down after a while, but it was strange that none of us were a good enough substitute tonight." She sits up in bed and eyes me curiously. "Ellie is staying for Thanksgiving?"

Nothing has been confirmed to my knowledge, so I'm wondering where she heard that. "Where did you hear that?"

"Is it true?"

"I know she's thinking about it."

"Well, apparently she told SJ and Isla and they are pumped."

I didn't realize she was planning to tell them this soon, but I'm wondering if they asked her outright and she didn't know what to say. SJ loves Thanksgiving, so if it came up in passing, I can see him asking her about whether she was planning to stay. "Okay, what's the problem with that? Ohio isn't exactly close, Margot."

"Isn't that kind of strange? I mean, she's the nanny. I wouldn't necessarily call her family. Why would she be staying for the holidays?"

I frown because at this moment I barely recognize my own daughter. Margot is considerate and typically very sensitive to other people's feelings and has never wanted anyone to feel left out. "Margot, what's gotten into you? This isn't like you and I don't like this side I'm seeing."

"I just think Isla and SJ are getting too attached to her, and what happens when she leaves?" Tears well up in her eyes, and I'm momentarily stunned by how much she looks like her mother. "Isla is so young and...Ellie is not her mom."

"No one said she was and Ellie is not trying to be her mom. No one can ever take your mom's place."

I hadn't expected this to be about their mother but it makes sense.

"Maybe not for me and SJ, but Isla barely remembers Mom

and her memories are going to fade more as she gets older. And… Ellie?" she says, probably shocked to hear me call her by her nickname when I've only ever referred to her as Elianna in front of them.

I move to sit on the edge of her bed. "Is this what's made you so upset lately?"

"I just don't want them to get hurt."

"No one wants that, Margot."

"Can't you see, if Ellie leaves, once again they lose another woman in their life who was supposed to take care of them? Even if mom were still alive, there's a reason why children bond so heavily with their nannies. It's because they see her as a mother figure. Dad, this isn't rocket science and I feel like you can't see that because you like her." I don't say anything because I don't know what to say, having not been prepared to have this conversation with anyone tonight. Margot must take my silence for confirmation because she continues much to my irritation. "That's what I thought…is something going on between the two of you?"

I get off her bed, not wanting to continue this conversation. "Margot, I understand your concerns, but it is not your job to worry about that."

She scoffs and blinks the tears away and I can see the anger all over her face. "Not my job to worry about what? My siblings? Somebody has to!" she says, raising her voice a little louder than she'd been talking.

Fury spikes in my veins. "First of all, watch your tone, young lady. You think I don't worry about your siblings? All I do is worry about you three."

"Answer my question, Dad." She stands up, crossing her arms over her chest.

"I don't owe you any explanation. I'm *your* father."

"When it's convenient, sure!" she argues and I am shocked by this overall reaction and her attitude.

I glare at her, daring her to continue. "You want to run that by me again?"

"Before Ellie started you were rarely ever home before eight, and now you're reading to Isla before bed and going to SJ's games all of a sudden? Coming home early? It's like you've adapted all these new behaviors because you're trying to impress her." She shakes her head at me. "And the fact that you won't deny it, tells me all I need to know. This is even worse! Now, you're what—dating her? And then when things go south, you expect her to just stay here working for you and looking after them? No, they'll lose her because of you. You can't honestly be that selfish."

Hearing her thoughts about me makes me feel like my heart is being ripped from my chest. I'm hurt that she's hurt and I'm angry that she's angry. I'm worried that she's right and that I have been selfish when all I've tried to do is be the best father to them. And because I can't make sense of my thoughts, I say the first thing I can think of. "You're grounded."

"For what? Telling you the truth that Uncle River won't?" she scoffs.

"No," I snap, "because you are so out of line and I don't know where you got the idea that you could talk to me like that."

"Fine. Someone needed to tell you this, and for the record, you guys could both use a lesson in covering your tracks. You guys both mysteriously are out of the house tonight, you both come home dressed like you were just on a date, and she smells like you and you smell like her." She glares at me before tossing pillows off of her bed. "And to your point, if you don't 'owe me an explanation,' then why lie about it?"

"Because you're not meant to know everything that's going on all the time. This isn't about you, Margot. It's between me and Elianna."

"That's exactly my point, Dad." She lies down on her bed and turns off the lamp on her nightstand. "I got it, I'm grounded. Can

I go to bed now? I have a history test first period." She turns her television off, turns her back to me and I hear a sniffle seconds later.

"Margot..."

"Just go, Dad, please."

I don't know what to say to her. At the end of the day, I had lied to her and I think that's driving some of her hurt. "Love you the most," I tell her before I slowly walk out of her room.

I'm stuck somewhere between sadness and anger when I see Ellie sitting on the steps. We weren't yelling, but we were certainly loud enough that she probably heard everything. The look on her face matches the one on mine and after checking on Isla and SJ and seeing them still asleep, I follow her downstairs. I usher her into my bedroom and she sits across from me on the bed.

"How much did you hear?"

"All of it," she says. "After the conversation we had when I got home, I thought there was more to her frustration."

I sigh, wondering what she could have said to Ellie and hoping it wasn't anything like what she'd said to me. "I'm sorry, you're tied up in this. What did she say to you?"

"Don't apologize. I'm just as involved. She didn't ask me if there was anything between us. She just mentioned that she thought Isla was getting too attached and about what happened at bedtime."

I pull off my jacket and toss it on the lounger in the corner before sitting on the bed next to her. "She thinks I'm selfish."

"You're not selfish, Rowan. I've never been in this situation so I'm not exactly sure how to navigate it either, but I think this is potentially stemming from seeing you with another woman that's not her mom while also being worried about SJ and Isla. I do think she is worried about them and I get that. It was some of my hesitation as well." She puts a hand on mine and squeezes it gently. "You are a good dad."

I let my eyes close slowly, feeling disappointment in myself replacing the previous anger and sadness. "Don't make me repeat it." *Especially because at the moment I do not feel like I am.*

"It's possible that you were going to have this conversation about anyone you were choosing to bring into their life. Maybe Margot thought she was prepared because she was fine with the idea of you dating. It's very different from actually seeing you with someone else." I know she's trying to cheer me up but all I can focus on is Margot calling me *selfish*. I stand up without another word and begin unbuttoning my shirt. "Can you tell me what you're thinking?" Ellie asks and I hate the nerves I hear in her voice. Like maybe she's thinking I'm going to take this situation out on her. I don't blame her and I hope I'm able to convey that properly.

"Their mother called me selfish. Often. Hearing my daughter say that…it just took me back, I guess. Bianca would say I cared more about work than her…than them…" I sigh, recalling the number of fights we had because I'd been late or missed something I'd promised the kids. "She told me one day I'd wake up and the kids would barely know me." I clear my throat. "I've really tried to be better about showing up for them. I guess it hasn't been good enough."

"Rowan, you're a single dad with a demanding job. You can only do so much. They have more of your time than I had with my dad growing up," she says, and while I know she isn't placating me, I can't help but feel like it.

"Yeah, and you wish you had more," I tell her while I pull off the rest of my clothes and put on a pair of sweatpants.

"Of course, but I know that wasn't his fault."

I go into my bathroom and stare at myself in the mirror. I don't know how long I'm in here before Ellie comes in and sits on the edge of the counter looking up at me.

"You are allowed to have a life, Rowan."

"But I'm not allowed to have you." I chuckle.

"Says who?"

"My almost seventeen-year-old daughter apparently."

She looks down at her hands and I can see the sadness written all over her. "Do you want to take a break..."

"No," I tell her, already knowing what she was planning to say. "She knows now. What would be the point of ending this?" The thought hits me hard and I turn my gaze to hers. "Unless you're planning to leave?"

"No..." Her bottom lip trembles slightly and when I turn her gaze to mine, her eyes are watery. "I've always tried to maintain a healthy distance with the kids I nanny for. There's always a plan in place for me to leave and...I try my best not to get attached." She rubs her nose and under her eyes. "And most of the time it works. I feel sad of course when I leave them but...with your kids..." She trails off. "The thought of leaving them—it hurts more than usual. And I feel like I've known this for a while. Since I met Isla in the grocery store when she teared up about her mother."

I stare at her in shock. "She cried?" I didn't know that. *No wonder she came to meet me.*

"Yeah...umm...I never really gave you the whole story. I wasn't hiding it, I just kind of forgot and I didn't want you to get mad at River." She chuckles sadly. "She was by herself; I think I mentioned she was climbing the shelves. I asked her who she was with, if she was with her mom and she said no and that she died." *I hadn't known Isla to talk about her mother at all, and it makes me wonder if there had been signs I hadn't seen.* "I told her that mine did too, and I don't know, maybe she felt comfortable or safe but she teared up and then she hugged me. I think I've been attached ever since." She shakes her head and looks up at me. "But I know I'm not their mother, and God, I hope Margot doesn't think I'm trying to take her place. Jacqueline thinks I took this job because a part of me was trying to rewrite the past. Do better for SJ and Isla than I ever did for my sisters...and be the person for Margot that I wish someone had been for me." She pauses before she raises her hand and lets it drop to her thigh in defeat. "But now she hates me. So..." A feeling of sadness washes over me thinking about Ellie as a child in the same situation that my kids are in now and how growing up without a mother is something I can't understand no matter how much I try to be there for them.

I shake my head at her and rest my hands on her shoulders, forcing her gaze upwards to meet mine. "She doesn't hate you, and listen to me, Ellie…I am so happy they have you. I know you are not trying to replace her, but Margot was right about one thing. You are a motherly figure to them and I'm glad it's someone who cares about them as much as you do." I pull her into my arms and press a kiss to her forehead and then her nose. "Please don't cry."

"I just don't want to be the cause of a strain between you and Margot. A good nanny doesn't—"

I pull back to look at her. "I think you are far past just being the nanny, wouldn't you say?" I interject.

"I guess."

I cup her face and stroke my thumbs over the apples of her cheeks. "There's no guessing. You're good for them. All of them. Margot included, even if she doesn't see it right now. And you're good for me. You make me want to be better for them and for me. We will work all of this out, but I'm not letting you leave us." I press my lips softly to hers. "That includes me, by the way."

"I don't want to…and even before I didn't mean a break for forever."

"I'm not letting you get away at all. Not even for a second."

I somehow convinced Ellie to stay with me last night, and I'm pleasantly surprised to wake up and find her still in bed with me. My arm is wrapped possessively around her middle with her back to me and I hope there will come a time when she's here every night. I kiss the back of her shoulder before trailing kisses slowly up her neck and to her cheek before she stirs against me, rubbing against my dick in the process.

"Mmm." She moans and the sound does nothing for the thickening in my sweatpants. She turns in my arms and her eyes flutter open slowly. It must take her a second to register that she's in bed with me because a sleepy smile finds her face and then they fly open. "Shit!" she whispers. "What time is it?" She goes to get up when I hold her tighter and drag my nose against hers. "Early. No one is awake yet."

She lets out a soft sigh. "I should go," she tells me but I have other plans for her.

"Not yet," I murmur as I slide my hands up her t-shirt and cup her breasts. "Five minutes."

She narrows her gaze at me. "Five minutes, Rowan," she says in what I imagine is the same stern voice she uses with SJ and Isla, and I chuckle.

"Ten at the most," I tell her as I pull her to straddle me. She crosses her arms over her chest and I put both of my hands up in surrender. "Hey, it's up to you how long you're in here. The sooner you come, the sooner you can leave." I grin at her and a mischievous look finds her face. She goes to pull my dick out of my sweatpants when I grab her wrist, halting her movements and she looks at me curiously. "I've been wondering…" I tell her while reaching my hand up and dragging my thumb over her covered sex. "If we can make you come like *this*."

"Like what?"

"With our clothes on. We didn't get a chance to explore this last week." I grip her thighs, pulling her tighter against me before rocking her slightly back and forth over my dick.

"Oh." The word comes out with a gush of air and she lays her palms flat on my chest to give herself some leverage. She begins to move her hips, chasing the high that I can already feel getting closer with every stroke. She moves herself back and forth and I trail my hands up her legs to her hips to help her move faster.

"You're doing so good, baby. Feels good, doesn't it?"

"Ye–yes…" she stammers. "For you too?"

"Fuck yes," I tell her. "You're going to make me come this way too, sunshine."

She slows down, teasing us both as she rocks slowly and my heart begins to beat in time with the throbbing in my dick. I start thrusting upwards when she grinds down, and soon we find a perfect rhythm. Her hands move up to my shoulders, shifting her weight and I slide my hands back up her shirt to find those pebbled nubs I wish were in my mouth. I rub my thumbs over both of them before settling on a continuous circular motion causing her to gasp.

"Oh my God." Her eyes squeeze shut as her movements become more erratic. "I'm going to come."

My balls are aching with the need to release and I know I won't be far behind her when she climaxes. "Rowan, oh God, right there."

"Take whatever you need, baby." She moves like she's riding me and then her mouth falls open and I watch as the orgasm washes over her, but she doesn't stop, she just continues to rub herself against me. I tighten my grip on her again as her hands move to my thighs and she begins to rub herself against me even harder. "Fuck, I'm there. You're so fucking incredible, making us come like this." I groan and just when I'm on the edge, she grabs one of my hands and slides one of my fingers into her mouth. She bites down gently before she winks in a way that is somehow both sexy and shy and then I come, shooting ropes of cum inside my pants.

CHAPTER TWENTY-ONE

Elianna

Leaving Rowan's room, my body is still buzzing from the orgasm I just had. I go to my room to take a shower and try to figure out how I'm going to approach Margot about this. I imagine she'll be a little cold toward me and I feel a rush of anxiety thinking about how to fix this.

Stop banging her dad might be a start.

The wayward thought flashes through my head and I try to ignore my snarky subconscious as I head into the kitchen to start on some breakfast. Around six-thirty, Rowan comes out of his bedroom dressed for work and I can't stop the sizzle that moves through me seeing him like this. He comes up behind me, pressing his chest against my back to pin me against the counter. He drops a kiss on my neck and then my shoulder before nuzzling my ear. "You can't look at me like that. It makes me want to bend you over this counter and we can't."

I shiver under his lips before turning around to look up at him. "You look nice," I tell him as I drag my eyes over the navy suit and white shirt he's wearing.

"That's not helping." He digs his teeth into his bottom lip and sweeps his gaze over me before he moves to the Keurig to make some coffee. "I know Margot should be down soon. Do you want me to stay until she leaves? Just in case..." He winces but I hear the implication. *It's possible, well probable, that there will be some residual attitude and he doesn't want her taking it out on me.*

I shake my head. "I think it's best if maybe I try without you here."

"Ellie..."

"I'll be fine," I tell him as I slide Isla's sandwich into her lunch box and turn to look at him. "I have to be able to talk to her. Especially if...I'm going to be here for...a while."

"Alright, let me know how it goes?" he says. "Call me if you need anything."

"I will," I tell him and then he's gone with a final kiss to my lips.

Twenty minutes later, I hear Margot come down the stairs and walk through the foyer completely bypassing the kitchen on the way to the front door.

"Margot," I call after her before moving into the foyer where I see her with her back turned and her hand on the doorknob. It stings that she wasn't even planning to say goodbye. I watch as her shoulders slouch and she turns to face me.

"Yes?" She has a blank expression on her face and her eyes look slightly red with bags beneath them.

"That was not...how you were supposed to find out," I tell her honestly and she chuckles.

"That's your opening line?" She shakes her head and I can feel the anger radiating off of her. "No, that's right. Your opening line was that you *don't want to be my friend or my nanny*. Didn't realize you were going for my stepmom." She lifts her chin slightly. "Well, don't bother, because I don't need or want one of those."

"I know you're angry at me and I am so sorry."

She forces a laugh. "For what? Lying to me? Let me guess. Dad knows all about the drama between me and Gabe."

"No, I wouldn't betray your trust. You asked me not to say anything about that and I didn't. And…I didn't lie to you, Margot. I didn't expect…I haven't been interested in anyone in six years. I certainly didn't expect to go into a nannying job thinking that would change." She doesn't say anything so I take a step closer to her. "What would make you happy? Tell me."

She scoffs. "Does it matter?"

"Your feelings mean a lot to your dad *and to me*, and for what it's worth, he is hurt by all of this. He hates that you're so hurt."

"I have to get to school." She opens the door before turning back to me. "I know I'm grounded, so I'll be home after practice," she says without another word before she's out the door.

It isn't long before Isla comes skipping down the stairs dressed for the day and I'm surprised she's downstairs before Sawyer. "Hi, Isla! Look at you all ready to go."

"I am!" She climbs up on one of the barstools just as I set some oatmeal in front of her.

"It's hot." I point at her and she nods before picking up the spoon. "How did you sleep?"

"Okay." She shrugs. "But I slept in Margot's room."

I look at her curiously at this revelation because it means she must have gone in there late last night. "You did? How come?"

"I woke up and I heard her crying."

"Oh?" Guilt slithers through me that I contributed to that. "Why was she crying?"

"I don't know. She didn't say. Sometimes she just does." She shrugs. "Probably because of Mommy. Only at night time though."

The fact that I didn't realize that nights were so tough for her makes me feel like shit. *Those nights that I was fooling around with her father she could have been crying herself to sleep.*

"Does it happen a lot?" I feel a little bit guilty using Isla to try and figure out Margot but I already know that she's shutting down and it would be good to know what she's thinking and how she feels before she completely shuts us out.

"Mmmm." She blows on her oatmeal before taking a small bite. "I don't know."

I take the seat next to her and look at her. "Do you cry? About your mommy?"

"Sometimes," she says before looking at me. "Do you? Isn't your mommy dead too?"

"Sometimes," I whisper. I tap the counter before pressing a kiss to the top of her head. "Well, you finish eating. I'm going to go check on your brother."

"Oh oh, Ellie!" Isla calls after me and when I turn around, she's practically brimming with excitement. "I know what I want to be for Halloween!"

"Oh?!" I tilt my head to the side because this has been an ongoing saga for the past two weeks.

"Tinker Bell!" she cheers. "Do you think SJ will dress up with me as Peter Pan?"

"Absolutely not," I hear from behind me and SJ walks into the room. "I told you; I have plans. We are being the Avengers and I already have my Spider-Man costume."

"Fine." Isla pouts.

"Maybe, your dad will be Peter Pan with you," I offer.

SJ snorts before sitting next to Isla. "Yeah, right. I'd pay big money to see that."

"Will you be Wendy?!" Isla's eyes light up and a huge smile finds her face.

"Sure, honey." Her energy is infectious and I find myself smiling despite the conversation we had just minutes ago.

It's been a week and Margot has barely spoken to me or her father. When she does, it's only because Isla and SJ are in the room. She's feigned a headache a few times and has even eaten in her room a few times which is why I'm shocked when one night after Isla and SJ are in bed she comes downstairs and into the living room and sits down on the adjacent loveseat. Rowan isn't home from work yet so I assume she only wants to talk to me.

"Do you want to watch something?" I ask her, holding the remote toward her.

"You know I was twelve when my parents divorced," she says and my extended arm lowers slowly. "That weird age when you understand enough on the surface level. I understood what a divorce was and that it meant my parents wouldn't live together anymore. I couldn't understand the whys of it all, especially because my parents hid their problems well. They didn't fight in front of me…" She shrugs. "I didn't feel the tension, you know? But again, I was twelve. But as I got older, I saw things differently on both sides. But still, I wasn't that kid who wanted my parents back together. That was SJ. He was only six and he was the one who made that wish when he blew out his birthday candles or put it on his list to Santa Claus when he still believed in him. My mom seemed so much happier, especially when she met Pete…that was her boyfriend. I didn't like him at first either. He was too…happy all the time." She scrunches her nose. "It was so annoying, but my mom told me in so many words to get over it because he was sticking around." She turns her eyes to me. "Are you planning…to stick around?"

"Would you hate it if I did?"

Her eyebrows pinch together and her lips form a firm line. "Don't ask me that like I have a say in this."

"No, but I would never want to be the reason for any kind

of rift in a relationship. When Sawyer and Isla find out, they are going to look at how you handle this."

"Isla adores you."

"Sure, but not more than she adores you, Margot. You're her only sister and in about two years, she is going to worship the ground you walk on even if she won't always show it."

"I won't hate it. I just worry about you hurting my siblings… or my dad."

I don't miss that she doesn't say anything regarding herself. "I won't hurt them, Margot, but what about you?"

"I'll be fine whether you stay or leave." She shrugs non-committedly before she's off the loveseat and I hear her footsteps retreating up the stairs.

"So, I was thinking…" Rowan starts as we sit on his patio. He has a fireplace out here as well, so it's keeping us warm on this colder than normal November night.

"Oh? About what?"

"That you and I need a night alone."

"I suppose we are due for another date." I prop my elbow up on the back of the chair and rest my head on it.

"Yes, but how about one that's overnight?" he says before grabbing my legs and draping them over his lap. I go to respond with a series of questions that he must expect because he continues. "River will come and stay with them."

"Wouldn't it be easier for them to just go to his house? How else will we explain both of us not being home if they're here?"

"I was thinking we should tell SJ and Isla. Margot doesn't usually stay over at River's and I don't want her staying here by herself or force her to make plans." While she had been grounded for a few days, Rowan lifted her punishment to try and get her to open up, but she didn't seem to care. She's been home every day right after cheer practice like she's still grounded.

I freeze because surely I hadn't heard him correctly. "You're ready to tell them?"

"Why not? It's been a week and I'm not even a hundred percent sure Margot hasn't told Sawyer."

"I don't think she has."

"I don't either, but I don't know how long that grace period is going to last. I assume she's trying to give us a chance to do it." He rubs my cheek and gives me a smile. "They're going to take it better than Margot is."

I nod, knowing he's right but still feeling apprehensive about it. "Okay, yeah, you're right."

"SJ is probably still awake. Do you want to tell him now and we can tell Isla tomorrow?"

I nod reluctantly because I really am nervous about telling them, but I do want to move forward and I'm tired of sneaking around.

When we get to Sawyer's room, he's awake, sitting up in bed, reading a comic book. He lowers it and looks at us over the top of it with wide eyes. "I didn't do it, whatever it is."

Rowan chuckles. "You know you give me more gray hairs than your sisters, kid."

"You wouldn't have me any other way." He sets his comic book down when Rowan sits on the edge of his bed and I lean against his desk. He darts his eyes back and forth between us. "What? You guys are freaking me out."

"SJ, we want to talk to you about something kind of important."

"Okay…" He raises an eyebrow in that same way Rowan does making him look even more like his twin than usual.

"So, first, I think your uncle is going to come stay here this weekend."

"SWEET. We're due for another Call of Duty marathon."

I gape at him in shock at the idea of him playing something so mature. Rowan puts a hand over his eyes while shaking his head, so I'm guessing this has been an ongoing battle. "I mean...Mario Kart?" he corrects, innocently.

"So, he'll be here Saturday after your game and he's going to stay the night."

"Okay, is that all?"

"Well, no...so I won't be here and neither will Ellie," he explains further.

"Ooookay," he says. "Where are you guys going? Dad, you got work? What about you, Elles?"

"So, that's the thing, SJ. We are going somewhere, *together*."

"Why?" he asks, and as smart as Sawyer is, I'm reminded of also just how young he is because he hasn't put it together.

"Well because, Son, we're...dating."

"No way!" he says, his mouth agape. He looks at me for a second before turning to his dad. "Aren't you kind of old for her?"

"Sawyer..." He glares at him but I see the humor lurking beneath his scowl.

"Listen, I'm cool with it. Does Margot know?" he asks, and I am not necessarily surprised based on the fact that he's a boy and only ten years old but I am relieved that at least one of the three is taking it well.

"She does," Rowan confirms.

"Oh, is that why she's been in such a shi–*crappy* mood?" He blanches.

"She's just a little concerned about some things," I explain and his eyes flit to mine.

He scratches the back of his head and looks at me "Like what?"

"She's worried about how you and your sister would take it if...things didn't work out," I tell him. "Obviously, no one wants that."

"Margot is always so worried about everything. We would be fine. Just like we've always been." He picks up his comic book and it's amazing how simple kids see the world at that age. So simple and yet, there's so much truth to his words. Because after all the shitty days I've had in my twenty-five years, I made it through all of them. "I mean it would suck, because, Ellie, I would miss your cooking," he corrects. "But I think it's cool that you love each other or whatever."

My cheeks heat at how easily that slipped out of him and Rowan seems to be just as flustered. "Right, well…ummm I'm glad to hear you're okay with this." Rowan clears his throat and I fight the urge to smile at how nervous he is. "We're going to tell Isla tomorrow, so just don't say anything for now."

Sawyer opens his comic book again and gives us a thumbs up.

The next day Rowan is home early and since Margot is home as well—a *rarity for a Friday night*—we are having dinner together. Even River is coming. I think his presence is supposed to lighten the mood, but I suspect it's also because Rowan told him I had made pot roast which happens to be one of his favorite meals.

We're sitting at the table in silence except for Isla who's just chatting away, mostly to herself or whoever is listening.

"Uncle River, are you coming to my soccer game tomorrow, or are you coaching?" SJ asks.

"No, we don't have a game tomorrow, so I'll be there," he says before taking a sip of his beer. "How many goals are you going to score?"

"Mmmm two," SJ says with his mouth mostly full.

"Holding you to that." River points at him. "Are you ready for tomorrow night?" SJ nods and gives a fist pump before River looks at Margot. "You have plans tomorrow night or are you going to be around?"

She tucks her hair behind her ear. "I'll be here," she answers, but her voice is despondent.

"Me too!" Isla cheers.

"Oh good, I figured you would be out at a dinner party or something. Cool," he says to Isla holding his beer out to her and she lifts her glass to clink it. A giggle escapes me because he really is the best uncle.

Obviously, the sarcasm goes completely over her head though, and she shakes her head. "No." Isla is sitting next to me, so she tilts her head to look at me. "Ellie, can we have a dinner party?"

"No, because they won't be here," Margot says looking at me and then her father.

"Hey, lay off." River, who's sitting perpendicular to her, nudges her elbow with his.

"Whatever," Margot mutters under her breath.

Sawyer, who's sitting next to her, rolls his eyes. "Dude, chill. You're so annoying," he says before taking a sip of his water.

"You won't be here?" Isla asks and I realize she didn't put it together that Margot said 'they' in terms of me and her father.

"Ummm, no not tomorrow, but I'll be back on Sunday."

"Oh, okay." She nods before turning back to her food and biting into one of her carrots.

"Can I be excused?" Margot asks.

"No," Rowan says without looking up from his food.

"Why?" she replies in a sullen tone.

"Because we're not done, that's why," Rowan says immediately.

"Go ahead," River says to her and Rowan glares at him.

"Are you kidding?" he snaps at his brother and I'm actually surprised that Margot didn't get up when her Uncle said she could.

"What? You think holding her hostage at the table is going to fix her attitude?" He rolls his sleeves up, revealing a bunch of tattoos on both arms and it's so crazy that despite how similar they look, Rowan and River are so different.

"No, but I am not going to let her think that this behavior is acceptable. I'm not rewarding a temper tantrum," Rowan says.

Margot's cheeks turn pink. "I am sitting here, you know."

Rowan turns his gaze to her. "Okay, I am not rewarding your temper tantrum." While his voice is calm and even, I can hear a bit of an edge in his voice. He's seated perpendicular to me at the end of the table so I slide my hand onto his knee and stroke it gently, trying to calm his nerves.

"Temper tantrum? You cannot be serious. I'm throwing a tantrum because I think this…" she says pointing between me and her dad, "is not a great idea? I'm so tired of having to be the responsible one. It's like I've always said, I'm the one person they can count on."

"Okay, first of all, I take offense to that," River interjects, cocking an eyebrow at her.

Margot sighs and looks at him remorsefully. "You don't live here, Uncle Riv."

"Doesn't mean you can't count on me. I've shown up for all of you every time you've needed me. So please, spare me the drama. Your dad and I worked hard so that most things didn't fall on you. Yeah, some things did, that's what happens when you're the oldest sibling and I know your dad is so thankful he had your help, but throwing it in his face now, like you did everything and he just wasn't around is not fair." He stares at her hard. "Margot, you're my girl and you know I will always be on your side, but I'm also going to tell it to you straight when you're out of line. And I think you have a skewed view of what's actually been happening around here."

I look down at Isla who's just watching what's happening with wide eyes and a mouth full of food.

Margot's anger seems to dissipate slightly before her eyes turn to her brother. "And you're just cool with this?"

"Cool with what? What's changed? Ellie was living here before and she's still going to live here."

"Because if they break up, she will *not* live here anymore. Am I speaking a foreign language? Why is no one understanding my concerns? Because what happens then?"

"We move on! Jesus, Margot. Not everyone and everything falls apart after a breakup. Remind me to stay away from you if you ever wise up and dump that loser, you're too good for," SJ says before taking a bite.

"Shut up," Margot growls, but I admit, part of me is glad he ended that dig with something slightly supportive. *She really could do better than that guy.* "I meant what happens with…" She looks at me. "The only person at this table that doesn't know what's going on. She is *not* going to move on that easily."

I look down at Isla again and notice that now she's not paying attention to us at all.

"Can you let us worry about that?" Rowan says. "I love that you are so protective of your siblings, but in case you forgot, I am too."

CHAPTER TWENTY-TWO

Eliana

I'M IN AWE THE SECOND WE PULL UP TO THE STUNNING LAKE house we have for the night. We'd driven out to Virginia, about forty minutes from home, and I'm so excited to spend a night alone with Rowan. "This is gorgeous. Where'd you find this?" I ask as he helps me out of the car.

"A guy from work. This is actually his lake house. He uses it for Airbnb mostly." He closes the door behind me and grabs our bags. "I've thought about investing in a lake house but I wanted to wait until Isla was a little older and was a stronger swimmer."

It's a two-story house that is mostly secluded with nothing but trees surrounding it except for the front which faces the lake. It looks almost like a log cabin with gray stones sprinkled throughout the structure and huge windows. It's like a house right out of a magazine.

"Wow," I say more to myself because I've never seen anything like this and I've been to my fair share of lake houses with families I've worked for.

"I'm glad you like it, sunshine," he says as we walk up the stone path to the door, passing a small pond with a fountain with fish swimming around. We make it inside and it's cozy and rustic with brown and cream couches and what looks like a ten-foot Christmas tree in the corner. I tilt my head to look at him. "Christmas tree already?"

He chuckles before turning to light the fireplace. "I think it's nice to have some festive decor for travelers. Besides, it is November and some people like to set up early. Not us. Pretty sure it was mid-December by the time we got the tree up last year."

I turn away from the silvery Christmas tree with twinkling white lights and put my hands on my hips.

"What? Oh my God, don't worry. I will get you guys together this year." He makes his way over to me and wraps his arms around me.

"I have no doubt that you will." He presses his lips to mine. "So, what do you want to do first?"

"You," I say while taking a step back and making an obvious gesture to his groin.

"Oh?" He smirks. "Because there's a hot tub out back."

"Shit, I totally forgot to bring a bathing suit!" I hadn't even thought about the possibility of a hot tub and with the temperature barely getting above forty-five degrees, I knew I wouldn't be getting in the lake.

"I didn't bring one either," he tells me and I'm pretty sure even if I brought one, I wouldn't be wearing it.

The idea of *delayed gratification or whatever* is how we end up in the hot tub before fooling around, although there's a good chance the idea of waiting until later seems to be coming to an abrupt halt with the way he's staring at me. We are both naked under the water, so while the bubbles from the jets slightly obscure our bodies, we know what *isn't* below the surface.

He turned on some music and it has just switched to a sultrier song that immediately sends a shiver through me.

"So, do you see yourself having more kids? Or are you done?" I'm on my second margarita which may be the reason behind my question, but thankfully so is he and when he downs the rest of his drink and stares at me with hooded eyes, I wonder if my question is just adding to the tension crackling between us.

"I thought I was done," he says before sucking an ice cube into his mouth and crossing the hot tub to where I'm sitting. He pulls me to my feet. "Now, I'm not so sure," he says low in my ear before using his lips to drag the piece of ice down my neck. The sensation of the hot water mixed with the ice is making me dizzy with lust and I grab onto his biceps.

"Oh?" I whisper as he drags the ice across my chest and up my neck on the other side. "Why aren't you sure?"

"Hmmm." He moans in my ear and then I feel his hand on my inner thigh. "I don't know. Do *you* want kids?" He drags a finger over my clit and presses his lips to my neck with the ice cube still in his mouth, sucking on the skin and sending another icy feeling through my body.

"Me?" I gasp.

He pulls back to look at me before pulling me so I'm pressed right against him. "I'm certainly not practicing how you get them with anyone else." Before I can respond, he lifts me in his arms and sets me on the edge of the hot tub. The hot tub is covered by the deck above us and on two sides so it's somewhat insulated, otherwise I'd be freezing.

"Spread them." I do as he says instantly, not feeling nearly as nervous as I did weeks ago the first time he told me to do this.

"Such a good girl. Always so eager to please me." He grabs his glass again and sucks in another ice cube. "Good thing you found someone who wants to please you just as much." He smirks and then his head is between my thighs pressing the ice and his tongue to my clit and I feel like I could pass out from the sensation. It's deliciously intense and I never want this feeling to end. I drag my fingers through his damp hair as he continues to eat me hungrily, lapping at me with the ice cube on his hot tongue.

"Fuck, Rowan!"

"Yes, baby?" he asks while he brings my legs over his shoulder. He pulls back, and a stream of melted ice or maybe spit connects his mouth to my pussy before he breaks it with his tongue. *Holy fuck, he's hot.* He looks up at me, dragging those hooded eyes up my body, letting them linger on my breasts with his bottom lip trapped between his teeth. "God, you're so fucking perfect," he says before diving back between my legs, his tongue fucking me faster as he laps at my clit.

My toes curl and my heart speeds up. "Don't stop."

"Stop? Hell no, baby, I'm just getting started." He raises a hand to keep the ice on my clit while his tongue pushes inside me and my head falls back, feeling my orgasm brew beneath my skin.

"Oh God, right there. I'm going to come." I moan as I push my sex harder against his soft lips.

"Let me hear it. No one is around for miles, baby. Scream for me."

"Oh fuck, Rowan!" I cry out *loudly* and then my climax washes over me hard and fast, knocking the wind out of me briefly.

I can feel my eyes twitch behind my eyelids and I expel a shaky breath just as I lift my head. When I open my eyes, they're hazy and when he steps closer to me, putting his hands on my face, I realize I'm crying.

"You're so beautiful," he says pressing his lips to each cheek, catching the two stray tears that have streaked down my face.

I throw my arms around his neck and pull his lips down to mine, swirling my tongue against his and tasting myself on him. "Fuck me."

He spins me around to face the edge of the hot tub and bends me over the edge. "Don't move," he whispers in my ear before I feel a smack on my ass. I gasp at the sensation and the sting his hand leaves in its wake. We'd had the jets on low but suddenly they've been turned up and the water is shooting out faster. He moves me over so I'm more in line with them and when he pushes me closer, I feel the pressured water hitting my clit.

"Oh my God."

He leans over and I feel his cock resting against me as he trails kisses up my spine. "I'm going to fuck you like this, okay?"

I nod enthusiastically because I want to do whatever he wants. "Yes. Yes *please*."

"Fuck. Your ass, Elianna." He groans. "Will you let me play with it later?"

"Oh fuck…I…yes!" I cry out when he moves me closer to the jets and it's now hitting my clit at full force. "Fuck me now," I say over my shoulder, and less than a second later I feel him push inside of my slick cunt that is already pulsing. "Rowan!"

"I know, baby, I know." He groans. "You're doing so well, taking my dick like this. You didn't know how good it could be in this position, did you?"

I shake my head because no position we've tried yet has felt like this. He grips my hips and continues to slam into me from behind all the while the jets are stimulating my clit and I feel like I'm in sensory overload.

"Rowan, oh my *God!*" I scream, slamming my hand down against the stone tiling around the hot tub as water splashes around us. I'm pushing back against him; my pussy feels like it's on fire with how hot it feels and I'm so close to the edge I can taste it.

"You're clamping down on me so damn hard, sunshine. Let go and make your pretty pussy come all over my dick. Do it now, fucking…*please*." He groans and I can feel his words in my clit. He slaps my ass again and it triggers my climax.

"Oh fuuuuck. Come inside me…*Mr. Kincaid*," I moan and the

growl I hear from behind me is so hot it already has me thinking about going again.

"Shit." His strokes are even faster now and I know he's close. I reach between my legs and drag my palm over his balls, squeezing them gently. "FUCK!" He roars and then holds me tight against him as I feel his cock pulse inside of me. Thoughts of the conversation we had earlier about kids has me thinking about his cum being stronger than my preventative measures leaving me pregnant after this weekend and my cunt throbs.

I don't even have time to contemplate that thought for long because he pulls out of me and then I feel his mouth back between my legs from behind before dragging upwards and rimming my asshole.

"Oh my God."

"I need this," he says as he squeezes one of my cheeks. "Need to claim you in every possible way."

I knew he was possessive but seeing this side of him is so fucking hot and I love that it's something only I see. "Okay…just… go slow."

"Not yet," he says, his tongue still tracing my asshole. "I need to prepare you better than this. I don't want to hurt you." He places a final kiss on my ass cheek before pulling me to stand and spinning me around. "I will never hurt you." He drops a light kiss on my lips and then my nose.

"I know."

"You want to go upstairs?" he asks, nodding toward the inside.

The bedroom is gorgeous with all-white bedding and a canopy, a fireplace that Rowan started while we were downstairs so the room would be ready when we were ready to move things to the bedroom. Rowan made us more margaritas, and I'm now feeling not only drunk on Rowan but a little drunk on tequila and it's making me horny as fuck.

"The first time I laid eyes on you, I knew you were going to be a problem for me, Elianna," he says against my lips. We're lying on the bed, a tangle of limbs, still naked and buzzing from our orgasms. "I've never felt such an instant attraction to someone."

"I felt the same...and Jacqueline called this after the first time I met you," I confess with a giggle.

"Did she now? I think I need to meet this best friend of yours."

"She's...something." I laugh. "But I love her. Even if she does call you Hot Daddy Rowan." I blurt out and my lips immediately form a straight line because I had *not* meant to tell him that. *Shit! Damn tequila.*

He pulls back and gives me a sly smirk. "Do you call me that too?"

"No." I shake my head. "She's just being silly."

"You don't think I'm hot?" He raises an eyebrow at me.

"Your ego doesn't need the stroking. You know you're hot, Rowan Kincaid. Have you seen the way women look at you? I don't even have to see it to know based on all the moms trying to get information from me about you." I laugh but he doesn't even crack a smile.

"I don't care about any of them. I care about the way *you* look at me." He pulls me closer and rubs my back.

"Of course, I think you're hot. I believe I frequently use the word *gorgeous* in my head, but semantics."

He moves to lie on top of me. "I don't know how I would feel about you calling me *Daddy*. Since you know...there's someone else that does? I'm trying not to think about that though." He chuckles. "Maybe we should try it. Just to see."

I raise an eyebrow at him. "How drunk are you?" I giggle and he shakes his head.

"I'm not." He narrows his eyes at me but I can see the haze in them.

"Sure about that...Daddy?" I say in a breathy voice and I feel his cock jerk against me.

I watch his pupils dilate and his mouth falls open. "Yep, we're good." He lowers his mouth to my neck and bites down gently. "I like it. Didn't think I would, but maybe it's because it's coming out of those perfect lips I haven't stopped thinking about since I met you."

"Did you think about them wrapped around your dick when you touched yourself?"

"Every fucking time." He kisses me slowly, trailing down my body, and running his tongue over both of my nipples before he gets off the bed. I follow him with my eyes and see that he's got a bottle of lubricant. "We don't have to do this," he says as he joins me back on the bed.

"I want to." I reach for his dick and stroke him slowly before gliding my thumb over the tip to collect the pearl of pre-cum that had formed. "Don't you want to fuck my ass, Daddy?" I purr and he wastes no time flipping me over and smacking my ass once.

"You're going to be a little tease with that, aren't you?"

"Not all the time." I giggle as he pulls me up on my knees and spreads my cheeks. I'm glad I'm a little drunk and feeling less inhibited or I'd definitely be feeling a little anxious over being this exposed to him. I gasp when I hear and feel him spit on my hole. "Did you just..."

I hear a chuckle behind me followed by the sound of squirting. "Just making sure you're extra lubricated."

I feel the cool gel and then his finger rubbing against me before he pushes slightly inside my asshole while another one of his fingers begins to rub my clit. I clench around his finger, never having felt anything inside before.

He lets out a breath and puts his other hand on my lower back. "Fuck, you are…this is going to be tight."

"You think?" I sass and he taps my ass gently.

"While I have a finger deep in your asshole, is probably not the best time for your smart mouth." I giggle when I feel more lubricant and then more pressure. "It's another finger," he tells me. "You're doing so well, baby. How are you feeling?"

"I'm okay." I moan, feeling the effects of that last margarita starting to kick in.

"You're perfect," he whispers, pushing even further inside and I feel my body start to build from all the stimulation.

"You're going to be so tight on my cock. Fuck…baby. You ready?"

I nod because my skin is buzzing and my pussy is wet and I feel like I'm in a state of complete euphoria. *Nothing has ever felt this good.*

"Fuck me, Daddy."

I hear a sound that might be a grunt or a groan as he slides his fingers out of me and I hear the squirt of more gel. "Tell me to stop if it's too much, okay, sunshine?" He trails a hand down my back and holds it at the base of my spine as I feel his dick at my hole and then he pushes in slowly and instantly I clamp down hard at the intrusion. "Rub your clit for me." I do as he says and I feel myself feeling looser as my orgasm begins to brew.

"Oh fuck…I can't believe you're…there. No one has ever…"

He's still inching in slowly and I feel his grip tighten on my hips. "And no one ever will be besides me," he says through gritted teeth and the possessiveness causes goosebumps to erupt everywhere.

"Oh, I think I'm going to come." I moan just as I think he's bottoming out inside of me.

"Yes, fucking come while I'm in your ass. I want you to feel good."

"It…feels…good…" I say through shaky breaths just as I

reach the peak of my high. He's begun thrusting slowly now and it still feels tight but the climax that's slowly moving through my body is lessening the pressure. "Yes yes yes! Oh fuck! Rowan!" I cry out.

"So tight, *fuck.*"

"Wait, I want to see you come," I tell him and he slowly pulls out and moves me onto my back. He lifts my legs slightly, so he can slowly slide back into my asshole and then his fingers go to my clit.

"I like this better anyway, so I can do this." He lets a stream of spit fall to my pussy.

"Oh. You are so…dirty." I bite my bottom lip watching his muscles flex as he thrusts. "I love it."

He gives me a sexy grin and picks up the pace causing his eyes to flutter shut but he never stops his assault on my pussy. He rubs my clit harder and faster and there's a good chance he's going to make me come again.

"Fuuuuuck, baby. I'm going to fucking explode."

"Yes yes, do that. I want to watch," I beg as I stare up at him watching him chase his climax. "Please, Daddy," I say as I grip his thigh hard. Lust flashes across his face and his eyes slam shut as he tightens his grip on my hip and slaps a hand down hard on my clit.

"Oh!" I cry out, the sting triggering a different kind of climax that makes me feel like everything is moving in slow motion. My limbs feel heavy and everything from the waist down tingles. "Wow," I whisper as he slides out of me and I *think* I feel him getting off the bed.

I feel the bed move and when I open my eyes again, he's staring at me with the sweetest expression. "Hi, gorgeous. I think you blacked out for a second. You feeling, okay?"

"That was…intense," I whisper as he wipes me gently with a warm washcloth.

"Did it hurt?"

"No, I think I'm okay. That smack at the end…" I trail off. "That was so hot," I murmur.

I feel myself moving and then I'm underneath cool blankets, resting on top of silky sheets. My eyes flutter open just in time to see Rowan cutting off the lights, leaving one on, and pulling me to rest on his chest.

"You're incredible, you know that? I feel so lucky to have found you," he whispers.

I think he may have said something else, but I'm asleep before I can ask him to repeat it.

CHAPTER TWENTY-THREE

Rowan

THE SOUND OF INCESSANT BUZZING WAKES ME UP THE next morning. I'm usually a pretty light sleeper with three children, but while last night was easily one of the best nights of my life, it was also pretty exhausting and I feel like I've been in a deep sleep for most of the night. Between the alcohol and all the orgasms, I was spent by the time I fell asleep. I'd never been more content though. Ellie passed out pretty much mid-sentence in my arms with her lips against my chest and I slept with her practically on top of me the entire night.

And now I want to spend every night in this position. The reminder that a phone ringing somewhere in the distance is what woke me up, prompts me to grab the device off the nightstand. When I see it's not my phone that's ringing, I look to the other nightstand where Ellie's is charging.

Ellie is still lying on top of me so I rub her back gently.

"Honey," I whisper. I press a kiss to her forehead and then her nose. "Ellie, wake up, baby."

I thought she was a light sleeper as well, but maybe she is just as exhausted. *She did end the night with a dick in her ass, after all.*

Memories of fucking her perfect ass come flooding back and I'm reminded of how good she felt. I've never had this kind of sexual chemistry with anyone. *Let alone with someone who hadn't had much experience before me.* It makes me wonder if there is such a thing as soulmates.

When her phone starts ringing again, I realize it must be important, so I push her to her back. I get off the bed, walk to where her phone is plugged in, and see she's got probably a dozen missed calls from her sisters.

Shit.

"Baby, wake up." I shake her awake more forcefully this time and her eyes flutter open finally.

"Hi, handsome," she says, stretching her arms out to reach for me. I grab one of her hands and press a kiss to her knuckles and then her lips. She must read the look I'm giving her because her face falls. "What is it?"

"I don't know, but your sisters have been calling."

She takes her phone from my hand and her eyes widen when she sees the call log. She puts her phone to her ear.

"Eden, what's up? Why are you and Em blowing me up? Are you okay?" Her free hand flies to her mouth and tears flood her eyes as the phone drops from her ear. I still hear Eden talking and she sounds a little hysterical. I gently take the phone from her and bring it to my ear.

"Hey, Eden. I think Ellie is going into a little bit of shock."

"Oh my God, who is this?"

"Ummm, I'm Ellie's boyfriend. Is everything okay? What's wrong?"

"Our dad had a heart attack. I booked the first flight I could get and I'm leaving school now but it's going to take me about two hours to get there from Connecticut."

"Shit, I'm so sorry," I look at Ellie who is staring straight ahead with a blank stare. I grab her hand and rub my thumb over her knuckles. "Do you know if he's stable?"

"I think he was when they got to the hospital? I'm not sure though. Emily is at the hospital. Call her."

"Alright, everything is going to be okay, Eden."

She sniffles and doesn't say anything in response before she finally speaks again. "What's your name, anyway? I didn't know she had a boyfriend. Fuck, I've been so busy this semester. I've barely talked to her or Emily."

"Well, Ellie can fill you in when she sees you." I wasn't sure if her sisters knew about me in the sense that I'm her boss and I don't want to be the one to drop the bomb that I'm now also her boyfriend amidst all of this.

Though I don't think I'll be her boss for much longer.

We get dressed, pack up the car quickly, and shortly after we are on our way back to the house. I haven't let go of her hand since we got in the car and though she isn't saying much, I feel like I can read her already.

"There's a two o'clock flight," she says finally. "I'm going to be cutting it close." She looks at her watch before turning to me. "Can you take me to the airport?"

"I can get River to take us."

"Us?"

"Of course, I'm coming with you."

"Rowan…"

"You're upset and I want to be there for you. I'm also a bit worried about you traveling alone while you're like this. I understand you may not be ready for me to meet your family; I don't have to come to the hospital but I want to be close by."

Tears well in her eyes and she brings my hand to rest over her heart. "You are so sweet, but I'm okay. We've been gone and we can't both leave the kids again."

"Baby, it's an emergency. They will be okay."

She sighs. "I need to go by myself."

"Why?"

"Because!" She wipes under her eyes. "Em said he's stabilized and he's going into surgery. I'm sure everything will be okay."

"I'm sure too," I tell her, doing my best to remain optimistic and help keep her spirits up. "But it doesn't change the fact that I don't want you traveling alone while you're feeling vulnerable."

"I don't want you to leave them. Unless you turn around and come back the same day, you'll more than likely be in Ohio overnight."

"Ellie, I've had to go away for work where I've been gone multiple days in a row. They will be fine. River comes and stays with them at the house." I can't tell if she's putting her guard up and pushing me away or if this is just about the kids, but it's looking more and more like I'm not going with her.

"That's not the point."

"What is the point?" I probe her gently, not wanting to argue but wanting to understand why she is so averse to having me come with her.

"Margot is still really sensitive about this and us and I just… don't want to take you away from them. I know you want to be there. I do, and I can't tell you what that means to me, but I don't want to be worried about them while I'm in Ohio." She shakes her head and tears flood her eyes. "This isn't about us or taking a step back, I promise. I just want to go by myself."

I relent because I don't want her to feel like this is about that. She has more important things to worry about and I don't want to be the cause of any additional stress.

I called River and briefly gave him the rundown while we were at the lake house as Ellie packed her things, so he pulled Ellie into a hug as soon as we walked through the front door.

"I'm going to go pack. I'll be ready in like ten minutes?" she offers weakly as she makes her way to her room. Her eyes are still red and watery and all I want to do is hold her in my arms and take every ounce of her pain away.

River winces when she disappears and we walk into the kitchen. "Are you going with her?" he whispers and I shake my head. "Why?"

"She doesn't want me to. Said I should stay here with the kids," I say while pulling a bottle of water out of the refrigerator.

"Oh man, I could stay if that's what she's worried about." He shakes his head. "I would just need to run home and get some stuff, but Margot's here."

"I told her that. I think Margot's attitude has her rattled and she doesn't want to give her another reason to be upset."

"Dude…I talked to Margot last night. For a while," he tells me as he leans over the counter. "I gave her a beer to mellow her out…" he chuckles. "Actually three."

"I could do without knowing that."

He snorts. "That girl could drink *you* under the table. Believe me, she was fine. You'd be proud. I drew the line at her wanting to take shots though." I glare at him but he continues. "It did get her to open up. Just give her some time. It's an adjustment and she's sixteen. This is really your first experience being around a girl this age since we don't have sisters, but as someone who deals with hundreds of them every day, they're a little moody," he whispers. "And we always thought she took Bianca's death the hardest. There are so many layers here. All that being said, she knows she has to work on her attitude."

I'm not surprised that River was able to get her to open up.

He has this way of always making people feel comfortable. Even strangers. He's personable and likable in ways I never felt I was.

I hear footsteps on the stairs and then I see Isla in one of her Princess costumes. I get the feeling she was just about to rope River into something when we got home.

"Hi, Daddy!" she runs toward me and I scoop her up in my arms, pressing a kiss to her cheek.

"Hi, Princess. Did you have fun with Uncle River?" I ask, doing my best to sound cheerful.

"Uh-huh! He let me stay up until eleven!"

"Didn't I say that was a secret?!" River points at her when he sees the look I'm giving him and then waves me off. "We were watching a movie and I let her finish."

"What movie?" I ask, wondering what my younger brother has subjected my youngest to now.

"Relax, some cartoon shit."

Isla giggles and presses a kiss to my cheek. "Where's Ellie?"

"In her room. Listen, angel—"

"Ellie!!!" she calls, kicking herself against me so I'll put her down before she takes off for her room. I was planning to tell her myself so Ellie wouldn't have to and I can only hope it doesn't make her more upset to have to tell Isla that she's leaving. I follow behind her and when I make it to her room, I see Isla already in Ellie's arms.

"I missed you!" she squeezes her and Ellie holds her tight against her chest.

"I missed you too! What did you do while we were gone?" she asks while she continues to pack some clothes into a small suitcase.

"Watched a movie and played Candy Land four times and I won six dollars and had pizza!"

I glare down the hall toward my brother at the thought that he's teaching my six-year-old about gambling and Ellie chuckles.

"Wow. Stakes have gone up since I was a kid." She looks at me in the doorway. "Your kids know how to gamble? I wish I would have known. My last job was with children of professional poker players and those eight-year-olds were *good*." She sighs and puts a hand over her face like she'd briefly forgotten what she was doing and now remembers that she's leaving.

"Honey, I'm leaving for a few days." She moves to Isla and kneels in front of her so she's at eye level.

"When will you be back?"

"I'm not sure. I have to go home."

"But you live here." A smile ghosts over Ellie's face and she brushes some hair out of Isla's eyes.

"I mean home to where my daddy lives."

"Oh. That's far, right?" Ellie nods and I can see the tears in her eyes before she blinks them away. "Why are you sad?"

She sniffles and puts on a smile. "I…I'm just going to miss you so much, that's all."

Isla's eyes well up too and I wonder if seeing Ellie upset is triggering her. "You'll come back, right?"

"Of course."

Her bottom lip trembles a little and I think it's hitting her that she's leaving for longer than the length of a school day. "Can we talk on the phone?"

"Yes, your dad has my number."

She presses a kiss to Ellie's nose before giving her a hug, and I feel the emotions building within because that was something Bianca always did and I'd never seen Isla do it to anyone.

"I have something for you," Isla says before she runs past me out of the room.

Ellie's eyes meet mine as she stands up and I don't waste a second closing the space between us to press my lips to hers. I feel her tears on my cheeks as my tongue moves against hers for no more than a second before I pull back to rest my forehead against hers.

"She's taking it better than I thought she would," she whispers. "You can call me if she wants to talk."

I rub the space under her eyes to wipe at the tears forming. "What about if *I* want to talk?"

"Anytime."

Isla comes running back into the room with what looks like a picture she drew and I realize it's the one of all of us. "Here," she says holding up the picture. "So, you don't forget about us."

Ellie drops to one knee. "Oh, Isla, I could never forget you guys." She takes the picture from her. "Thank you so much. I love this, but are you sure you want me to have it?"

Isla nods. "Did you talk to Daddy about the puppy?" she tries to whisper and Ellie laughs before looking up at me.

"Not yet, but I'll work on it when I get back," she whispers back before she stands up. "We should go," she says looking at me.

Isla's brown eyes move to mine before narrowing slightly and I see the worry on her face. "Daddy, you're going too?" I know this is what Ellie was worried about and while I hate that I'm not going with her, I know it's for the best.

"I'm just taking her to the airport because she has to get on a plane. I'll be back in a little while."

She nods and I'm surprised she doesn't ask if she can come too.

SJ comes into the room a second later. "Uncle Riv says you're leaving?" he asks and Ellie nods.

"Yes, but just for a little. You're in charge, 'till I get back." She points before she crosses the room, pulls him into a hug, and kisses his forehead.

"You got it. I'm…uhh…sorry about your dad," he says while looking at the floor. SJ doesn't show emotion often so I feel like he may be struggling with his feelings a little.

"Thank you. He's going to be fine…I just need to be there."

"Yeah." He nods.

"I have to go, but I will let you guys know when I get to Ohio, alright?"

SJ nods and we all move out of the room. "Where's Margot," I ask them, looking around for my oldest daughter.

"Taking a nap," Isla answers.

"She's hungover." SJ snorts and I shoot a murderous glare at River.

"I didn't let him have any. Relax," he says before shooting a glare at SJ.

"What's hungover?" Isla asks and I turn to River.

"Handle this...like an adult please," I say as I usher Ellie out of the door.

CHAPTER TWENTY-FOUR

Elianna

THE FLIGHT TO OHIO IS QUICK AND EASY EVEN THOUGH I spent the majority of it trying to keep my tears at bay, thinking about my father and saying goodbye to Rowan even if it was only for a short time. The thought of not seeing his smile every day sent a wave of sadness through me that I hadn't anticipated.

Emily texted me while I was in the air that my father made it through surgery and that they removed the blockage. I feel so much relief that he's fine, but I know I won't feel completely better until I see and talk to him. I make it to the hospital quickly and push through the doors of the waiting room to see Emily, her husband, their daughter, and my mom's mom.

"Ellie Bellie!" my grandma says, practically jumping out of her seat. I'm in her arms instantly and I feel comfort in that way only grandmothers can provide.

"Hi, Grandma!" She kisses my cheek and puts her hands on my shoulders.

"You are prettier every time I see you. You are glowing." She narrows her eyes at me and gives me a sly smile. "I need to hear all about this boy because you look in love, girl. And why I'm hearing about it through the grapevine is unacceptable." She pinches my arm and I wince at the pain.

"It's…kinda new."

Emily stands up to engulf me in a hug and it stuns me to see how much she looks just like our mother. Mahogany eyes that sit behind square frames stare at me and I feel like we are transported back to a time where we could have a whole conversation with just our eyes.

"Hey," she says and I see the exhaustion all over her face. She'd ditched our natural curls and color in our teen years, opting to straighten her hair and dye it a jet black.

"Hey, Em." While I'm staring at her, something seems off, and on their own accord, my eyes drift to her stomach before moving back to her eyes curiously. Her eyes widen before she nods once and tears flood my eyes. "Oh my God, Emily," I whisper as I hug her again and she chuckles in my ear.

"I hate how well you can still read me." She puts a hand over her eyes. "Ten weeks," she confirms.

"Auntie El!" My niece comes to sit in my lap the second I sit down and I squeeze her tight. She's almost seven now and I suddenly have a vision of her and Isla being the best of friends.

Remembering that I told Rowan I would text him when I got to the hospital, I pull out my phone and shoot him a text telling him I will call him in a bit.

"Hi, honey."

"We are still waiting for them to let us see him, but new guy?" Emily asks with a quirked eyebrow. That's the thing about Emily; she only allows vulnerability to show for a moment before she's back to having her tough exterior. "So, where'd you meet him?"

"Ummm…" I sigh, knowing there's no sense beating around the bush. "He's the dad I nanny for."

Emily's husband, Trent, who'd been quiet since I got here because he's not a big talker, looks up from his phone and stares at me with wide eyes. "Okay, Ellie."

Figuring he's thinking something salacious; I clarify. "He's not married, you fool. Their mom is not alive."

"Aren't you living there?" Emily asks, with her eyebrows raised to the ceiling, and I glare at her for bringing that factoid up in front of our grandma.

"Can you not?" I ask her. I'm annoyed that even at a time like this and after the moment we just had, my sister can still successfully irritate me.

"Emily, don't be a prude. You were barely out of diapers before you started shacking up." Our grandma interrupts. I bite my lip to hide the grin because I should have known my grandma would come to my defense. *Being the favorite grandchild does have its perks.*

"It just happened…he's amazing though. I think I may actually be in love." I look at my grandma who's looking at me over the top of her glasses as if to say *I knew that.*

"How many kids does he have? Three, right? That's a lot," Emily says, and I hear what sounds more like support than judgment.

"Yes, three amazing kids, and I am crazy about them."

"Are they crazy about you and their dad?" Emily asks while itching her nose ring.

I tilt my head. "His oldest daughter is warming up to the idea. His youngest daughter is too young to really grasp it; I think? And the middle is a boy and he is fine with it."

"Wow, the oldest daughter being difficult? Where have I heard that before?" Emily says and while a smile pulls at her lips, I know it was meant to be a dig.

"Not today, Emily Nicole," my grandmother warns.

She sighs and turns back to me. "Well, I'm glad you're happy," she says with a noncommittal shrug.

The doctor walks into the waiting room and spots us before coming to sit in a nearby chair.

"So, your father and son-in-law are doing fine." He turns to look at me. "Hi, I'm Dr. Johnson. Are you Elianna?"

"Yes, that's me." I nod immediately.

"Great, your father wanted me to check to see if you were here. I'm supposed to bring you back first."

"Heaven forbid, not the daughter that's been here," Emily grumbles.

I wince and look at the doctor who looks old enough to be my grandfather with kind eyes and a sweet smile. "Emily can go first."

"He requested you," he says as he stands up.

I sigh, knowing this is going to be a problem. "I'll be quick," I tell Emily and she rolls her eyes.

"Whatever."

We're walking down the hall in the intensive care unit when Dr. Johnson speaks up. "She must be the middle daughter. He mentioned he had three."

"That obvious, huh?"

"I have three daughters as well. It happens. But as the father, there's a reason why we choose a certain child first. It means you're the toughest and the first person you see after a significant health crisis will see you at your weakest." He pats my back and nods toward the room with a smile.

I push through the door to see my father sitting up and looking good for someone who just had a heart attack followed by immediate surgery. His eyes find mine, and for a second, they get a little glassy before he smiles.

"If this was all just to get me to visit, I am not amused," I tell him before a smile pulls at my lips.

"Ellie."

"Hi, Dad," I whisper as I move through his private room and

lean down gently to hug him. I search for that familiar scent to trigger my nostalgia brought on by my father's hugs but I only smell the faint smell of the hospital. "How...are you not eating well? Are you exercising?"

"Wow, you've been here for five seconds and you're already on me. That has to be a record."

"Dad, I'm serious." I stare into his warm chocolate eyes and shake my head. "I'm still not ready to be an orphan," I repeat the words I'd said to him years ago when my mom died. He'd smoked cigarettes for years and once she died, I made him promise to quit because I was scared of what would happen if something took the only parent we had left. He'd quit after much badgering and crying and months of temper tantrums.

Truly, I delivered some Academy Award-worthy performances.

"I know," he tells me with a nod. "I'll do better, Ellie. Please don't cry." He reaches for my hand and squeezes it.

"I thought when I left..." I sniffle as a tear falls down my cheek. "You said you'd be fine."

"And I am."

"Clearly not!" I exclaim before letting out a defeated sigh. "I wasn't planning to move back yet." I bite my bottom lip thinking about how I would uproot my life back to Ohio. Transferring schools would be easy, but the thought of leaving four people I'm very attached to feels like it would be impossible.

"And I don't need you to. Honey, sometimes things just happen when you get older. Could I be taking better care of myself? Yes. But I don't need you to do that for me. You did that for long enough."

A sad smile pulls at my lips. "I met someone...in Maryland."

"Oh?" The biggest smile crosses his face because he's been asking me for a grandchild for about two years now. "Is he here?" He nods toward the door.

"No, he wanted to come. But...I told him I wanted to come

alone." *I'll give him the rundown on the details later...juuuust in case he's not thrilled about his age.* "I think you'll really like him."

"Honey, if he's got your stamp of approval, I love him like a son already."

Later that night, only Emily and I are left at the hospital. My grandma left and Trent took my niece home. Eden came straight from the airport, but once she found out he was okay and saw him, she went home to change and drop off her stuff. So, Emily and I are sitting next to each other in the waiting room while they do some tests on my father when she speaks up.

"We're moving," Emily says sadly and I turn to look at her.

"What?"

"We're moving...", she repeats. "Trent is getting transferred."

"To where? Tell me you mean like down the street."

She shakes her head. "Chicago."

"Chicago!?" I say. "You...when?!"

"Next month?" she offers weakly. "They said they could put it off for a few months but we agreed to go because we wanted to move before I got too pregnant."

"Put it off! Our father just had a heart attack!"

"You think I don't know that? I didn't know this was going to happen when we agreed, Ellie. God," she says before putting her hands over her eyes. "You think I would have said yes if I did? You're not the only person who cares about Dad," she snaps.

I ignore the last part because I refuse to let her goad me into an argument. "So, you have to go?"

"Unless I'm planning to live in a different state than my husband, yeah? He has to be there the first of the year. That's why we were having Thanksgiving at my house. I heard you weren't thrilled about that," she grumbles.

"It wasn't about you," I whisper.

"Oh?" Emily says. "Seems like it's always been about me. What I'm doing wrong. What I could be doing better…" She trails off.

"We just always have holidays there and…it made me think about Mom." She doesn't say anything and I just shake my head.

"Weren't you planning to move—" She starts and I turn to look at her.

"So, we're right back here again? It's like six years ago all over. You make a decision and everyone just has to be on board? I have to change my entire life because you did?"

"I never asked you to drop out of school, Elianna. Stop with the martyr bullshit." She turns her narrowed eyes to look at me, giving me a cold stare.

"Odd way to say thank you."

"This is just so you. No, Ellie. I'm not saying you have to move home—"

"You basically are in not so many words. Eden is at Yale and that's not close and Grandma is getting older. They need support." I argue. Emily would never blatantly say I should, but she knows I would if she weren't here.

"Grandma is fine and she has Allie and Indy," she says referring to my cousins on my mom's side. "I know about Dad. I just thought since the plan was always for you to come home that you would. You've never mentioned wanting to stay in Maryland. I wouldn't have suggested it otherwise." She crosses one leg over the other and huffs. "I'm not the bad sister you think I am."

"But I am?"

"No. I never said you were." She snaps. "You're the one that is always so tough on me. Not the other way around."

I lean forward letting my arms rest on my thighs. "I was only ever trying to help. You say you didn't ask me to come home back then, but what would you have done if I didn't?"

"I would have figured it out." She sighs. "I know you just wanted to help and I'm glad I never had to know what it was like to do it alone. I've never doubted that you were in my corner, Ellie." Tears well in my eyes hearing words I'd heard many times from Eden who is the most sensitive out of the three of us, but not from Emily, who in my opinion, is the toughest. "I love you... even if you are a pain in my ass." I laugh through my tears and pull her in for a hug and I can feel her pulling away after only a second. "Okay that's enough. This is why I don't say anything nice to you!" She rolls her eyes before giving me a smile.

After a few minutes of silence, she speaks up again. "I know you've felt comfortable staying away because I was here and this changes everything. That's why I've been dreading telling you this, but maybe we can talk to him. He can move to Chicago with us."

"Do you think he'll leave his house?"

"I don't know." She shrugs. "But we could ask."

Later that night, I'm at my father's house in my old bedroom by myself. Eden, wanting to keep herself busy, went out with some of her friends who I will probably be picking up later from the bar. I pick up the phone to call Rowan and he answers on the first ring.

"Hi, sunshine."

"Hey."

"Are you at your dads?"

"Yeah." I pull one of my dad's beers to my lips and take a healthy sip. "Having a beer."

"As you should. It's been a day. Are you there alone?"

"Yeah, Eden went to get drunk with her friends. You remember what it's like when you're home from school for the first time since graduating. Also, I mean...he's fine. There's no need for anyone to worry." Even as I speak the words, I feel as if I'm holding back tears because... *my dad had a heart attack.*

"I'm so happy to hear that, baby. God, I've been so worried about you. We all have."

"Tell everyone I'm fine. I'm okay." *Sort of.*

"I hear it in your voice, baby. Talk to me. What's going on?"

I sigh, knowing I'm going to have to broach this subject at some point. "Can we FaceTime?"

"Yeah, of course." My phone rings and I instantly prop it up in front of me. "Hey, beautiful." He shoots me that perfect smile and I hate that what I'm about to tell him, will probably cause it to fade.

"So…" I rub my forehead. "Emily dropped a pretty big bomb today." I sigh. "She's moving to Chicago. Her husband got transferred and he has to be there the first of the year. They're moving after Thanksgiving."

He must know where my head is at because he winces but nods. "Tell me what you're thinking."

"I don't want to leave him here alone. Especially after a heart attack…" I run a hand through my hair and put my head in my hands.

"What if he moved?"

"He's not going to want to leave this house," I tell him, and part of me doesn't blame him. Not only did he live with his wife and raise his three children here, but it's a gorgeous three-story Victorian house in a prime location that has been paid off since before Eden was born. The number of offers he's received and turned down over the years is a little crazy.

"You can't put a price on memories," my dad would always say.

"Do you want to move back to Ohio?" Rowan asks.

"No…not really. I…I've grown to love Maryland, but I feel like I don't have a choice. I mean I do…I know I do. But…the right choice doesn't have me leaving him here alone." I ramble because I'm still not sure what to do in this situation.

"I get that."

"I haven't made any decisions though." I shake my head. "It's just a shitty situation."

"I could move," he says softly, and of all the things I thought he would say, that was not one of them.

"What? No. What about your job? And you're going to uproot Margot during her senior year of high school? God, she'd really hate me." I chuckle darkly.

"I meet most state requirements; I can probably waive into Ohio, and if I can't, I'll take the exam. I am pretty sure I'll pass…" he chuckles. "and Margot will get over it."

My heart squeezes thinking about how much this man must care about me because I can't believe what he's willing to do for me. "I can't ask you to do that."

"You're not asking."

"Okay, well, like I said, I haven't made any decisions."

He nods slowly. "We will figure this out together. Okay?"

The next morning, Eden and I are sitting in the kitchen having breakfast before visiting hours at the hospital begin.

"God, I forgot how well you cook," Eden says as she bites into the French toast I made knowing it's her favorite. "Elles," she says when I don't respond and I look at my youngest sister who really could be my twin. "Don't feel like you have to move back."

"Eden…"

"Don't do it. Not if you're happy in Maryland. You know Dad wouldn't want you to." She takes a sip of her coffee. "We'll talk to Dad and it'll be three against one. We'll make him go to Chicago." She says before taking a bite.

Our doorbell rings and I frown wondering who that could be.

"Emily has a key, doesn't she?" I frown because I don't know who else would be here at this hour. I suppose it could be one of the neighbors coming to say hello or to check on us. What I do not expect is to see the man I'd cried myself to sleep over last night because the thought of leaving him felt like a weight on my chest.

"Hey, sunshine." He has a little more facial hair than usual, like he hadn't shaved and maybe a little tired like he didn't sleep well last night. My fingers itch to touch his face.

"Rowan?" My eyes move to the person next to him and see Margot staring at me with soft eyes and a kind smile. "Margot? Wha–what's going on? How do you know where I live? Where's SJ and Isla?"

"You got it from here." Margot smiles at her dad before squeezing me in a hug and walking past me. "Hi, Ellie."

She goes inside, closing the door behind her and he slides his hands into his jacket pockets. "That was a lot of questions, so I'll start with the most important first. "SJ and Isla are okay. They're in school and River has it under control. They don't know Margot came with me and Isla is going to throw a fit that she couldn't come. She asked to call you three times after you left, by the way." He grabs my hand and drags his lips over it. "I knew I needed to be here. After last night…I talked to Margot and…asked her if she hated the idea of moving."

"Rowan…"

"I told her, I'd respect her decision whichever she chose and I knew it was a big deal and would understand if she really didn't want to. But…you see she's here right." He smiles. "Are you getting it now? I need to be where you are. *They* need to be where you are. So, if you need to move here to be closer to your family then we're coming with you because you're our family."

Tears are sliding down my face and I take a step closer to him. "Rowan. I…can't believe you did this."

"I asked you once who was strong for you while you were being strong for everyone else and…I want to be that person. I love you and I'll be strong for you. Forever, if you let me."

I'm in his arms a second later, pressing my face into his neck as the tears fly down my face. "I love you too," I murmur against his neck and then his lips are on mine, kissing away the pain of last night and everything I've felt since I talked to my sister yesterday. "Wait," I pull back to look at him. "You didn't answer me. How did you figure out where I lived?"

"Your file. I figured that was obvious." He laughs.

"Oh, duh." I smack my forehead. "That's right." I kiss him again and a wicked grin finds my face. "So… since you love me and all, does that mean I get a raise?"

EPILOGUE

Seven Months Later

"That one," Isla says as she points at the third one in the past thirty seconds.

"I thought you liked the other one?" I ask her as I point to the front of the store.

"Nuh-uh, this one is better." She points at the glass case.

"I don't like that one as much," Margot interjects. "I still like the first one at the last store."

I sigh, thinking about driving back to that other store at this hour. *Traffic is going to be insane and Isla will be ready to have a meltdown.* "You mean the one all the way in Fairfax?"

"I told you that was my favorite! I don't know why we left," she says about the *Tiffany* store we'd been at before this one. She crosses her arms over her chest.

"It just didn't feel right," I tell her. I'm waiting for a ring that reminds me of Ellie. A ring that I know just by looking at it that it is the one for her.

"Daddy, can I have a snack?"

I sigh and nod at her as Margot pulls a bag of Goldfish out of her purse and hands it to her. "Why are you stressing? Ellie is going to say yes. It doesn't matter what the ring looks like."

I had been thinking about putting a ring on her finger the second Margot and I flew to Ohio after her father's heart attack. Knowing I wanted to be with her for the rest of my life, was what prompted me to get on that plane. I'd been shocked but so proud of my daughter when she asked to go with me so that she could apologize in person and also prove to her that she really was okay with moving to Ohio. "I want it to be perfect."

"It will be. Ellie loves you so much. She would be laughing at you stressing out this much, honestly."

She absolutely would.

I'd told Ellie that I was taking the girls out for the day, and SJ, who is also a part of the plan but had zero interest in helping me choose a ring, asked her and her father to take him to a baseball game in the city. SJ's behaviors vastly improved and I can't believe he starts middle school in just a few months.

We didn't move to Ohio. After Ellie's father got wind of what I was willing to do, he'd been moved that I'd do that for her and told me he wouldn't have me uprooting my whole family just because he was being a stubborn old man.

His words.

I had his permission to marry her about five seconds later.

With the money he made from selling his house *which for the record was a fuck ton*, he decided to buy a condo in Maryland to be closer to Ellie—we'd asked him to come live with us to which he declined so he wouldn't 'be anywhere that close to where my daughter has relations'— and an apartment in Chicago so that he could go back and forth between his daughters. Eden, when she comes home, comes to Maryland because in the fifteen minutes I'd been talking to Ellie on her front porch, she and Margot had bonded. I'm happy that they did but now Margot has been begging me to let her go visit Eden at Yale without any parental supervision. I may have agreed but I'd overheard Eden telling her this summer about all of the guys that would make her forget all about Gabe *who she'd dumped right after prom.*

I really need to get the full story about what happened there.

We go back to the front of the store to look at the first ring that all three of us liked. I look down at the three-carat oval-shaped diamond ring. "I do like this one too." I say and Margot nods in agreement.

All three of my children had been more than on board with me asking Ellie to marry me and I am surprised that Isla has been able to keep it a secret as long as she has. "Now you know you can't tell Ellie I have this."

Isla nods between chewing. "I know! I *need* a new Barbie's Dreamhouse." *Okay, so I had to bribe her a little bit for insurance.*

"She's going to be so psyched," Margot says excitedly. "I'm really happy for you, Dad."

"Thanks, honey." I wrap an arm around her and press a kiss to her temple. "Love you the most."

Later that night, Ellie climbs into bed next to me and I immediately pull her against my chest. "I missed you today." I press a kiss to her lips. I rarely spend a Saturday without her. Usually all of us do something and it's amazing how much she's brought our family together.

"Me too," she whispers. "So…" She presses a kiss to my bare chest and looks up at me with those innocent doe eyes. "Can I see it?"

My heart begins to race and I pull back slowly to look at her.

"Can you see *what?*" *Please tell me she means my dick.* She raises an eyebrow at me and I blink at her, wanting her to clarify.

"I don't know why you told her. She can't keep secrets from me."

I let out an annoyed breath and shut my eyes as I count backward from ten. When I get to five, I give her a side-eye. "I bribed her. How did you get it out of her?"

"Bribed her with something better." She blinks at me several times. "I still have so much to teach you."

"Isla Kincaid. God, these kids," I grumble.

"For the record…" She climbs on top of me and kisses my lips. "My dad told me too."

"What?!"

"Sorry, he's still pissed you beat him last week at golf. I told you to let him win!" I let out a sigh followed by an annoyed laugh and she moves to straddle me. "So…can I see it?" she asks while grinding down on my dick.

I groan in response. "Don't try to seduce me, Elianna."

She feigns shock and giggles. "I would never."

"And no, now I'm going to make you wait even longer." *Lie.*

"Oh, good one." She puts her hands on my chest and moves herself up and back. She's wearing a tiny silk two-piece set and I can already see the dark spot forming between her legs as the wetness forms. "Please?"

Get her off before she breaks you down, Rowan. "No. That's anti-climactic."

"I'll let you stick your dick in my ass tonight," she purrs.

My dick throbs and my eyes find the ceiling while I consider her offer. "No, you're waiting so I can get on one knee and tell you that I love you and I'm utterly obsessed with you and I want to spend the rest of my life with you."

"Fine," she says with an eye roll before she goes to move off of me. I grip her hips to hold her in place and give her a smirk.

"Can I still put my dick in your ass tonight?"

She scoffs. "That was not the deal I posed!" She grins and rolls her eyes again. "I mean, yeah."

I push her onto her back and kiss her, pouring every bit of love and devotion I have for this woman into it. "Don't worry, you won't have to wait long."

Because I'm already planning to ask her tomorrow.

THE END

Stay tuned for River's forbidden romance:
The Cheerleader is Off Limits
coming Fall 2025

ACKNOWLEDGEMENTS

Thank you so much for reading! As always, it takes a village to deal with my chaos, so just a few thank yous! I have to start off with thanking **Rachel Baldwin** for not only reading this in its rawest form, but all of the feedback regarding the kids, especially Isla! Thank you so much for being on this book's journey with me through every step. Love you!

Tanya Baker, for always being in my corner and being there for me through it all. Love you big.

Kristen Portillo, thank you for helping make this book perfect! One day I'll get my tenses and my timelines right the first time around. Until then, I'm grateful I have you to catch them. I appreciate you immensely!

Stacey Blake, thank you for always making the interiors so gorgeous and exactly what I want! Thank you for making my books so pretty!

Ari Basulto, I would be lost without you. Thank you for all that you do to keep me organized! Thank you for running all of my teams and overall Q.B.'s life better than I could. A million thank yous.

Pang Thao, it's safe to say I am utterly obsessed with these covers and everything else you make for me! You're so good to me and I appreciate everything you do!

Giana, I am so thankful for you and your friendship. I love you and our chats so much! Thank you for always cheering me on.

Extra special love to all of my author friends, and while I couldn't possibly name them all, I wanted to name a few that are always so encouraging and supportive: Marni Mann, Sara Cate, Sierra Simone, Julie Murphy, Dylan Allen, Kandi Steiner and SE Rose: thank you for your endless support, love, (and early copies of your books!) I love being on this ride with you all.

To my producer Jenna Taplin and the Lyric Audiobooks

team, thank you so much for all of your help with bringing this to life and embracing my chaos! I appreciate you all!

To the babes on my street team and ARC team, thank you for your excitement! Thank you for your love for me and my books and that you're always willing to let me take you over a cliff. The reason I can do what I do is because of you guys in my corner. Thank you for always clapping the loudest. I love you all!

To all of the bloggers and bookstagrammers and TikTokers, thank you for your edits and your reels and your videos and always sharing my books! For still talking about books I wrote two and three years ago and loving them so much. For sharing with your friends (and sometimes your family? Ha) Thank you for everything you do. (Because seriously? Videos are so hard.) Thank you for your reviews and chatting with me online. You make my days so much brighter.

And finally, and most importantly to YOU, to the readers, thank you for letting me into your minds and your hearts again with another book. I hope you enjoyed it! I love you all. See you in a few months, for River's book?

ALSO BY
Q.B. TYLER

STANDALONES

My Best Friend's Sister
Unconditional
Forget Me Not
Love Unexpected
Always Been You
What Was Meant to Be
Keep Her Safe

THE SECRETS UNIVERSE

The Worst Kept Secret
The Season of Secrets
Our Little Secret

BITTERSWEET UNIVERSE

Bittersweet Surrender
Bittersweet Addiction
Bittersweet Love

CAMPUS TALES SERIES

First Semester
Second Semester
Spring Semester

ABOUT THE AUTHOR

Bestselling author and lover of forbidden romances, tacos, coffee, and wine. Q.B. Tyler gives readers sometimes angsty, sometimes emotional but always deliciously steamy romances featuring sassy heroines and the heroes that worship them. She's known for writing forbidden (and sometimes taboo) romances, so if that's your thing, you've come to the right place. When she's not writing, you can usually find her on Instagram (definitely procrastinating), shopping or at brunch.

Sign up for her newsletter to stay in touch!
https://view.flodesk.com/pages/6195b59a839edddd7aa02f8f

Qbtyler03@gmail.com

Facebook: Q.B. Tyler
Reader Group: Q.B.'s Hive
Instagram @qbtyler.author
Bookbub: Q.B. Tyler
Twitter: @qbtyler
Goodreads: Q.B. Tyler
Tik Tok: author.qbtyler
www.Authorqbtyler.com

Made in the USA
Columbia, SC
09 July 2025